Taking Leave

"Well," Sindri said after a moment. "I think I should probably go." He grabbed his hoopak staff and scooted out of the booth. Maddoc watched him silently.

Sindri turned around and met Maddoc's eyes. "I guess if I don't ever see you again, I should say . . . thank you. You really did help me."

"So glad to have been of assistance," Maddoc said, his tone clearly sarcastic.

Sindri shrugged. "Well, I guess despite everything, I don't regret being your apprentice. Just . . . I can't be around you anymore."

Not waiting for a response, Sindri turned and walked away.

THE NEW ADVENTURES

SUNCATCHER TRILOGY

BY JEFF SAMPSON

Volume One
THE WAYWARD WIZARD

Volume Two
THE EBONY EYE

Volume Three
THE STOLEN SUN

THE NEW ADVENTURES

SUNCATCHER TRILOGY

VOLUME THREE

THE STOLEN SUN

NORFOLK COUNTY
PUBLIC LIBRARY

JEFF SAMPSON

COVER & INTERIOR ART
Vinod Rams

MIRRORSTONE™

Dragonlance®: The New Adventures

THE STOLEN SUN

©2007 Wizards of the Coast, Inc.

Cover art by Vinod Rams
Cartography by Dennis Kauth
First Printing: September 2007

Library of Congress Cataloging-in-Publishing data is on file.

9 8 7 6 5 4 3 2 1

ISBN: 978-0-7869-4291-6
620-95957740-001-EN

U.S., CANADA,
ASIA, PACIFIC, & LATIN AMERICA
Wizards of the Coast, Inc.
P.O. Box 707
Renton, WA 98057-0707
+1-800-324-6496

EUROPEAN HEADQUARTERS
Hasbro UK Ltd
Caswell Way
Newport, Gwent NP9 0YH
GREAT BRITAIN
Save this address for your records.

Visit our web site at www.mirrorstonebooks.com

FOR ANGEL

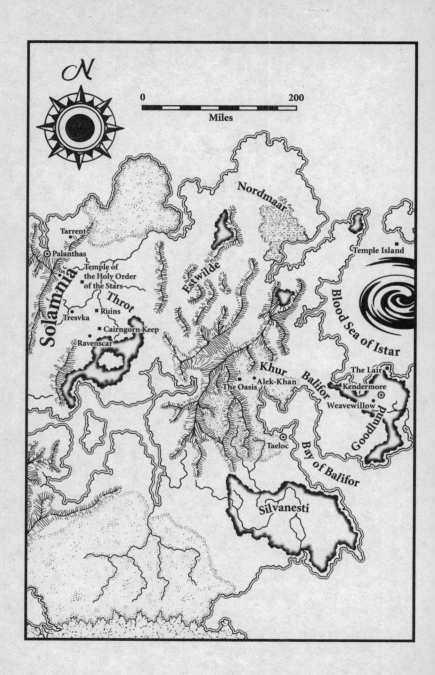

TABLE OF CONTENTS

PROLOGUE

Wilden watched Sindri—the lone kender wizard in all of Krynn—as he slept. The little mage snorted, scratched his nose, then turned on his side. He pulled his purple cloak tight around his shoulders and let out a little snore, seeming perhaps the least-threatening supremely powerful chosen one that Wilden could imagine.

Slivers of red moonlight seeped through small windows and cast strange shadows along the slatted walls of the wagon. The night was silent save for the sound of crickets outside, the rumbling of the wagon's wheels, and the clomping of horse hooves.

In the wagon also rode Wilden's traveling companions. Aside from the kender—Sindri Suncatcher—there was the short and feisty girl, Tayt, who lay sprawled in a corner with her jaw slack and her hand limp atop her chest. Next to her, curled in a furry ball, was a small creature named Rizzek that was part lizard and part cat, clearly created by magical means.

In the corner opposite Wilden, sitting straight up and with his eyes closed, was the old wizard Maddoc. The man's black robes made him seem a part of the darkness, his silver beard like the

1

half-moon of Solinari on the shadow of his face.

Wilden knew he should sleep as well, but he could not take his eyes off Sindri. The little wizard had at first seemed so ordinary, so much like every other kender. How was it that he, of all people on Krynn, had been chosen to rebirth an ancient magic onto the world?

And how was it that Wilden was aiding him?

Wilden knew the Wizards' Conclave, for which he worked, was angry with him. He'd spent years being trained by them, living with them, hunting down renegade magic-users for them, only to abandon them after they'd trusted him with capturing the "renegade" Sindri.

"Us, *not* them," Wilden reminded himself, realizing quite suddenly that he had started to separate himself from his old order in his mind.

"Ahem."

Wilden looked into the shadowy corner where Maddoc sat. The older wizard was in the same position as before, but his eyes were open now. His features were unreadable.

Wilden smiled. "Can't sleep either?" he whispered. "Not sure about you, but my mind is still very much on what happened at Anica's keep."

Maddoc's expression did not change. Wilden noticed that Maddoc's gloved right hand was clenched.

Shrugging, Wilden looked away. "I suppose sleep will overcome me eventually. It always seems to, then goes away long before I want."

Maddoc grunted. "You do realize we are heading for an entire countryside filled with kender?"

Wilden chuckled. "I do. You're saying I'll need all the rest I can get?"

"I would say that, yes."

The older wizard fell silent, closing his eyes once more. Wilden wasn't sure if Maddoc had actually gone back to sleep or was just making a show of dismissing him.

Wilden scooted down the floor and lay down. Splinters poked through his shirt and into his back, but he'd experienced worse resting conditions. Closing his eyes, Wilden tried not to worry about the conclave and about what the revelation of Sindri's powers meant.

And Wilden dreamed.

Sparkling stars spread out in front of Wilden on a field of black, dots of silver arranged in the shape of godly constellations. The red moon cast a hazy pink glow in tiny drops of water that hung in what Wilden assumed was cold air.

Assumed, because he could not feel a thing.

Hmm, he thought. *I've left my body.*

This wasn't a rare occurrence—but rather, an uncontrollable magical gift that had always been a part of him. Foresight, his mentors at the Wizards' Conclave had called it—the ability to sense events that were happening or were about to happen, usually in distant locations.

Wilden twisted so that he looked down away from the stars as he waited for his power to take hold and lead where it would. Far below him, winding along a path in a dark field, two horses pulled a small wagon. It was the wagon in which he and his companions now traveled.

The wagon's driver chewed on a long blade of grass. They'd hired him back in Alek-Khan, a small trader village near Anica's keep. Even from his distance high above, Wilden recognized the signs of the man's weariness: slumped shoulders, bowed head. He'd been trained to notice every small body motion of others in order to anticipate when and how to use his many skills in battle.

Before Wilden could feel too sorry for the tired driver, he felt a tug. It were as though someone were pulling thin cords at his wrists and ankles to get his attention. As usual, he allowed himself to go slack, the invisible cords tugging harder and harder until, in a flash, he was flung halfway across the world.

Wilden blinked (or what passed for blinking, considering at the moment he had no body) and took in the location where his foresight had taken him. Wherever it was, it was not yet fully night—probably somewhere back west, in Solamnia. Dying light from the sunset streamed through fir trees that towered toward a sky writhing with gray clouds. Wolves stalked birds that squawked and darted between branches.

Scanning the ground, Wilden noticed that a good portion of the earth had caved into what appeared to be an underground cavern. It looked as though someone had taken a giant dagger and gouged a path through the forest. It was a relatively fresh wound too—needles still clung to trees that had toppled into the underground cavern.

Willing himself to float over the gouged earth, Wilden followed the destruction deeper into the forest. More wreckage lay here, more dark and dirt-filled holes where the ground had collapsed in. Wilden didn't have to see the remnants of an old keep's walls to know where he'd been taken in his dream: the remains of Cairngorn Keep.

Cairngorn Keep—where it had all begun, where Wilden had come to capture Sindri for the conclave, and where a dark beast created by a more dangerous force had been sent to kill them all. In the end, Wilden had fought alongside Sindri, the renegade he

JEFF SAMPSON

was supposed to have captured. And in so doing, he had set himself down the path he was on now—the path he was certain he had to take, though he was just as certain it might lead to his undoing.

Branches crunched indelicately through the underbrush. Knowing he was taken back to this place for a reason, Wilden willed his incorporeal body to turn so that he could watch as a figure came into view.

Instinctively, Wilden tried to stiffen in surprise as he saw who it was, though it was rather difficult to do so without muscles to clench. The figure was a tall man of about sixty years. He was dressed in pearl white robes that glowed in the growing darkness. Faint symbols embroidered in silver along his sleeves and hems revealed his power. His wispy gray hair had been cropped short, and dark stubble shadowed his lined face.

It was a face Wilden had known since he was a child: It was Garin, his master at the conclave, his mentor in the art of high sorcery, his friend.

Garin did not look pleased.

A swatch of black separated from the darkened trees behind Garin, and another figure stepped forward. Save for his blue eyes, the man's entire body was covered in form-fitting black clothing—the clothing of a renegade hunter.

The renegade hunter stepped to Garin's side. He was muscular and lithe and towered above even Garin, who himself was a tall man.

"Cairngorn Keep," Garin muttered. He shook his head, then scratched musingly at his stubbly chin. "It seems Wilden's story checks out."

Eyes stoic, the renegade hunter nodded, so slightly most would have missed it.

Garin sighed and lifted the hem of his robe as he rounded a mound of weed-strewn rubble. "It does not make sense. What could have happened to take Wilden from his path? I trained that boy, and I trained him well!"

The renegade hunter lowered his head and muttered something into Garin's ear that Wilden couldn't hear. Garin shook his head.

"No," he said, glaring back at the renegade hunter. "The kender is a renegade, no matter who or what was after him and caused this destruction. And anyone who aids him is a renegade himself."

The renegade hunter did not respond. Instead, he bounded gracefully over a few tumbled blocks of black stone that had once belonged to the keep's walls. He leaned down and dug through the dirt, then stood up to show Garin what he'd seen: a green leather book with gold writing embossed on its cover.

Garin crossed to where the renegade hunter stood. He was clumsy as he climbed, his boots almost slipping from the stone blocks. Yet somehow he managed to keep his robes pristine during his climb.

Garin took the book and flipped through its pages, furrowing his brow. "Strong magic is buried here," he said. "All over here. We will need to send members of the conclave to gather these artifacts before more renegade magic-users can get their hands on them." Tucking the book inside his robes, Garin straightened his shoulders. "In the meantime, you and I will need to head east to Khur. If the tale of Cairngorn Keep's destruction is true, it is likely Wilden's story about Anica and what happened at her keep is true as well."

The renegade hunter nodded. The two wizards began to walk deeper into the remains of Cairngorn Keep, looking for more artifacts.

Wilden willed himself to follow so as to hear the rest of their discussion, but he heard another crunch of underbrush beside him. A young man and a young woman walked through the darkened trees, whispering between themselves playfully.

As they grew closer, Wilden saw them more clearly. A tall young man in green leather armor walked beside an elf girl, her hair a cascade of golden curls. His muscles were honed from much sword work, probably with the rather ugly sword that hung from his belt. She, too, wore leather armor, her sleeves pulled tight in an archer's fashion. An artfully carved longbow, its ends capped with blue jewels, hung from her shoulder.

The boy stiffened as he saw the ruins of Cairngorn Keep. The elf girl's beautiful features fell into concern as the boy stopped teasing her and took in the destruction with unbelieving eyes.

"Davyn," the elf girl said. "What—"

And then, the unseen magical tethers around Wilden's wrists and ankles snapped him away. The continent flashed by in a blur of trees and mountains and stars. Quite suddenly, the wagon in which his sleeping body rode reappeared beneath him. He tumbled through the sky, falling faster and faster toward his body. In moments he would be awake.

There was a flash of red just before Wilden hit the wagon's roof. An image filled his vision, a terrifying image of a mound of crimson flesh writhing as though hundreds and hundreds of people were trapped beneath, trying to escape. The flesh bubbled and bulged into creases that looked quite a bit like faces—the scarred, sharp-toothed, pointed-eared faces of countless goblins. As one, the mangled faces in the mound of flesh shrieked.

Then, everything went black.

Wilden's eyes snapped open as the whole wagon jostled. Hanging packs slapped against the walls, and wooden supports creaked in protest. Outside, one of the horses whinnied in distress as the driver called out for them to slow down.

Wilden sat up and looked around the wagon. Everyone was where he had last seen them, and everyone still slept.

Wilden lay back down, but he did not close his eyes. What he had seen at Cairngorn Keep hadn't been expected, but at least how he'd seen it was usual. He'd had many, many dreams of the same sort in his life. All it meant was that at that very moment, his old master and a renegade hunter were after not just Sindri, but *him*. He'd completely disobeyed his orders, and now he would need to be captured. It was how things were done.

What had not been usual in the least was the image that he had seen just before waking—the terrifying image of what appeared to be hundreds of goblin bodies melted together into a ruddy, disgusting, fleshy mess. The vision had been more similar to the foresight he'd had when awake—quick flashes of moments that were happening elsewhere.

Wilden did not know what the image of the goblins meant. All he knew was that somehow it was tied into Sindri's journey, and that it meant something bad for them all.

Wilden couldn't worry about the conclave now. Though it went against everything he had ever been told, he knew that Sindri's unusual magic and his journey were important, and he had to stay by Sindri's side, no matter the outcome.

Closing his eyes, Wilden willed himself back to sleep, the dream—and its messages of dark forces still after them all—shoved to the back of his mind.

JEFF SAMPSON

CHAPTER

1 GONE FISHING

I see it!"

Sindri sat atop the front of the rumbling boxcar wagon, hand over his eyes to block out the glaring sun as he scanned the horizon. He'd been waiting to see this all day—the distant green tops of the birches and maple trees that were the beginning of the Kenderwood.

Legs dangling over the wagon's side, Sindri kicked against the wagon in excitement. Beneath him, the wagon's driver hunched his shoulders and scowled as dirt fell from Sindri's boots into his hair.

Sindri peered down over the side of the wagon. "Hey, did you hear me?" he called into the open window. "I see it! We're almost to Kendermore!"

Tayt's head of cropped black hair popped out of the window and she turned to look up at Sindri. "Yes, we heard you," she said with a smile. She smiled a lot these days, Sindri noticed. It made her light brown face lovely. She continued, "You're awful excited. I thought all a kender ever wanted to do was get away from home and travel."

Sindri tilted his head. "Of course! But I haven't got to tell Mother and Aunt Moonbeam and Grandfather Hephdeezee and everyone else about all that's happened to me, and sometimes retelling the stories of an adventure is the best part. And I haven't tasted bloodberries in years, though I don't think they'll be quite ripe yet, and though I think we're too late for the Harrowing festival we may be in time for Midyear Day, so we'll get to catch fireflies with everyone for Midsummer's Eve. Oh, and I'll get to show them all my magic!"

The wagon's driver snorted. "A kender wizard," he muttered, then slapped the reins to keep his horses trotting down the path.

Sindri leaned over the front of the wagon, his long and shaggy black hair falling around his face. "That's right," he said, "a kender wizard." A familiar warm glow pulsed inside Sindri, a constant power that hadn't left him since the adventures in Anica's keep. Focusing on that power, Sindri wiggled his fingers in the direction of the wagon driver's wide-brimmed hat, which was set on the seat next to the man.

The hat popped up from beside the driver and fluttered in the air, bits of golden magic sparkling around its edges. As the driver sputtered in surprise, the hat spun in figure eights around his head and between the oblivious horses before it fluttered into an apple tree off the path, knocked an apple inside, and then twitted back to the driver.

"I thought you might like a snack," Sindri said with a grin.

The driver looked up at Sindri, his jaw slack. Sindri smiled wider and gestured for the man to take the apple out of his hat.

Grabbing the apple, the driver muttered a quick thank you, then plopped the hat firmly on his head and resumed his course.

Sindri fell back atop the wagon, arms outstretched. The edges of his purple cloak fluttered in the wind. Above him the sky was a clear robin's egg blue, and the unfiltered sun warmed him from his pointed ears all the way down to his toes.

Sindri couldn't help but laugh. The spell had of course been simple—he figured all he did was move the air around the hat to make it dance the way it did—but how many times had he heard over the years that same irritating phrase, "kender can't do magic"?

But he *could* do magic. And not only that, according to lost lore that he and his companions had recently discovered, Sindri's magic was a resurgence of an old magic that had long died out, one that wasn't reliant on the whims of moon gods.

He didn't have to remember magic words if he didn't want to, or use spell components, or lose energy when he cast his magic. The old power welled from within him, always ready to be tapped for anything from the smallest cantrip to the biggest defensive spell he could think of.

And only he had the power. He, a kender. A kender wizard. *The* kender wizard!

A gentle knock sounded from inside the wagon. Wood scraped against wood as a small window behind the driver opened. Then came the sound of someone muttering instructions, and moments later the clomping of the horses' hooves slowed and the wagon jolted to a stop.

Sindri sat up and again looked over at the trees of the Kenderwood. Home was so close, and so was the final leg of his journey.

The wagon's door opened and Tayt stepped out, stretching and breathing deeply. The short girl adjusted her pack over her shoulders and headed toward the trees where Sindri had magically plucked the apple.

Sindri gripped the edges of the wagon's roof and leaped down to follow Tayt. But just underneath him, another person emerged. Wilden wasn't prepared in the least as Sindri landed on his back with a heavy thud, and the two fell to the dirt.

"Oh!" Sindri said, leaping to his feet and dusting off his trousers. "Sorry, Wilden. I didn't see you!"

Flat on his back, Wilden laughed, his long blond hair tousled. "Quite all right, Sindri," he said as he held up a hand. Sindri helped the young man get to his feet. "I was just thinking that I had never had a kender fall on me out of thin air before, and now I'll never be able to say that again."

Sindri laughed as well. "You know, that sounds like something a kender would say."

Wilden grinned and shrugged. "Well, we are heading to the land of the kender. I figure I should practice fitting in."

Brushing off the sleeves of his white shirt, Wilden walked around the front of the wagon to offer his assistance to the driver, who was unhitching the horses.

Sindri looked happily at his friends. Together, he, Wilden, and Tayt had discovered ancient temples that revealed the secrets of Sindri's powers. One temple still remained, and Wilden claimed that he didn't want to travel so far with Sindri and then miss out on the journey's end.

But that didn't seem right, Sindri realized as he watched Wilden lead one of the horses toward a nearby stream. Wilden was a renegade hunter for the Wizards' Conclave and his goal had been very clear: capture Sindri, no matter the cost. Now Wilden had turned his back on the conclave, and he'd even taken to teaching Tayt more about magic than what she'd already picked up on her own.

"I sorry!"

A flash of brown and black fur darted from the wagon's interior, swirled around Sindri's feet, then leaped to his shoulders. Sindri looked to his left to find a small, furry, triangular head peering at him with wide amber eyes.

"What's wrong, Rizzek?" Sindri reached up and patted the furry lizard creature.

Rizzek whimpered, then buried his head in Sindri's cloak. Sindri scratched behind Rizzek's ear and the creature purr-clicked in contentment. His long tail flicked against Sindri's cheek.

"Huh, Rizzek?" Sindri pressed. "What is it?"

A shadow appeared in the wagon's doorway and Sindri frowned.

Maddoc stood there, tall and imposing, his ornate black wizard's robes melding with the shadows in the wagon. The old man's face was tight with irritation, his blue eyes twitching.

"I'm afraid your friend Rizzek disturbed me while I was resting," Maddoc said in his deep, regal voice, his calm tone not revealing any of the annoyance so clear on his face. "I instinctively began to cast a spell. I caught myself, but I'm afraid he was already frightened by that point."

Sindri shrugged and looked away. Tayt and Wilden were laughing with each other next to a stream a little ways off, and he longed to run off and join them.

"Sindri," Maddoc said as he stepped down from the wagon. Sindri looked back to see the wizard wince as though the effort was too much for his old bones. "I have something for you."

Sindri tilted his head. "What is it?"

Reaching into his robes, Maddoc produced the golden dragon scale that Sindri always carried inside his cloak pocket. It was the scale that was given to Sindri by a mysterious benefactor who sent him a map to the first of the ancient temples, and it was one of the keys to the answers Sindri longed to know about his powers.

Sindri patted at the pockets that lined his purple cloak and scowled. "How did you get that?"

Maddoc took a step forward and held the scale close enough that Sindri could grab it. "I found it in the wagon the night before last," the old man said, his face stoic. "It appeared to have fallen from your pocket. I decided to fix it so that you wouldn't lose it again."

Only then did Sindri notice a shimmering band of silver attached to the scale, forming a necklace. Sindri took the scale and hung it around his neck, careful not to disturb Rizzek on his shoulder. The scale sparkled in the bright sunlight.

"Thank you," Sindri muttered.

Before Maddoc could say anything else, Sindri turned and walked off toward Wilden and Tayt. Maddoc grunted behind him, but did not follow.

Sindri absently fingered the golden dragon scale as he stomped through the grass. Sindri had trusted Maddoc as much as he trusted his mother and father, but Maddoc had lied to Sindri, hid what he knew about Sindri's powers. He wanted to trust Maddoc again, but the day rapidly grew close when Sindri would have to have a talk with the old wizard. Though Sindri had never before been unwilling to take on any task, this one he was actually dreading.

Just ahead, there was a splash and Tayt said, "Oh, I did it!"

Sindri plopped down on his knees next to the stream, tilting his head as Tayt laughed and clapped her hands. Disturbed, Rizzek readjusted himself around Sindri's shoulders, but still did not remove his head from the folds of Sindri's purple cloak.

Wilden grinned and slapped Tayt on the back. "Good show!" he said. "You're certainly picking this up fast. A natural, my master would have called you. It's no wonder you managed to teach yourself the spells you did."

Tayt smiled shyly and shrugged. "Yes, well, those spells were easy. And I have a good teacher this time around."

Sindri scooted closer on his knees and tilted his head the other way. "What did Tayt do?"

"Well," Wilden said, "I'd have Tayt show you, but she'll have to restudy the spellbook before she can." He gestured toward his lap at a small leather book open to reveal loopy handwriting scribbled on yellowed pages. "So I'll just show you myself."

Wilden shoved back the sleeves of his white shirt, revealing the magic symbols tattooed in black on his forearms. As Wilden pulled free some spell component from a pouch at his waist, Sindri reminded himself to ask Wilden about the tattoos, which also covered the renegade hunter's chest.

"*Berair dentaya*," Wilden intoned. "*Lingkaran bentuk, namba dalam sentana.*"

As Sindri watched in wonder, part of the rippling stream in front of them grew still. The water bulged up from the stream, and with a *pop*, a large bubble of water rose into the air.

Sunlight reflected off the shimmering water bubble as though it was faceted like a diamond. A dark shape flitted inside the shimmery globe and Sindri laughed when he saw it was a green-scaled trout.

"You caught a fish!" Sindri said. "What a handy trick."

Wilden grinned. "I thought so, yes," he said. A wave of his hand sent the water globe collapsing back into the river, setting the trout free with a splash.

Tayt ran her hand through her close-cropped hair. "Well, it's not exactly a spell that'll get me out of a jam in a hurry," she said, "but it's a start."

Sindri was hardly listening. Instead, he stood and stretched his hands toward the stream before he even thought to do so. Wilden and Tayt's talking and the sound of the horses sipping at the stream faded as the pulsing power in Sindri's stomach coursed to his fingertips.

In a flash, two dozen globes of water burst from the stream. They hovered above it in a long line like a row of pumpkins set out at harvest time. Inside each globe was a trout.

"Neat." Sindri grinned.

Sindri looked over at Wilden and Tayt only to find them looking at the sudden appearance of the globes with concern. Both shook it off as Sindri lowered his hands and the globes landed back in the stream, splashing water droplets on his arms.

"Your powers are growing," Wilden said, almost to himself. He looked away, his blue eyes lost in thought.

Sindri wasn't sure what had bothered the two of them, but he didn't have time to think on it, because Tayt leaned forward and fingered the dragon scale hanging around Sindri's neck.

"Nice," she said. She let go of the scale and reached up to scratch behind Rizzek's ear, which peeked up from beneath Sindri's hood. "Now you won't lose it. When did you make this?"

Sindri scowled despite himself and glanced back over his shoulders. Maddoc stood by himself next to the wagon, looking away from them.

"I didn't," Sindri said quietly, all his worries about Maddoc suddenly crashing down upon him once again. Not waiting for Tayt to respond, he walked over to a nearby apple tree and sat down.

Leaning back against the trunk, he sighed.

Tayt looked at him knowingly, but didn't follow. Instead, she turned back to Wilden and opened her pack. She pulled out a hunk of crusty bread as Wilden thumbed through his self-written spellbook to continue their lessons.

Rizzek purr-clicked and shifted himself on Sindri's shoulders, his tail slapping Sindri in the cheek. Sindri patted the little creature, his eyes on Maddoc over near the wagon.

I'll be home soon, Sindri thought. And then I'll be able to figure everything out.

Sindri's stomach growled and he thought about eating with Wilden and Tayt. One more glance at Maddoc and the hunger immediately went away.

Something moved in the trees near Maddoc, something large and lumbering. Maddoc didn't seem to notice, and Wilden, Tayt, and the wagon driver were busy around the stream.

Sindri tilted his head so that his pointed ears aimed toward the trees. He heard heavy, booted feet clomping through the underbrush—several large people were heading through the forest. As they walked, metal clinked, and Sindri realized that they were wearing armor.

"Oh neat, Rizzek," Sindri whispered. "We have visitors."

That feeling of excitement quickly went away as Sindri caught sight of one of the visitors through the trees. He must have stood seven feet tall, and his chest was as broad as two of the most muscled men Sindri had seen put together. His skin was a sickly greenish yellow and his piecemeal armor was covered in rusty stains. A jagged scar crossed his hideous face, and tusks jutted from his lower lips.

"Ogre," Sindri spat. Ogres—and worse, ogre slavers—lived to the northwest of Kendermore. The vicious brutes rarely bothered the kender, but they'd been known to kill innocent adventurers for absolutely no reason and to kidnap wandering kender for slaves.

The filthy ogre barbarian sniffed at the air. Scrunching his large, bulbous nose, he looked over at Maddoc. "Hey!" he bellowed. "We got us a wizard!"

Everyone turned to stare at the ogre. As they did, the ogre's companions—three other ogres, just as burly and ugly—clomped out of the woods.

The ogre who had spoken curled his scabby lips into a smile. "Now we can have us some fun," he snarled.

Sindri jumped to his feet as Wilden and Tayt abandoned their meal to aid Maddoc. With one look at the ogres, Rizzek yelped and leaped from Sindri's shoulders. He darted behind an apple tree to hide.

Sindri's power boiled inside of him as his companions readied for the forthcoming skirmish. "Yes," he agreed with a grin as he flexed his fingers in anticipation. "This is going to be *loads* of fun."

CHAPTER

2 Up and Away

Wilden had snapped to attention at the sound of the ogre's husky voice. He dropped his spellbook and looked back toward the wagon.

Maddoc stood motionless in the wagon's shade. Standing among the trees in front of the wizard was a burly, hideous ogre.

"Oh great," Tayt said as she shoved the chunk of bread she'd been eating back into her pack. "Can't we ever take a wagon ride without getting attacked by something? First the dark beast, then the tylor, now ogres."

Wilden looked back at her and grinned. "You realize who they're up against, right?"

Tayt looked over at Sindri, and Wilden followed her gaze. The kender's shaggy black hair had fallen in front of his face, but it didn't hide his gleeful smile.

Near Wilden and Tayt by the stream, the wagon driver shouted as the horses reared back, having no doubt caught the ferocious scent of the unbathed ogre.

Wilden looked back at Maddoc, whose flat regard of the ogre barbarian looked very much like boredom. Three more ogres crept from the trees, and the ogre who had spoken grinned wide, making him look a bit like a toad with tusks.

The ogre laughed.

"Come on," Wilden said to Tayt. He leaped to his feet and heard the girl do the same. Sindri didn't seem to be in any rush to help, but Wilden couldn't just stand there and let Maddoc get pummeled.

As he ran from the stream back toward the wagon, Wilden instinctively studied each ogre. The act of doing so had been ingrained in him since he was a child, and the details of each ogre popped out at him in seconds.

The ogre who had spoken stood taller than the other three, and he jutted his chest forward and his arms back as though daring Maddoc to make an act of aggression. His armor was hideous and unkempt, but was more elaborate than those of his fellows. It had shoulders of thick animal fur and a ragged, bloodstained sash that stretched from his shoulder to his waist. His axe was also the biggest, the handle almost as long as Wilden was tall, and with a double-bladed head the size of a wagon wheel.

Clearly, he fancied himself the leader.

Two of the other ogres stood hunched forward, their eyes devoid of thought, their sick smiles revealing rotten teeth. They were more slender than the leader, and both carried chipped swords crisscrossed with spiderweb cracks. In a race where a smattering of brains and some muscle could take you from a grunt to a warlord, these two were clearly little more than lackeys.

The fourth confused Wilden, but just for a moment. He was shorter than the other three, and like the lackeys, he was slender, wore ill-fitting armor, and wielded a barbed mace that had surely seen better days. But his eyes weren't dim—they were sharp and wary, flitting among Maddoc, Wilden, and Tayt curiously. His ears were a bit too perfectly pointed, and Wilden wondered if the ogre had a bit of elf blood in his family line.

Wilden didn't think on it long, as he and Tayt had finally reached Maddoc's side. In the few moments it took for him to run from the stream to the wagon, Wilden had formed a complete plan of attack.

"The leader is cocky," Wilden whispered to Maddoc and Tayt as he leaped into the wagon. "I'll take him out before he expects anything, because if he's prepared he'll be a wall. The lackeys to his left and right will take a moment to realize what happened, and you two can easily disarm them." Wilden started to turn to collect his weapons, then stopped to look back down at Maddoc. "The one in the back is smart. We'll need to save him for last so that we outnumber him."

"What is we got here?" the lead ogre grunted from outside as Wilden leaped to his pack and pulled free his weapons—two hand-held scythes, the crescent blades glitteringly sharp.

"What we have here," Maddoc responded in his cool tone, "are four ogres who might want to continue on their way."

"Is that so?" The ogre snorted and Wilden rolled his eyes. Always so arrogant, these brutes.

"It is," Wilden heard Tayt say. He looked over his shoulder and saw the girl put her hands on her hips and stare at the ogre. "You've stumbled upon a wagon full of powerful wizards. I mean, if I were in your place, I'd turn and run away before I got hurt." She paused, crinkled her nose, then said, "And then I'd go take a bath."

The ogre growled, and Wilden heard one of his companions— likely the one in the back—laugh.

Good, Wilden thought. Keep them distracted.

He twisted his scythes between his fingers, waiting for the right moment. The ogres seemed to be taking their time in making any sort of move, and for all Wilden knew they'd think better of it and move on.

A flash of foresight jolted Wilden, and a vision appeared in his mind of occurrences outside. He saw Sindri floating several feet in the air near the grove of apple trees, something that tended to happen when he tapped his magic for big spells. Rizzek was nowhere in sight, and the wagon driver by the stream was too busy trying to calm the rearing horses to be of any help.

Sindri's expression was part elated, part devious, and Wilden furrowed his brow. He still hadn't had a chance to really, truly take in the information they'd discovered—that Sindri was going to bring about magic that would make the moon gods, wizards, and the Towers of High Sorcery obsolete. The power Sindri wielded was far stronger than Wilden had anticipated from the temple etchings, and Wilden had seen many times that that power could be incredibly deadly. Even spells that would stretch a powerful wizard didn't phase the little kender—like causing a whole river to bend to his will.

Wilden heard a roar in the distance, then the *thunk* of a weapon hitting the hard-packed ground in anger. The vision of Sindri dissipated and Wilden turned back to the doorway to see the lead ogre's shadow looming over Tayt.

"I don't like the way you talk," the ogre grunted. "You know who I am?"

Tayt shrugged.

The ogre let out another guttural roar. "I am—"

Now, Wilden thought.

The spell came to him in a flash, and the words seeped from his lips faster than most people could hear. *"Cepat tanda, perubahan*

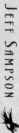

ayun." He focused on his destination, stretched out his arms, and let the magic overtake him.

And Wilden burst apart.

The sensation was so familiar by now that Wilden had almost forgotten what it was like when he'd first been trained to teleport. It was an unusually complicated spell that many wizards had trouble mastering. But Wilden had no trouble remembering the words. His master, Garin, had once told him that his ability to teleport so well was tied into his foresight ability, though Wilden wasn't quite sure how they were related.

The bits of magical energy that comprised Wilden zipped through the air, so fast that no one would be able to see him. Then, with a flash of shadow, he reassembled, the pieces of himself falling back into place with a snap only Wilden could feel. As always, his teeth itched.

He'd transported directly behind the lead ogre. The brute hulked in front of him, oblivious as he shook his axe at Tayt and Maddoc.

"—Magam, battle lord of the Rorgash tribe!" the ogre finished. "And you will show me respect!"

Wilden tried not to gag at the ogre's rotten smell. Tayt hadn't been joking when she said the ogre needed a bath.

"Uh, Magam," one of the ogres behind Wilden said, only just then coming to his senses and realizing someone had teleported directly in front of them.

"What!" Magam bellowed.

Wilden tapped the ogre on his shoulder, and Magam turned around, sneering.

"Hello," Wilden said and nodded sociably.

"How did—" Magam started to say.

Wilden didn't let him finish. With a quick swipe of his scythe the ogre's sash fell free, and with it came the ogre's leather belt. The belt, covered in pouches and knives, landed about the ogre's feet in a heap.

Magam roared and lunged at Wilden, axe held high. Wilden sidestepped the ogre—who promptly stumbled because of the belt around his ankles—then spun around to punch the ogre in the back of his head.

Magam's eyes rolled back into his head. For a moment, he swayed like a sapling caught in a heavy storm. The ogre battle lord's lackeys watched on in dimwitted shock. Magam promptly fell backward. He landed with a clang of metal armor, and his heavy axe thumped beside him. Beyond the fallen ogre, Maddoc and Tayt smirked.

Wilden grinned and eyed the remaining ogre lackeys. "So, who's next?"

The smarter ogre said nothing, choosing instead to step back as his two stupid friends roared and waved their half-destroyed swords in front of their faces. Ogre spittle hit Wilden's cheeks and he grimaced.

Before the ogres could attack, Maddoc and Tayt struck. Maddoc's spell was quick, a flash of red light that burst against the hand of the ogre to Wilden's left, causing the brute to drop his weapon and yelp in pain.

Tayt, meanwhile, leaped forward and slid in the dirt. She hit the ogre to Wilden's right with a sharp kick to a knobbly knee that was stupidly exposed through his armor. As the ogre howled, Tayt leaped to her feet, snatching what appeared to be a coin purse from the ogre's waist. As she deftly pocketed the purse, she twisted behind the ogre, grabbed his wrist, and twisted it until he dropped his sword.

JEFF SAMPSON

Then Tayt swooped down to grab the ogre's sword as she jumped to Wilden's side.

"No magic, Tayt?" Wilden asked.

Tayt raised an eyebrow. "Sometimes a little brute force is easier. Don't you agree?"

Wilden grinned. "Of course."

Maddoc cleared his throat behind them. "Children, if you'd focus?"

Wilden winked at Maddoc, then faced the ogres with his scythes held ready. The smarter ogre crept back even farther, and there was no mistaking the smirk on his face. His two friends, however, loomed over the unconscious form of their leader, their teeth bared as they favored their wounded limbs.

"You no normal wizards," one of the ogres spat. "You die!"

Tayt reached into a pouch at her waist and pulled free a handful of colored sand as Maddoc rustled through his own spell components. Wilden readied himself to attack as soon as both their spells were cast.

"Hey now," Wilden said as the ogres leaped forward. "No need for death to be involved."

"You die," the ogre repeated, "you stupid—"

A thunderous boom echoed between the trees.

The air cracked with the deafening sound, and the ogres stopped ranting as confusion settled in. Wilden spun around. The sound had come from where Sindri was standing, but he couldn't see the little wizard with the wagon in the way.

The earth trembled. Tayt began to fall and Wilden caught her even as he struggled to maintain his own balance. Maddoc clung to the side of the wagon, looking angry.

In an explosion of soil, the ground directly in front of Wilden burst into the air, rising higher and higher into the sky like a massive pillar. The ground atop the pillar was the section of grass and trees upon which the ogres stood. Now those trees, the three lackeys, and the unconscious ogre leader perched on a precariously small island fifty feet in the sky.

Wilden tilted his head back and looked at the newly risen pillar. Roots stuck out from its side, as did the heads of some undoubtedly confused worms. The ogres peered over the side of their little platform in the sky, trembling in fear.

"Huh," Wilden said. "Would you look at that."

"Wow! Did you see that?"

Sindri raced around the side of the wagon, his purple cloak and shaggy hair fluttering behind him. He seemed not the least bit exhausted despite the fact that he had just used quite a bit of magic to bend the shape of the earth to his will. In fact, he seemed more energetic than ever, his violet eyes sparkling with glee.

Sindri skidded to a stop in front of Wilden and Tayt, then gaped up at the massive pillar of earth. Catching sight of the ogres, he waved.

"Hello up there!" he shouted. "Have a good trip?"

The ogres roared and shook their fists, but they were so far up that they seemed about as threatening as a litter of kittens.

"Glad to hear it!" Sindri called, then laughed.

Tayt smiled at Sindri, then shook her head. "You know, every time I think I learn something big about magic, you go and do something like this."

Sindri tilted his head. "But it's neat, right?"

Wilden hooked his scythes on his belt, then patted Sindri on his shoulder. "Neat is one word for it," he said. "Right Maddoc?"

The old wizard didn't answer. Instead, his features unreadable, he

JEFF SAMPSON

turned from Wilden, Sindri, and Tayt and climbed into the wagon. After a moment, he said, "We should continue on if we expect to make it to Kendermore before nightfall."

Sindri scowled and Wilden patted him on his shoulder again. "No worries, Sindri," he said. "You really helped us out, but Maddoc's right. Shall we gather our things and continue?"

Sindri sighed, then shrugged. "We should." He turned to head into the wagon himself, calling over his shoulder, "Hey, Tayt, got anymore food? I'm famished! I've always wondered what it would be like to starve to death, but I'm thinking I should wait awhile before I give it a go."

"Oh," Tayt said, her eyes constantly glancing up at the ogres atop the pillar of earth. "I left my pack at—"

Wilden placed a hand on her shoulder. "I'll get it. You get settled in." Leaning in close to Tayt, he whispered, "And judging by Maddoc's expression, you should try and make sure Maddoc and Sindri don't go off on each other."

Tayt shook her head. "It's going to happen sooner or later," she whispered back. "I really don't trust that man, anyway. Especially not with the way he treats you."

"If I recall, you didn't think you could trust me either."

Tayt rolled her eyes and punched him lightly in the shoulder. "Well, you changed. He hasn't."

Wilden shrugged. "Maybe you can give him some of that steel you stole from the ogre to help him get on his way."

Tayt smiled sheepishly and fingered her pocket. "You saw that?"

"I did."

She shrugged. "Old habit. I'll kick it eventually." She bit her lip in thought. "Well, maybe. Anyway, the pack?"

Wilden stood straight and saluted. "Right away, mistress!"

Tayt rolled her eyes again, then climbed into the wagon.

Wilden looked back up at the ogres high above him. One of them dangled precariously over the edge of their little plot of land in the sky, trying to grab hold of the roots and make his way down. Behind him, the smart-eyed ogre laughed.

Wilden headed back toward the stream. He gathered Tayt's packs as the wagon driver finally calmed down the two horses. As Wilden bent down to pick up his spellbook, he caught sight of a thick and furry tail swaying behind the trunk of an apple tree.

"It's all right, Rizzek," Wilden said. "We're safe now."

With a tiny yowl, the little creature darted from behind the apple tree and raced back toward the wagon. Shaking his head, Wilden leaped across the stream and grabbed the reins of one of the horses.

The wagon driver nodded his thanks, then met Wilden's eyes with a look of awe. He gestured toward the giant pillar of earth that loomed above the wagon. "By Paladine, I've never seen anything like that. It sure is something."

Wilden turned back to look at the pillar of earth and the wagon. He caught sight of Sindri leaning out the window and looking ahead toward Kendermore, none the worse for wear despite his massive spell, and completely dismissive of it as though it were an everyday occurrence.

Sindri's powers were big. Bigger than big. A deep, old urge told Wilden he needed to take Sindri to the conclave to be studied. An even deeper urge told him that it was the last thing he should do.

Wilden shook his head, readjusted his and Tayt's packs over his shoulders, and began to lead the horses back to the wagon.

"Yes," he said at last to the wagon driver's comment. "It sure is something."

CHAPTER

3   WEAVEWILLOW

*S*indri sighed in contentment as he and his companions grew close to the line of trees that were the start of the Kenderwood. Again he sat atop the wagon's roof, and he took a deep breath, pulling in the fruity, earthy scent of the woodland morning.

Several hundred years before, after the lands to the north were destroyed by the gods during the Cataclysm, the kender came from all over Krynn to explore the area that was now known as the Kenderwood. The countryside had once been wide and open, dotted with ruins of human towns and farmland, and the empty homes were just asking to be poked through—and settled in.

As kender legend told it, a kender by the name of Oletta Maplekeys, who had come to live in the far eastern edge of this abandoned land, had one day discovered her pockets overflowing with seeds. No matter how much she emptied her pockets, the seeds kept coming and coming, making her dress rather bulky and heavy. Figuring it best not to be wasteful and throw the seeds away, Oletta decided to donate the seeds to the birds.

Oletta left her home and headed west, tossing the seeds along the 29 ground as she went, not realizing that while the terrible Cataclysm had brought the kender in droves, it had sent most animals fleeing for safer ground. As such, the seeds were not eaten, and eventually they took root. Trees and bushes and vines sprouted from the once fertile farmland soil, and the animals which the seeds were meant to feed slowly began to return.

Thus, the Kenderwood was born.

"Oh, it's beautiful here."

Sindri looked over the side of the wagon and saw that Tayt had peeked her head out. "Isn't it?" he said. "It's not as stuffy or overgrown as the woods back west in Solamnia, so there's lots of room to run around. There are no woods like the Kenderwood, I've always said."

Tayt laughed. "I have never once heard you say that."

Sindri thought for a moment, then said, "Well, I'm pretty certain I thought it."

The wagon driver followed the looping path through the trees that led through the center of the Kenderwood to the main city of Kendermore. Sindri and his companions were headed to a town that had sprouted up not too far from the main city—the town in which Sindri grew up, Weavewillow.

They trotted through the woods at top speed all through the day. Sindri lay on his back, smiling in contentment as they passed willow trees with long branches that flowed like curtains in a breeze, thin white birches with black leopardlike markings, and an apple orchard in the middle of which sat a stone cottage. Ferns and bushes sprouted between the trees—the bloodberries upon them sadly not yet ripe—as squirrels and birds darted among the branches of the sparse canopy above.

They passed a few kender towns as they made their way

through the woods, and Sindri waved at the little kender children who ran up to watch the wagon pass. They stopped for lunch in a small clearing dotted with white petunias and poppies the color of raspberries. While Sindri, Tayt, Wilden, and the wagon driver had a bit of a picnic, Maddoc chose to eat alone inside the wagon.

Sindri hadn't spoken to the man since the fight with the ogres. Maddoc had tried to say something about the spell Sindri had cast, find out from Sindri how he'd done it, but Sindri had changed the subject and spoken with Tayt instead. Maddoc, being Maddoc, scowled and grew silent.

Lunch finished, the companions rode forward. As early afternoon hit and butterflies began to dart through the trees, Sindri saw wooden palisades surrounding another kender town. Rising above the palisades was a tower with five other towers hanging off of it—Weavewillow's town hall.

"We're here!" Sindri called down, practically shaking with glee. He leaned over the front of the wagon. "Hey, we're here, stop the horses!"

"Whoa there," the wagon driver called as he pulled back on his reins. The horses reared their heads as they clomped to a stop, the wagon slowing behind it. Sindri leaped down from the roof and landed with a thump next to the driver on his perch.

The driver started in surprise, and Sindri gave him a bow. "Thank you for the trip," Sindri said as he stood back up. "For some reason, no one else in Alek-Khan wanted to give us a ride here."

The driver cast a nervous glance toward the wide open gates of Weavewillow. "No offense, but if the pay wasn't so good, then I probably would have declined too. Last time I gave a ride to kender, they somehow managed to steal two of the wheels off my wagon and replace them with a dinner platter and a blacksmith's anvil."

Sindri waved a hand. "Oh, I'm sure those other wheels just got lost," he said. "But it's a good thing those kender found something to fix the wagon with!"

The driver shook his head. "Sure, sure," he muttered.

Sindri leaped down to the ground to find Wilden, Tayt, and Maddoc standing in front of the open wagon door, Rizzek darting between their feet. Wilden and Tayt both had all of their traveling gear, though strangely, Maddoc held only Sindri's pack and hoopak.

"This is where you grew up?" Tayt asked as she looked over the town. "How come that building is missing a wall?"

Sindri took his belongings from Maddoc's outstretched hands, not meeting the old wizard's eyes. To Tayt he said, "Oh, walls often just get in the way, so sometimes we just don't put them up at all. Makes it easier to get around."

Wilden laughed. "Sindri, I never knew any kender before I met you," he said, "and so I never knew if all the stories about kender were true. I'm glad to see that some of them are."

Sindri bounced around to face the gates. "Well, come on!" he said. "Let's go! Mother will be so glad to see us."

With Rizzek scrambling at his feet and Wilden and Tayt behind him, Sindri headed toward the wide open gates that led to the cobblestone streets of Weavewillow. Only after Sindri was partway there did he realize Maddoc hadn't followed.

Sindri turned back and gave Maddoc a questioning look. "Are you coming?" he called.

Maddoc stood with his arms crossed, eyes narrowed, and lips pursed. "I have paid this driver to take me into Kendermore so that I can find a place to gather my thoughts," he called back. "I

32

JEFF SAMPSON

do not believe I would fit in at your homecoming. I will find you tomorrow."

Sindri shrugged. "Oh. All right."

Without another word, Sindri turned and continued his course to Weavewillow's gates. Wilden quickened his pace to come to Sindri's side.

"Maddoc isn't coming with?" Wilden asked.

Sindri shrugged again. "I suppose not," he said. He didn't want to discuss it. Maddoc had seemed angry with him ever since the spell back with the ogres and Sindri's subsequent refusal to talk about it. He didn't want to worry about the shady old wizard now, not when he was home. But despite himself, Maddoc's lies would not leave Sindri's thoughts.

Sindri, Wilden, Tayt, and Rizzek reached the gates to find the lone guard sitting in the grass and leaning back against the wooden wall that surrounded the town. He'd flopped his topknot over so that his hair covered his face, and he appeared to be sleeping.

Sindri chuckled. "Some things never change," he said.

Rizzek darted ahead of the group, his muzzle pointed up as he sniffed the scents of the city—sweet rolls baking for dessert, meat roasting in fire pits.

"Food here," Rizzek rasped. "I get food!" With a happy little yowl, the small creature darted through the kender that milled in the stone paved courtyard of the town and into the row of stalls where kender sold their wares.

Rizzek zipped between the legs of one kender woman who was browsing the stalls. She was dressed in poofy blue trousers and a billowy orange shirt, a pair of goggles resting comfortably atop her head. Her golden topknot cascaded down her back, a curl at its end.

"Aunt Moonbeam!" Sindri called as he recognized her.

Aunt Moonbeam shaded her face with her hand and squinted as she peered between the milling kender shoppers. With a gasp, she jumped and clapped her hands. "Sindri! You've come home!"

"Sindri?" another voice called, a sweet voice Sindri recognized immediately.

"Mother!" Sindri cried. He turned to see her holding up the hem of her yellow dress as she darted across the courtyard, other kender laughing and ducking out of her way. Sindri dropped his hoopak and pack and raced to meet her as Wilden and Tayt looked on with smiles.

Sindri grabbed his mother in an embrace, and they laughed and hugged for a long time. Sindri never wanted to let go. He hadn't realized how much he'd missed her.

Sindri pulled back, holding his mother at arm's length to look her over. She was the same as he'd left her, right down to the yellow dress, though there now seemed to be a few extra silver hairs in her dark brown topknot. She smiled so wide that wrinkles creased around her violet eyes.

"Sindri, I don't know what to say," she said. "I never expected you here. I thought you were out adventuring still! I want to hear everything that's happened, and—"

She didn't get a chance to finish, for at that moment Aunt Moonbeam barreled into Sindri so hard that he would have fallen if she hadn't simultaneously caught him up in a bear hug.

The stout woman lifted Sindri from his feet and practically shook him, she hugged him so fiercely. Finally she dropped him and Sindri laughed.

Aunt Moonbeam put her hands on her hips and gave Sindri a once over. "Still insisting on wearing your hair like that, I see!"

she said. "But by the looks of you, you've had yourself a lot of traveling." She elbowed Sindri's mother. "I always told you he was a boy after my own heart. Just like his father."

Sindri's father, who was Aunt Moonbeam's brother, had stayed in Weavewillow only long enough to help bring Sindri into the world before his eternal case of wanderlust sent him out into the world again. He hadn't forgotten his family back home, though, and over the years he'd sent Sindri all sorts of letters and souvenirs from the exotic locales to which he'd traveled. Sindri had only vague memories of his father from when he was younger, the most vivid of which was his father regaling him with a tale about a king and a pig, but he was sure they'd cross paths again one day.

"Did you get my book, Aunt Moonbeam?" Sindri asked with a tilted head.

Aunt Moonbeam shuffled in close as other kender started to crowd around, drawn by the commotion. "I did indeed," she said. "Dragons! Why, as soon as I got that I wanted to head to the nearest lair I could find. If it weren't for this blasted bum knee of mine—"

Sindri patted her shoulder. "You'll get to see them, I'm sure of it. No one adventures better than you!"

"Oh Sindri," his mother said even as muttering kender shoved up behind her. "We really should talk, I—"

"Sindri, my boy!" The voice boomed across the town square and kender were positively tossed in the air as an old, bald kender huddled over a cane shoved past them.

"Grandfather Hephdeezee!" Sindri cried. "Oh, I haven't heard your stories in years." Sindri began to bounce on his toes, looking over the crowd of mingling kender. "And I need to see Grandmother Trumbauer and Uncle Turtledove and Jandy and, wow, there are so many people here, and hey! Those are my friends!"

Everyone turned as Sindri pointed across the now crowded town square to Wilden and Tayt. They stuck out like maple trees in a carrot field, positively towering over the diminutive kender. They waved shyly.

"Tayt! Wilden! This is my family!" Sindri shouted, pointing to his mother. "My mother, Senna Suncatcher, my aunt—"

"Ah ha!" Grandfather Hephdeezee interrupted as he looked up at Sindri's friends. "Wizards, by the looks of 'em. But from what we've heard, you're on your way to being the greatest kender wizard since your Great-Great-Great-Great-Great-Great-Great-Great-Uncle Mildred."

"Oh!" someone called from the crowd. "The wizard has come home!"

Other kender started calling the same thing, and Sindri spun around to take it all in, giving up on the long-distance introductions. Though he recognized many faces in the crowd, Weavewillow was still a rather large town, as kender towns went. He expected his family to be excited to see him, but it seemed the whole town had heard of his exploits.

"You know what this calls for?" Aunt Moonbeam shouted, her hands on her hips. "A party! The biggest homecoming party the Kenderwood has ever seen!"

The kender whooped and laughed, since even if they didn't know Sindri, everyone enjoyed a good celebration, and Aunt Moonbeam shoved through the crowd to get her party started. Sindri vaguely saw some kender darting out of the gates shouting about a party as they ran down the road toward Kendermore, but he was quickly distracted by kender shaking his hand and shouting questions at him.

Sindri looked at his smiling mother and then over at his overwhelmed friends. Troubles with Maddoc or not, this was turning out to be the best day he'd had in a long while.

It was many hours later, and golden afternoon had settled over Weavewillow. The party had begun almost immediately, with drinks and food passing from kender to kender as everyone enjoyed the thrill of the impromptu celebration. At the crowd's request, Sindri had stood on a stage that was hastily created out of several empty crates and regaled everyone with the tales of his adventures. He leaped and flung his cape and, as the big finish, cast a spell that made dots of light appear all around the darkening street.

Grandfather Hephdeezee took over the telling of tales as Sindri was passed from relative to acquaintance and back again, answering the same question hundreds of different ways and enjoying every minute of it. Tayt and Wilden, meanwhile, sat as near to the crate stage as possible, eating roast beast and laughing at Grandfather's expertly told tales. Rizzek darted around them, the energy of the festivities affecting even him.

As Grandfather Hephdeezee bellowed out another rousing tale and the last relative shook Sindri's hand (Aunt Trutkoff, who was known for her viselike grip and as such was always asked to shake hands last), Senna pulled Sindri away from the crowd.

"Where are we going?" Sindri asked.

Senna turned to look back at him, proud tears welling in her violet eyes as her lined face creased into a broad smile.

"Oh Sindri, I just wanted some time with you all to myself," she said. "It's been so long since we've seen each other, and look at you now." She reached out and tousled his long, shaggy hair. "All grown up, and a wizard! I knew you'd do it, Sindri."

Sindri beamed. "You always said I would. And you were always right."

Sindri's mother took in a deep, happy breath, shaking her head slightly as she looked over Sindri. Then, regaining her composure, she smoothed out her dress and turned to lead Sindri back to their home.

The sounds of the kender's laughter at Grandfather's story and the delighted shrieks as games were played faded away as Sindri and his mother walked around Old Thessily Milkweed's general store and headed back to where a row of small cottages sat between the trees.

Sindri's home hadn't changed a bit. The picket fence that surrounded their yard was still pristinely white, and the gate was wide open, as any proper gate should be. The entire front yard was alive with color—tall and leafy plants with juicy red tomatoes and bright green peapods dangling from their ends, trees dotted with fat purple cherries that had yet to fall, rows of bushes glistening with all sorts of berries, mounds of plump yellow mushrooms of varying sizes. His mother's garden had never looked better.

"You remember that plot, don't you?" Senna said, gesturing toward a little empty spot of earth as the two of them walked across the cobblestone path to the cottage's doorless entry.

Sindri looked down and saw that the empty spot was not that empty at all—a square-cut stone sat there, with words chipped into it.

"I do!" Sindri said. "That's where you had the vision of me being a wizard while you were planting carrots."

Sindri's mother nodded. "You should have seen how many people

JEFF SAMPSON

came to see that little bit of dirt when Aunt Moonbeam got your latest letter and your book."

Sindri laughed, then crouched down next to the stone. It read:

> *There once was a kender named Suncatcher*
> *Who was the greatest wizard on Krynn.*
> *But many years have passed,*
> *Something something something-ast,*
> *And he was all but forgotten.*
>
> *But here in this spot,*
> *A vision was got,*
> *That the Suncatcher wizard would rise again!*

Sindri laughed and clapped his hands. "That's neat!" he said. "Who made that up?"

"You remember your friend Niblet Trunkthumper?"

Sindri nodded. "Good old Nibbles! He never was much of a poet."

Sindri's mother kneeled down and brushed dirt off the engraved stone. "Well, Nibbles has been traveling around with a band of gnomes and a half-elf bard, and let me tell you, that was the most fascinating group I ever did see. The elf sang beautifully and the gnomes played these massive musical contraptions that looked a bit like shells on wheels covered with all sorts of tubes and boilers."

Sindri's mother stood and brushed off her skirt. "Anyway, they visited to give us a show, and I told them all about you and the vision I had about you being a wizard, and Nibbles made up that little ditty on the spot. Grandpa Rex had it engraved on that stone, and we made sure to firmly plant it in the ground so it wouldn't get lost."

Sindri shook his head, a smile on his face. "Wow, that is amazing," he said. "I never knew a gnome bard, though I did know a gnome *Barb* once. I'd like to see Nibbles and his group sometime." He looked down at the stone again. "And the song is great too. I'll have to make a rubbing of it later to carry around with me."

"Of course!" Senna grabbed Sindri's hand. "Now, let's get inside so we can talk! I want to hear all about your adventures!"

Sindri tilted his head. "Even the ones I already told everyone?"

"All of them!"

She dragged Sindri into the cottage before he even realized they were moving. He took in a breath, as for the first time in years, he saw the inside of his home. It wasn't a bit like the last time he'd seen it—all of the knickknacks were different, as were the tables and chairs and lamps. The last rug in the living room had been a woven wool rug with a fish design, and now there were several circular rugs that were painted brown and red.

The only things that had remained the same were the smell of lilies that never seemed to leave the house and the stone fireplace, since it was a bit difficult to move. Though, now that Sindri looked closely, there did seem to be a few stones missing.

"The furniture switched itself again, I see!" Sindri leaned his hoopak staff against a plush armchair, then plopped atop the seat. Something seemed a little strange about the seams of the chair—they appeared to have once had buttons on them, though the buttons were now gone.

Senna busied herself in the kitchen, preparing tea. "Well, it all just disappeared over time. But I always seem to find replacements, so I'm never without a place to sit!"

She bustled back into the living room with a little tray, atop which was a spindly vase and two brandy snifters.

"The tea set disappeared too," she said as she set the tray on a low table in front of the fireplace. She sat down and poured tea into their glasses from the vase. "Now, tell me your stories!"

Sindri started from the beginning with his adventures with Catriona and the minotaur Jax, who insisted Sindri had stolen his coin purse (though Sindri had only conjured one of his own). He quickly moved on to the battle with the green dragon Slean at the Temple of the Holy Order of the Stars, then regaled her with the fascinating story of the haunted kingdom of Arngrim.

Then came the part about the dragon well and the spirit dragon that had given Sindri a gift, and all of the business with Asvoria, including his side trip to the wizard school in Palanthas.

Sindri finished the thrilling tale of Elidor's flight from an undead king of thieves and started in on his discovery of the Temples of the Sun, when his mother interrupted him.

"Oh," she said, "I think you missed a part."

Sindri took a sip of his tea. It smelled flowery, like roses, but had a nice bitter edge to it that Sindri found quite tasty. "Did I?"

"Well, weren't you staying with a wizard named Maddoc for many months?" she asked. "As his apprentice?"

Sindri swallowed and looked down. "Well . . ."

Sindri's mother leaped to her feet, her yellow dress flouncing around her feet. "You know, I'm sure of it. It's in your book!"

She dug into the pockets on the front of her dress, pulling out and tossing aside a deck of playing cards, a spool of thread, a bag of marbles, three gold-plated butter knives, and a brass figurine of a monkey reading a book before she finally found what she was looking for—a hammer with a clawed end.

"Aha," she said. "This'll do."

Sindri twisted in his chair and watched as she went to the wall behind him. He hadn't noticed it before, but hanging from the wall with a rather large nail pounded through it was a leather-bound book with a painting of a green dragon on its cover, titled *A Practical Guide to Dragons*.

"Hey!" Sindri said. "That's the book I sent Aunt Moonbeam. How did you get it?"

"I'm not sure," she said with a shrug that sent her gray-streaked topknot bobbing. "Moonbeam lost it, and one day it just appeared under the mattress of my bed. I figured it was best to nail it down so it wouldn't get lost again."

Tongue between her teeth and one leg propped against the wall for leverage, Sindri's mother hooked the clawed end of the hammer around the nail and tugged with all her might. The nail pulled free and flew across the room to clatter against the opposite wall, and Senna snatched the book before it could fall to the ground.

"Here we are," she said as she came back around Sindri's chair with the book hugged in both arms. She shooed him over with her fingers, then plopped into the armchair next to him. Flipping through the book's pages, she said, "Let's see . . . ah, here it is, your aunt pasted your letter in the front of the book. It says right here, 'I've met a wizard named Maddoc who has agreed to teach me everything he knows.' And you talk all about what you learned from Maddoc in your notes throughout the book!"

Sindri took a sip of his tea and tried very hard not to look sullen at the mention of Maddoc's name. He'd *accidentally* left out mentions of the wizard when telling his tales, if only because he wanted to avoid thinking about the old man's intentions, at least for the day.

JEFF SAMPSON

"Oh, him. Yes, I spent some time with him. Nothing exciting happened." Sindri turned in his chair. "Mother, can I ask you
something?"

She smiled, the edges of her lips and eyes crinkling. "Of course,
my little wizard. As long as it isn't a question about the bathing
habits of ogres, as I've had that question rattling in my head for
many years and not a single ogre I've come across has ever given
me a chance to find out."

"Oh, it's not about ogres," Sindri said. "Though we met some on
the way here and I can tell you they probably don't bathe at all. I
have a friend, and this friend was lied to by another friend that
he thought he could trust. And this friend still wants to trust the
other friend, because he's helped my friend a lot, but he's pretty
sure that the other friend is just using him, though he's too upset
about it to really decide what to do."

Sindri's mother nodded along as she listened, then bit her lip
in thought as Sindri finished. "Well, I've never personally met
anyone I didn't think I could trust," Senna said after a moment.
"In fact, usually I'm the one being accused of lying, though I can't
fathom why. I *am* something of a seeress after all. One would think
I would only tell the truth! But I suppose if your friend feels so
uneasy around someone that he can't talk to his friend about it and
straighten things out, that friend may not be much of a friend to
your friend, and they shouldn't be friends any longer."

Sindri nodded grimly. "That's what I thought."

Sindri's mother didn't hear him. Instead she pointed in the air
and mouthed what she'd just said. "We said a lot of 'friends' there.
I think I may have answered wrong. Oh dear."

Sindri stood from the chair and shook his head. "No, you
answered exactly right," he said as he grabbed his hoopak. Leaning

forward, he gave his mother a hug. "Thanks for your help, Mother. I'll see you later."

Senna tilted her head. "Where are you off to?"

Sounds of the town's laughter filtered through the open cottage door while Sindri paused. Then he sighed. "There is someone I need to talk to."

CHAPTER

4   TRANSFORMATION

The Oasis had seen better days.

The keep was a massive structure constructed of blocks of white stone, the lower levels more temple than castle, with flowery pillars in place of walls.

The keep was located behind a tall, cracked wall of white sandstone, deep in a thick jungle of a desert oasis. It may have once been well tended, this keep, but now vines had begun to overtake the walls. A once beautiful fountain was broken in two, water trickling from its base. Frames and artifacts were stripped of their precious metal and gems, and vases and dead plants lay scattered across the tiled floor.

Davyn stood with Rina in the keep entrance. As they watched, a creature that looked like a giant earthworm slowly pushed its way through a curtain of vines that divided the rooms, lowered its featureless head to study the fountain's small stream of water, then continued on its way.

"Two keeps destroyed in as many months," Rina said. "Sindri has been busy."

Davyn looked over at the elf girl and couldn't help but smile. **45**

She grinned back, and again Davyn realized just how beautiful Rina was.

Davyn turned back to the keep. "I would say that, yes. I just hope we find him before . . ." Lowering his voice, he gestured over his shoulder. "Before they do."

They both glanced back to see the white-robed wizard and the black-clad and silent bodyguard that they'd accompanied here. Garin, a member of the Wizards' Conclave, and his renegade hunter.

Davyn hadn't expected anything good to come of Sindri's time with Maddoc, but he certainly hadn't expected *this*. He and Sindri had gone their separate ways a year ago, after they'd fought and destroyed their original foe, an evil and ancient sorceress named Asvoria. Sindri had proclaimed his intention to become Maddoc's apprentice, and Davyn had gone on to other adventures while helping their friends Nearra and Jirah break a family curse.

With that quest over, Davyn had planned only to stop by Cairngorn Keep to show Rina where he'd grown up, and also to check in with Sindri and see how the kender was doing. After that he was going to go visit his adopted blood brother—Rina's real brother—Elidor, whom Rina had heard was now living in the wasteland of Khur.

Of course, as Davyn had learned many times in his life, nothing was ever that simple. He should have expected to find Cairngorn Keep destroyed and Sindri and Maddoc off on some trip to the other side of the continent—and with the Wizards' Conclave and who knew who else on their heels.

But he *hadn't* expected it. Worried about Sindri's fate and about the possibility that Maddoc was somehow involved, he'd asked to come with Garin to search for Sindri.

Davyn studied the old wizard. Though they'd traveled far, the aging man's robes were as pristine as ever, the unfiltered sunlight reflecting from its silvery hems. Garin studied the walls of the keep, one hand rubbing a wrinkled chin that seemed eternally dotted with gray stubble.

Garin had been relatively tight-lipped during their trip, and the renegade hunter seemed to be mute as far as Davyn could tell, so Davyn wasn't entirely sure what they were up to. All he knew was that they needed to find Sindri for some unspecified reason. Having lived with Maddoc for many years and knowing all about the Wizards' Conclave, Davyn was fairly certain that by "find," Garin probably meant "capture." It was all the more reason to not let the wizard and his black-clad companion out of his sight.

"There doesn't seem to be anyone here," Davyn called down the entrance's steps to Garin. "Looks like this place was more or less abandoned."

Garin looked up and smiled. "It would appear that way, yes, and it does match up with what I was sent by the renegade hunter accompanying your friend Sindri."

Rina crossed her arms and tossed her golden curls over her shoulder. "So, the woman who owned this keep, she's supposed to still be here?"

Nodding, Garin climbed the steps to their side. The renegade hunter followed.

"That's right," Garin said. "She apparently kept slaves for many years and performed much dark magic, including going after your friend. Your friend, however, staged an uprising with her slaves and the woman was stripped of her powers."

Davyn turned to look back at the broken fountain. "Anica was her name, right?"

"Correct. Marten is with me to help collect her so that she can stand trial before the Wizards' Conclave for being a renegade magic-user."

The renegade hunter—Marten—stood at Garin's side. His only visible feature was his blue eyes, which revealed no emotion. He nodded ever so slightly at the mention of his name, but made no other move.

At the renegade hunter's waist hung two handheld scythes, their blades shaped like crescent moons. Davyn had admired the weapons when he'd first seen them, but he hadn't seen the renegade hunter use them yet.

Davyn gestured toward the interior of the keep. "We should see if we can find Anica. She was the one who destroyed Cairngorn Keep, the letter said, which means she was after Sindri. You think she can tell us where he's gone?"

Garin smiled as he stepped between Davyn and Rina to enter the keep. "That would be the plan, son."

Garin walked past the fountain with Marten at his side. Davyn grabbed the hilt of his sword as he watched them walk toward a spiraling staircase that led to the upper floors.

Rina lowered her head and whispered, "You don't trust them?"

Davyn shook his head and scowled. "It's this whole situation I don't trust. Garin only tells us bits and pieces about what's going on. Maybe it's because that's all he knows, or maybe it's because it's all he wants us to know. Better to be safe than to be too trusting."

Rina raised an eyebrow. "Oh, you're only saying that because he's a wizard."

Davyn scowled further. "Am not."

"Yes, you definitely are. You have a vendetta against wizards."

Davyn thought about it for a moment, then shrugged. "All right, yes, that's true. Can you blame me?"

Rina unhooked the decorative longbow from her shoulder and dramatically unfurled her free hand to gesture toward the retreating figures of Garin and Marten climbing the stairs. "Not at all. Shall we follow?"

Davyn unsheathed his sword. "Of course."

They climbed the white stairs, Rina running her fingers across the green metal railing. Its supports were shaped like leafy vines. The upper story was more traditional than below, since it actually had walls, but it was just as destroyed. Farther down the hall, Garin and the renegade hunter stood at the doorway to a room, looking in curiously.

Davyn and Rina came to their side and looked in. It was a bedroom with the standard affair: canopy bed, small table, open window. A chair sat in the center of the room, severed ropes hanging from its armrests.

"Hmm," Garin muttered. He scratched at his chin.

Rina leaned forward and peered into the room. "Am I missing something?" she asked as she took a tentative step past Davyn to get a better look. "I—"

She started and looked down at the bow clenched in her hand. Davyn couldn't be sure, but he thought the gems at its ends had momentarily flashed a brilliant blue.

Rina's nose scrunched as though she smelled something awful. "Something's not right in here."

Concerned, Davyn, too, stepped forward. The hilt of his sword shivered in his hand and he felt it too—a feeling like something was brushing ever so slightly along his spine, a sense that the corners of the room seemed a little too distant, the angles of the bed not quite right.

Again Garin said, "Hmm." Davyn looked over his shoulder to see the wizard still staring thoughtfully into the room from the doorway. At his side, the renegade hunter had pulled free his blades and held the scythes ready.

Unable to stand the nausea that had begun to tingle in his gut, Davyn gently grabbed Rina's arm and stepped out of the room. Almost immediately the feeling passed.

"What's wrong in there?" Davyn asked.

For a moment, Garin didn't answer. Then, as though hearing the question several moments later, he shot his head toward Davyn, a solemn expression on his face.

"Anica was supposed to be here," he said, "bound with no way to free herself."

Davyn looked at the empty chair in the middle of the room. "They just left her here to starve to death?"

Garin didn't answer, instead turning back to the room. He raised a hand and reached into the doorway. He shuddered.

"There was immense power in this room," he said. "Something I have never experienced before. Anica was not working alone."

Meeting Davyn's eyes, he said, "I don't believe your friend is out of trouble just yet."

Davyn turned to look at Rina. She swallowed, then smiled. Anyone who had just met her would have been distracted by the pure beauty of her smile. Davyn had known her long enough to realize she was nervous.

Davyn took in a breath, then looked back at Garin. "We need to find Anica. Would she have had any way to escape the keep?"

Garin lowered his hand from the doorway. "Not likely. The letter we received said that all of Anica's slaves had left her here, taking with them all the transportation that was available. She was left with some other wizard, a man by the name of Derry, but I was told his magic was so limited that he would be of no help. So no, she wouldn't have starved to death, necessarily, but she wouldn't have been able to leave the Oasis. *Shouldn't* have, at least."

Derry, Davyn thought. Why does that name sound so familiar?

Garin turned abruptly away from the room and walked back toward the spiral staircase that led to the main floor. "No, she and the other wizard must still be here, hiding from us."

Marten followed Garin, silent as a shadow and still prepared for battle. With another look at one another, Davyn and Rina followed as well.

"It looks like you have some idea where they might be," Rina said with a raised eyebrow.

Garin stopped at the top of the stairs and looked back at them. "That I do. Anica was apparently obsessed with something hidden beneath her keep, and it was that which caused her to take slaves and capture your friend Sindri in the first place. Being blinded and mad, I imagine she'd turn to what she longed for. It is the way of some wizards."

Rina raised her other eyebrow. "And what is this thing hidden beneath her keep?"

Garin turned away. "Let us find it and you will see."

The group traveled past overturned chairs and a ransacked kitchen before heading down a long, plain tunnel that led deep under the keep. At the end of the hall lit only by glowing bluish white moss that dangled from lamps along the ceiling was a rusted metal door that opened to reveal a cool, dark, stony tunnel.

Garin led the way through the tunnels almost as though he'd been there before, a ball of light he conjured letting them see where they were going. At first it seemed the tunnels were naturally formed caverns within the same mountain from which Anica's keep was carved, but as they traveled deeper, Davyn saw giant metal gears lying on the floor and pipes that oozed white steam sticking from the wall. Wrenches and other tools lay scattered in piles, as though someone had set about dismantling whatever contraptions had lined these walls but then left them in a hurry.

They seemed to have been walking for an endlessly long time when Rina reached out and grabbed Davyn's shoulder. She stopped, her head tilted toward the direction in which they traveled. With her other slender hand she brushed her golden curls behind her pointed ear so as to hear better.

"Hey," Davyn called out to Garin and the renegade hunter. "Wait a moment."

The two wizards stopped and looked back silently. Rina narrowed her green eyes in confusion.

"What do you hear?" Davyn asked.

Rina shook her head slowly, the look of confusion not leaving her face. "I'm not sure. It sounds sort of like . . . gurgling, I suppose. Like a vat of boiling fat. And there are other sounds too. Like voices, but *not*. And a cracking sound like twigs breaking." She shook her head, her golden hair falling back to cover her ear. "I don't know what it is, but it doesn't sound natural."

Garin scratched his chin and looked ahead. "Anica and the other wizard must be down here. We will approach with caution. Rinalasha, you can see well in this darkness. If I snuff our light, you would be able to lead us, yes?"

Rina seemed taken aback for a moment at the use of her full name. She had of course introduced herself as such, as was only

JEFF SAMPSON

proper for a Silvanesti elf, but to Davyn's ears the name seemed so *formal*. And Rina was anything but formal.

"Yes," Rina said. "You want me to lead us toward the sounds?"

Garin nodded, then looked at Davyn. "You should have your sword ready, Davyn. Marten will have his weapons handy as well. We have no idea what might await us."

Davyn nodded and pulled free his sword. Its overly ornate hilt and blade were dull and ugly, but he'd come to grow fond of the weapon. It didn't hurt that the sword was more than a bit magic.

"Lead the way," Garin said to Rina. Then he waved his hand over the ball of light that had lit their path and said, "*Shirak*."

Darkness flooded over them. Davyn reached forward his free hand and gripped Rina's tunic. He felt a hand grab his belt—Garin or Marten, he wasn't sure—and they started forward.

Davyn didn't like this feeling of being blind, but he trusted Rina. He stood close to her, so close that he could smell the scent of summer blossoms on her hair. He focused on that reassuring smell, trying to disregard the thought that they were heading in pitch black toward something Rina had described as *unnatural*.

It didn't take long for Davyn to hear the sounds as well. There was a sickening gurgling noise, like some beast drowning in a well of viscous fluid. He could also clearly hear the snaps that Rina had described, but they were more like bones breaking than twigs cracking, he thought.

"We're in a cavern now," Rina whispered. Davyn sensed it at the same time she said the words—gone was the oppressive feeling of rock walls closing in on all sides, replaced instead with a feeling of a vast, empty, mysterious place. Rina's whisper echoed farther than it would have in a tunnel.

The sounds were louder here, and Davyn momentarily wondered

if perhaps the noises were of something *eating*. He didn't get to think on it long, for Garin chose that moment to point a finger right next to his face.

"I see a light," the old man said. "Ahead. Rinalasha?"

Davyn heard Rina swallow. "Yes, I see it. There's . . . something next to it."

"Something?" Davyn whispered. "What kind of something?"

Rina only said, "What in E'li's name *is* that?"

Davyn strained his eyes to peer into the darkness. He saw the pinprick of light, which seemed to be coming from a small lamp. But he could see nothing else.

"Rinalasha," Garin whispered. "Can you—"

Light filled the cavern.

Davyn immediately shielded his eyes, blinded by the sudden brightness after traveling through the dark for so long. He held his sword ready as he blinked rapidly, trying to regain his vision.

At first all he saw was the cavern itself, a vast dome-shaped room of sorts that was much larger than he would have thought. Broken statues, surrounded by the picked-clean skeletons of what had once been rather large beasts, littered the floor. Floating in the ceiling was a ball of peat that had been set aflame, filling the room with light as bright as the sun's.

Deeper in the cavern, to Davyn's left, stone pillars rose from the floor like the spines of some massive monster. At the back of the cavern were more pillars that surrounded a dark space he couldn't quite make out. A pair of tall metal doors stood ajar in the center of the row of pillars.

Rina stiffened and in a flash she had her longbow fitted with an arrow. Davyn followed her gaze and only then did he see what she was looking at.

In a back corner of the cavern, sitting on a toppled statue of a person's torso, was an old woman. She was dressed in black robes that were tattered at the edges and muddy. Her face, wrinkled like an apple left out in the sun too long, was curled into a devious smile, and a puff of white curls clung to her aged scalp like a mound of mold.

The woman, who Davyn guessed was Anica, at first appeared to have two blank, black eyes. It didn't take long for Davyn to realize that she in fact did not have eyes at all—just two open, empty sockets.

She held her left hand outstretched, a piece of green and decaying meat dangling from her fingers. Beneath the dangling meat was a giant, pulsing mound of red flesh.

"Hello," the old woman called across the cavern, her tone pleasant and grandmotherly. The disturbing smile did not leave her face as she let the piece of meat fall from her fingers.

A face bulged up from the mound of red flesh, a monstrous face with beady black eyes and jagged yellow teeth. It snarled and spat, then opened its mouth wide to let the piece of meat land inside with a sickening splat. The face—that of a goblin, Davyn realized—gnawed and gnashed on its sickening meal. Around it, arms and legs appeared, clawing at the air. In moments, the creature's meal was finished and the head and limbs disappeared back into the writhing mass of flesh.

"What in the gods' names is *that?*" Davyn whispered.

Garin scratched his chin as the renegade hunter crouched into a fighting position at his side, scythe blades held ready. Garin looked between Anica, who still sat smiling, and the blobby mound of skin.

"I have absolutely no idea," the wizard said after a moment.

The mound shuddered, a small jiggle that quickly grew to a splattery shake. Anica looked down at the mound and clapped her hands.

"Oh good," she said. "So glad you're done gestating, my dear. I just picked the last corpse clean and had nothing left to feed you."

The red, fleshy blob responded by spontaneously sprouting several dozen goblin faces that opened their mouths wide in anguished screams. The mass bubbled and sloshed, then inflated into a lopsided bubble, with jagged limbs poking through it in odd and terrifying angles.

Davyn and his companions could only watch in shock as the fleshy mound doubled in size, its insides containing a hundred or more deformed goblin bodies. Certain it would burst and send gore flying through the air, Davyn prepared to duck.

Instead, the mass stopped growing, looking a bit like a misshapen and giant mushroom that towered over Anica. The faces and the limbs stopped slapping at the air as the goblin heads opened their frightening, jagged mouths as one and whined, a grating, high-pitched sound that set Davyn's teeth on edge.

Then, as fast as Davyn blinked, the fleshy mass collapsed in on itself, compacting and sloshing and squishing together until it suddenly slopped into the shape of a wet, shivering, and naked old man.

The man stood and, as he did, Anica stood as well. The man was short and stout, with a squarish head, jowly cheeks, and small black eyes. Davyn recoiled as he realized that he knew who the mass of goblins had turned into: the Goblin Man, a vile and crazy little wizard who had been an old cohort of Maddoc's.

But that wasn't his real name, of course. His real name was Arvin. Arvin *Derry.*

JEFF SAMPSON

Everyone stared as Arvin blinked his two beady eyes once, twice. He was covered in slime, and he made no effort to hide the fact that he was completely and disgustingly nude. Anica, however, picked up a black robe and tossed it over his shoulders. Davyn noticed for the first time that she never blinked, which made sense, seeing as she didn't have eyes.

"Look, my dear," Anica cooed. "We have *visitors.*"

Arvin blinked again and looked across the cavern at Davyn, Rina, and the two conclave members. He twisted his jowly face into a lecherous smile. "How delightful."

"It appears," Anica said while guiding Arvin toward them, "that there is a white-robed member of the conclave and a renegade hunter here, perhaps to capture us."

Davyn wasn't sure how Anica was able to see them, considering she had no eyes. He wasn't sure he wanted to know.

Arvin shook his head like a dog shedding water, sending little splashes of pale red goo flying from his hair to hit the statues and bones they walked past.

"My my, well that just won't do," Arvin said. "You see, they are also with two young people I'm afraid to say I've met before, and who are cohorts of that Sindri fellow I've vowed to destroy." He tilted his head and grinned even wider, looking more than a little like a toad. "I suppose killing them all would be a good test of my new power. That is, if I don't screw up its use."

Anica laughed. "I suppose it would."

Davyn held his sword ready to slice through the two Black Robes. Out of the corner of his eye he saw the renegade hunter prepare to attack as well. Rina nocked an arrow.

"Run," Garin said between clenched teeth. "Through those metal doors when I say."

"What?" Davyn whispered. Anica and the Goblin Man had stopped to whisper slick spells. "We need to kill them!"

"Run!" Garin shouted. He shoved at Davyn's shoulder, throwing him off balance and into Rina. The renegade hunter did not hesitate in obeying his master and ran past them.

"What are you—" Rina started to say.

Garin ignored her and raised his hands. "*Sintana keclaksin,*" he incanted. "*Min da santek!*" White light flared over his gnarled fingers.

But Davyn didn't have time to see what spell the old White Robe was casting. Instead, he grabbed Rina's hand and raced to follow the renegade hunter as tendrils of black magic burst from the Goblin Man's fingers and spiraled across the room, dissolving everything it touched along the way.

Behind them white light flared and Garin cried out. Rina tried to turn back to help, but Davyn tugged her forward. "Just run," he gasped between breaths.

They leaped over stone statues and wound past skeletal remains, their eyes focused on the metal door. The renegade hunter had just gone through, disappearing into the darkness beyond. Davyn had no idea what was in there, but the back of his neck tingled with the black magic spell that swirled through the cavern, eating everything it passed.

Then, they were through. Davyn skidded to a stop, almost slipping on a small stream that cut through the room they'd entered. Rina tried to regain her composure beside him.

Cackling laughter wafted through the open door and for a moment all Davyn could do was breathe and wait. He had no idea what had just occurred, but what he did know was that the Goblin Man had always been, by his own admission, an inept wizard.

He'd been transformed. And he was after Sindri.

A figure appeared in the doorway and Davyn stiffened, his sword held high and ready to slice down the attacker. But in the blazing orange light that still flared in the cavern, he saw that it was Garin. The old wizard stumbled in, his face scrunched in pain though he did not seem to have any visible wounds.

Marten, the renegade hunter, appeared from the darkness to stand protectively next to Garin. Beyond the injured White Robe, Anica and the Goblin Man strode forward, arm in arm and still smiling.

"Now now, that doesn't seem very fair," the Goblin Man said, then giggled maniacally. "We can't go in there!"

"That's a shame," Rina said from Davyn's side.

"No matter," Anica said. She bowed to Davyn and his companions. "I am sure we will meet again. For now, we have a kender wizard to destroy."

With that, the deformed black-robed duo left the cavern, leaving Davyn cowering with his companions and wondering what, exactly, had just happened.

CHAPTER

5   Parting Ways

Moonshine Pub sat in a corner of Kendermore, between a tower that looked like a lop-sided and much shorter version of the Tower of High Sorcery in Palanthas and a house several stories high that appeared to be abandoned.

Though not many people in the mishmash and haphazard city of Kendermore knew Sindri, the festivities of Weavewillow spread all through the Kenderwood like a wildfire, and now the streets of Kendermore were crowded with revelers clinking drinks and wearing pointed party hats, celebrating as only kender could, all without particularly knowing why.

Because everyone had taken their fun to the streets, the pub was pretty much empty when Sindri finally made his way out of the crowded nighttime alleyways. A few plump and giggly barmaids with kegs hoisted upon their stout shoulders raced from the back-room of the pub, shoved past Sindri, and headed out to keep the partiers soaked in their drinks.

Sindri grinned as he watched the pub's door close behind them.

The sounds of the partiers outside quickly became muffled, but the joyful sound of kender still filled Sindri's ears. It really was good to be home, even if just for a little while.

But Sindri was on a mission—he needed to find Maddoc and speak with him, and he figured the wizard would have retreated someplace quiet. So far Maddoc hadn't been anywhere Sindri had looked—not the library or the arcane trinkets shop or any of the inns. This was his last stop in Kendermore, and then Sindri would have to search elsewhere.

The tiny pub was reminiscent of one Sindri had visited in Ravenscar, a town near Cairngorn Keep. The floors, the walls, and the tables were all crafted from dark wood, and few lamps were lit, causing the corners to fill with shadows.

As far as Sindri could tell, there was only one person in the entire pub, an old kender man behind a bar that ran along the left wall. Though half bald, he still pulled up what little hair he had left into a respectable topknot. Atop his large nose sat a pair of glasses almost as big as his head, the lenses magnifying his eyes so that he resembled an owl.

The bartender nodded sociably as Sindri came close.

"Hello there, young'un," he said, his voice surprisingly high pitched. "Glad you could visit. I thought with all the partying outside I'd have to spend the night by myself, and I was just thinking about how dull that'd be. Care for a drink?"

Sindri climbed onto one of the stools and set his hoopak staff against the bar. Readjusting his purple cloak so that he didn't sit upon it, Sindri shook his head.

"I'm not thirsty, but thank you," he said, then tilted his head. "Is this your place? It's fantastic."

The old kender beamed and stuck his chest out proudly. "It is indeed, and thank you! The name's Macaphee Moonshine, but you can call me Mac—that's what all the regulars do. This here is my life's work." Mac walked around the bar to the nearest table and began to stack the chairs atop it. Sindri twisted in his chair to watch him.

"I remember when I was about your age and got the wanderlust," Mac went on as he quickly dusted off a table and then put another chair atop it. "I always found myself in pubs just like this. I had so many good times in those pubs—winning at drinking games, getting chased around by the bar owners, and clapping along as the drunken brutes threw chairs at one another." Mac sighed, a faraway look in his magnified eyes. "Those were the days, yes sir. We don't get much by way of fights here, of course, but I made it look just like I remembered, for old time's sake."

Sindri propped his elbows on the counter and rested his head in his fists as Mac came back around the bar. "That sounds amazing."

Mac turned away from Sindri to grab a rag from a bucket, then turned back to scrub at the counter. "It was, it was. So . . . ?"

"Sindri. The name's Sindri."

Mac nodded. "So, Sindri, what's your story? Why aren't you out there having a good time? Most of my customers are old folk like me who've long since settled down, but you seem around the age to be out and about exploring the world, if not making a ruckus here in the city."

Sindri leaned back and shrugged. "Oh, I did have fun earlier, and I have been exploring. I got the wanderlust really early—Mother was so proud—and I've been out on the road for a few years now. I've been studying to be a wizard, and—"

"A wizard?" Mac dropped his rag and put his hands on his hips, a smile spreading across his face. "Well, I'll be. You're the kender wizard! I should have guessed it by your funny hair. I've heard all about you!"

"Really?" Sindri smiled.

Mac nodded. "Oh, sure. It was all just rumors, of course, but your family must have been talking about you for months, and everyone tells stories here. Why, a kender wizard! I never thought I'd live to see the day. 'Bout time someone showed those stuffy wizards in Palanthas that we can be just as magical as them."

Sindri laughed. "That's what I always said!"

Picking up his rag, Mac shook his head. "I'll be, the famous kender wizard here in my pub." Resuming his washing, he asked, "So, why is it that you're back home? Shouldn't you be off fighting beasties or taking a magical test at one of those wizard towers?"

Sindri lifted his elbows as Mac washed beneath them. "Well, I'm sort of on a journey right now, actually, and it just happened to take me by the Kenderwood. I think the partying going on here in the city sort of happened when my mother and Aunt Moonbeam and everyone went a little overboard, not that I mind of course, because festivals are always loads of fun. But I sort of have a really important conversation I need to have with someone—my old master—and I haven't been able to find him. I figured he'd be someplace quiet, since he can be a bit stodgy at times, and he does like Solamnian brandy, so—"

"So you ended up here," Mac finished. "You don't suppose that master of yours is the human man in the black robes sitting in the back corner who seemed rather upset when I told him the only brandy I had was not Solamnian?"

Sindri spun in his chair, following the direction Mac had gestured with his eyes. Just as the old bartender had said, hidden in the shadows of a booth in a back corner was Maddoc, nursing a drink.

Sindri swallowed. "Yes," he said. "That would be him."

"Oh, well don't let me keep you," Mac said. "Go on ahead, go have your talk. Just let me know if you need anything."

"All right."

Sindri jumped down from the stool and grabbed his hoopak. With a deep breath, he focused his resolve and marched toward Maddoc.

The old wizard sat hunched behind the table, his knees crowded in close and high—the booth had been made for kender patrons, and the normally regal Maddoc looked awfully funny sitting there. Dark bags hung heavy under his glassy blue eyes, as though he'd been sitting here awake for some time.

Maddoc raised his glass, which contained a brown liquid Sindri guessed was not Solamnian brandy, as if to toast Sindri.

"You managed to tear yourself away from your fans," Maddoc said in his low voice.

Sindri shrugged, then scooted into the booth opposite Maddoc. "Well, yes. I wanted to talk to you."

Maddoc snorted, then took a sip from his glass. "Really? Why, Sindri, so glad to hear you're deigning to speak to me once again."

Sindri scowled as Maddoc set the glass on the table. The old wizard pulled his gloved hands back, his left hand fingering the right.

"Things aren't very right, Maddoc," Sindri said quietly, figuring he should just dive in and get this over with. "I thought I could trust you but . . . I don't think I can."

Again Maddoc snorted, but he said nothing.

Sindri swallowed. "When Asvoria took your powers, and you said you'd help me learn magic, everyone told me to be careful. They all figured you were out for something from me, but I didn't believe them. I thought you actually liked me."

"I do," Maddoc said.

"Well," Sindri continued, "I don't know that. I mean, I thought I did. But you kept things from me, Maddoc. You didn't tell me my magic was something different, and I could have learned so much more if you would have just told me. I thought that's what masters did for their apprentices, taught them how to use the magic that was their very own. That's what Wilden said his masters taught him, and that's what he's teaching Tayt."

"Wilden," Maddoc scoffed, again rubbing at his right hand. "That boy has done more to harm you in recent times than I ever did."

"Maybe," Sindri said. "But he never lied to me about what he planned to do."

Maddoc grabbed his glass and downed the remainder of the brandy. He slammed the glass against the table, then raised a hand. "Bartender, another, if you would."

Sindri looked over at the bar. Mac grinned and waved, then proceeded to pour Maddoc another glass.

"I have dedicated much time to you, Sindri," Maddoc practically spit. Sindri stiffened at the unmistakable sound of anger in his voice. "More time than I have with anything except my studies of Asvoria. I took you in and trained you when no one else would. And now, you pull away and practically ignore my advice. *Now*, when your powers are more unpredictable than ever and you need all the help you can get. I would have made you great!"

"And made yourself greater in the process, right?" Sindri said, feeling the anger rise within him as well. "I guess that's what I always was to you—some sort of experiment. You took me in to study me and make yourself more powerful, just like you tried to resurrect Asvoria to learn her magic, and just like you tried to gain the power of that crown you put on Elidor."

Maddoc waved his hand dismissively. "Is that so wrong, Sindri? Do you not quest for knowledge yourself? Were you not using me as I was using you, to learn magic you could not otherwise have learned yourself?"

"You two having a good time, I hope?" Mac appeared next to the table with Maddoc's new glass of brandy. Sindri fell quiet and looked down.

"Yes," Maddoc said. He grabbed the glass from Mac, then slipped the bartender a steel coin in payment. "Now, if you'll leave us to our conversation . . ."

Mac nodded. "Oh, of course."

When the bartender was gone, Sindri looked up again, a scowl on his face. He felt himself shaking—so much pent up frustration was built within him, mingling with the constant power in his gut, and it felt as though he would burst.

"It's not that you tried to learn from me, Maddoc. I guess I expected that." Sindri fingered the warm, golden dragon scale that dangled from his neck. "It was this scale. This and the map. You said you'd help me examine them, and then you tried to destroy them both. You wanted to keep me from my destiny."

Maddoc took a sip from his glass, then raised one of his bushy eyebrows. "For your own good, Sindri. I did it for your own good."

"Yeah," Sindri said as he let the golden scale drop and thump against his chest. "You already told me that before, that you didn't want me to get hurt. I guess you never thought that lying to me would be the thing that would hurt me the most."

Maddoc sighed, a deep aggravated sigh that shut Sindri out yet again. Closing his eyes, he propped his elbows on the table and steepled his fingers in front of his face.

Sindri's lip trembled as he went on. "I thought you were my

JEFF SAMPSON

friend. I even thought you were part of my family. But my family and friends would never do what you did. Never."

Maddoc did not open his eyes. "I don't suppose anything I say will change your mind?" he said, his voice muffled behind his fingers.

"No," Sindri said. "I don't think it will. I didn't want to believe Tayt or Catriona or anyone else when they said I couldn't trust you. And I felt bad about what happened to Cairngorn Keep. That's why I wanted to travel with you, see if maybe I was wrong, if maybe I could understand you. But I don't think I can, Maddoc."

Lowering his hands, Maddoc opened his bright blue eyes and stared directly into Sindri's own. "The last few months have meant nothing, then? My risking my life to help you on your journey, our battles at Anica's keep, all I have taught you—it means nothing to you?"

Sindri looked down. "Oh, it does," he said. "I really, really, really appreciate it. If it weren't for you and Wilden and Tayt, I don't think I'd have gotten this far." Sindri looked back up and tilted his head. "Thing is, those two are helping me because they want to help *me*. And I'm pretty sure you're helping me only to help *you*."

Silence. Maddoc stared into Sindri's eyes, and Sindri stared right back. He had no idea what Maddoc was thinking. He never knew what Maddoc was thinking. All Sindri knew was that when he used to look at Maddoc's face, he saw a mentor. Now, he wasn't sure what he saw.

"This is it, then," Maddoc said finally, his voice low. "We go our separate ways."

Sindri swallowed, feeling uneasy by how simple it was for Maddoc to agree to this. "Yes," he said. "I think that'd be best for all of us. I'm really sorry about your keep, Maddoc, and you can stay in Weavewillow as long as you want. I don't think Mother would mind. But I need to finish my journey myself."

"You mean," Maddoc drawled, "you need to finish it with only Wilden and Tayt, correct?"

Sindri shrugged. "Well, yes. That's right."

Again they both fell silent. Maddoc steepled his hands in front of his face again, his eyes not leaving Sindri's.

"Well," Sindri said after a moment. "I think I should probably go." He grabbed his hoopak staff and scooted out of the booth. Maddoc watched him silently.

Sindri turned around and met Maddoc's eyes. "I guess if I don't ever see you again, I should say . . . thank you. You really did help me."

"So glad to have been of assistance," Maddoc said, his tone clearly sarcastic.

Sindri shrugged. "Well, I guess despite everything, I don't regret being your apprentice. Just . . . I can't be around you anymore."

Not waiting for a response, Sindri turned and walked away. He wasn't sure how he felt. He thought it'd be like a weight had just fallen from his shoulders, and that he'd feel so light he could practically float without needing to cast a spell first.

Instead, Sindri sort of felt hollow. He'd known a lot of people in his life, and made a lot of friends. Not once had he ever distrusted any of them. Not once had he ever considered telling any of them that he never wanted to see them again.

He didn't like this feeling, not one bit. He knew deep inside that this was the right thing to do, that despite all the good Maddoc had done, something dangerous still lurked in the man.

It didn't make it any easier.

With a wave to Mac as he passed the bar, Sindri opened the door to the pub. The sounds of the rowdy partiers met him in a wave of laughter and conversation. Trying to focus on the path ahead, Sindri dived into the sea of kender and disappeared into the night.

Maddoc watched Sindri go without moving from his rather uncomfortable spot behind the table.

He had expected this for some time. Sindri had grown bold and angry as his new powers took hold. Maddoc immediately recognized the inevitability of this day and the conversation that had just occurred from the moment he learned Sindri had discovered the burned map.

If only Sindri could have waited until they had discovered the last temple before casting Maddoc aside.

With a grunt, Maddoc picked up his drink. His mind was not only on Sindri. He thought back to the ordeal in Anica's keep, to poison-induced hallucinations he had of Sindri's original companions reading to him a list of his sins.

He'd continued to have dreams of those moments, of those five children: Sindri, his adopted son Davyn, the fledgling wizard Nearra, the warrior Catriona, and the elf thief Elidor.

Maddoc never put much stock in destinies. He'd always planned to be the one in control of his path. But it seemed inevitable that one day Maddoc would be tried for whatever crimes those around him felt he had committed. And it was all starting tonight, with Sindri renouncing him for good.

Maddoc thought for a moment, then raised his hands and muttered a few words of magic. The shadows around him twisted and turned, forming into the wispy shape of a falcon with glowing red eyes: the new Shaera, his undead familiar.

The bird hovered in front of Maddoc's face, its black feathers trailing behind it like smoke.

"I need your eyes," Maddoc whispered. "I must know how this plays out. Take wing, Shaera. Follow Sindri."

The bird cheeped, almost sounding like a quiet songbird, then flapped its wispy wings. It flashed through the darkened pub and out through an open window, into the nighttime city filled with unruly kender.

The bartender looked over at Maddoc and tilted his head. "Are you all right there, my good sir?"

Maddoc closed his eyes and leaned back. "Yes," he muttered. "Now, how about another drink?"

CHAPTER

6   Moving On

So that's Kendermore." Tayt craned her head back to take it all in. "Huh."

Wilden looked at her and grinned. "You know, you read so much about the cities on Krynn, but you can never get the full flavor of a place until you actually go there."

Tayt shook her head. "This place has most definitely got flavor."

They'd only seen the city from afar before, as they traveled through the woods to Sindri's village. It was surrounded by a fifty-foot wall, which hardly seemed handy since the massive gates were wide open.

The city sprawled beyond the gates, and it was quite unlike any place Tayt had seen before, if only because it was sort of like *every* place she'd been before—the storefronts, the homes, the streets, they were all mismatched and arranged without any sort of scheme, as though the kender who'd built it had picked their favorite details of the cities they'd traveled to and smashed them all together.

Night had fallen, but the wide stone courtyard beyond the open gates was clogged with kender dancing and singing and telling tales, 71 all at the top of their lungs. Lamps were lit and fireflies darted into the sky, making it seem as though stars were falling. Tayt found it to be oddly pretty, this strange little city filled with kender celebrating for no apparent reason, but the prospect of navigating a sea of kender to find Sindri wasn't exactly the most appealing.

"Do you think that kender really saw Sindri go this way?" Tayt asked Wilden. "I mean, he did seem like he'd had a bit to drink. And his name was *Hinky*. Can someone named Hinky really be all that trustworthy?"

Wilden laughed. "Well, let's give it a shot. This could be fun."

Tayt shook her head. "You are enjoying Kendermore far too much for someone who was supposed to be some wizard warrior."

Wilden shrugged as he strode toward the wide open gates and the throng of kender. "What can I say?" he called over his shoulder. "I've always had a soft spot for the underdog."

Tayt smiled to herself, then followed. It was funny how life worked out, she thought. From what she'd heard, renegade hunters were supposed to be completely devoted to the conclave and their duty. Having a soft spot for anything was probably frowned upon.

But Wilden had never really seemed like a normal renegade hunter, not even when he was following his duty. She wondered how he'd managed to end up with the job in the first place, then decided maybe it wasn't her business. He was helping her and Sindri, and that's all that mattered for now.

The roar of the kender crowd took over Tayt's ears as they grew close, making it impossible to hear anything else Wilden might have said. The gates opened to a massive town square, and kender dressed in garish clothes all colors of the rainbow were spilling from the gates and onto the tall grass outside. Three young male kender sang a song at the top of their lungs as they walked drunkenly in circles near a guard who was laughing so hard that he was lying on his back, hands clutching his stomach and tears streaming down his face.

Tayt sidestepped a few kender playing a game of cards, then squeezed into the crowd to follow Wilden. The tall man was easy to see, since he towered over the short kender, but actually following him through the throngs proved to be rather difficult. Tayt was bumped around, once so hard that she ran full speed into an old kender woman guzzling purple wine from a goblet bigger than her head. The wine ended up on Tayt's shirt, smelling oddly like soap, and the old kender laughed long and hard.

Tayt grimaced, then looked up to see Wilden waving her forward as he mouthed something she couldn't hear. She nodded and pushed her way through the crowd.

Wilden led her from the well-lit town square toward a side road that looped off around a row of buildings all missing half their walls. There were fewer kender here, and no hanging lamps had been lit so it was a bit darker. Tayt breathed a sigh of relief. The crowd, though amusing at first, was hot and more than a little smelly.

Tayt darted past a group of kender rolling little dice. They'd drawn a pattern of squares on the stone road and were playing some strange combination of games Tayt couldn't make out. When she got to Wilden's side, she wiped her hand across her forehead and flicked off sweat.

"I guess we didn't miss Midsummer's Eve after all," she said, looking over her shoulder at the multicolored scene of revelers. "I know kender are happy-go-lucky, but I've never seen anything like that."

Wilden shook his head, an amused smile on his face. "Midyear Day and Midsummer's Eve won't happen for another few weeks.

I think the celebrating in Sindri's town just sort of spilled over."

Tayt raised her eyebrows. "Wow," was all she could think to say.

Wilden laughed. "Yes. These are interesting folk. It's nice being around a family—extended though it may be—that is as caring and fun as Sindri's."

Tayt looked down at her feet. "Yeah." She thought for a moment, then continued. "I suppose at one time I thought of the other slaves at Anica's keep as something like family, but they were nothing like this. I suppose I didn't really know what a real family might be like, until—"

"Until Sindri." Wilden patted Tayt on her shoulder. "I know what you mean. My parents were never in the picture, though my brother and I were close. We trained together at the conclave since we were very little, but he . . . he died. I always sort of thought of the members of the conclave as my family after that, but after meeting Sindri and you, I'm not so sure. Nothing so far compares to the two of you."

"You're getting mushy," Tayt said, grinning despite herself.

"Well, yes. Sorry. I've been in an odd mood lately." Wilden turned back toward the darkened street. "Back to the task at hand? Let's hope Sindri sticks to the side streets to travel, or we may not find him."

Tayt looked up at a sign dangling from a pole at the street's end. "Cherrystone Boulevard," she read. "Well, let's go."

The road proved to be as loopy and incomprehensible as a small child's scribbled drawings. Tayt and Wilden found themselves rounding a corner only to meet another corner, then a loop, three bridges, and a path that went under a house before continuing on as a road. The designs of the buildings were as inconsistent as the rest of the city, with tiny cottages sitting cozily beside an exact replica of a temple of Mishakal—inexplicably half-built to also resemble a temple to Hiddukel.

The farther along Cherrystone Boulevard they went, the fewer kender they encountered and the more distant the sounds of the partying became. Tayt was fairly certain they couldn't have traveled too far away from the town square, since Kendermore hadn't seemed *that* big, but for all she knew they'd traveled miles along this odd little road.

Wilden stopped and gripped Tayt's shoulder, then pointed down the street. Tayt looked to where he was pointing and saw a kender staring up wistfully at a tall, decrepit house. His purple cloak and shaggy black hair fluttered in the light summer breeze, and the top of his hoopak was lit with magic light.

"Sindri," Tayt said. "Hey, Sindri!"

The kender shook his head then turned to look over at Wilden and Tayt. He smiled and waved.

"We didn't know where you went," Tayt said as she and Wilden came to Sindri's side. "Your grandfather was telling the funniest story about your uncle Wimbogchaser chasing something called, well, a wimbog around the center of Palanthas, and when he was done we looked everywhere and couldn't find you. Your mother said you'd left very suddenly, and then someone else said they'd seen you head this way."

Sindri nodded, then turned back to look at the big old house. "Yes," he said. "I needed to find Maddoc. It was time I had a talk with him."

Nodding knowingly, Wilden kneeled at Sindri's side. "Are you all right?" he asked.

Sindri shrugged. "You know, this is an awful nice house," he said.

"I always imagined myself on the road, but I suppose eventually I'll grow too old to wander and will need to settle down. This seems like a mysterious and creepy enough place for a kender wizard, don't you think?"

Tayt looked over the house. Shutters dangled precariously from its windows, and it seemed the wooden walls were about ready to collapse from rot. "It sure is," she said. "But what happened with Maddoc, Sindri?"

"I just told him everything," Sindri said, then sighed. "I told him how I felt and that I couldn't travel with him anymore. And so he's not coming any farther with us."

Tayt didn't know how to react. It's not like they hadn't expected this, and she had never once trusted Maddoc. In her view, all Black Robes were inherently evil. But she also knew how much Maddoc had meant to Sindri, and she didn't like the idea that the happy little kender wizard was now feeling so bad.

"Well," Wilden said after a moment, "I suppose it needed to be done. So what next, Sindri? Off to find the last temple?"

Sindri looked back up at the dark house. "I suppose," he said. "But I think maybe I'd like to stay here for a little bit. I only just barely got to catch up with Mother, let alone Aunt Moonbeam and Cousin Dorny and Uncle Oliver and, oh, Cousin Phadri too."

"Good idea," Wilden said as he stood to his full height. "That'll give us time to plan. And hey, maybe we'll be around for Midsummer's Eve after all. If it's anything like the impromptu celebrating going on now, I'm sure it's something."

Tayt looked over her shoulder and in the direction of the town square. Even from the darkened crook of Cherrystone Boulevard she could make out the glow of the hanging lamps. She scrunched her eyebrows when she saw several kender had climbed a tower

JEFF SAMPSON

and were now dangling precariously from various buttresses and flagpoles.

"Yeah," Sindri said as Tayt turned back around. "It sure is something!"

"We should head back to Weavewillow before it gets too late." Wilden ran his hands through his hair and looked up at Sindri's house. "And I think this place would be perfect for you when you get older."

Tayt followed their gaze, then narrowed her eyes. A wispy shape fluttered over one of the house's several chimneys.

"It even has giant black birds hovering about," she said. "Maybe a wizard lives here already."

Sindri bit his lip thoughtfully as he, too, looked at the shadowy bird. "I wonder. . . ." he said, then shook his head. "Shall we head home?"

With Sindri leading the way, they headed back down the looping road toward the main gates, none of them giving another thought to the black falcon that quickly drifted away with the wind.

By the time morning came, the impromptu celebration of Sindri's return had finally died down. Tayt was surprised to find the streets of Weavewillow mostly immaculate. She'd expected to see empty cups and streamers littering the cobblestones. It wasn't until Sindri's cousin Dorny ran by with her pockets bulging full of party favors that Tayt realized what had happened to the mess.

Still, Rizzek was able to find many bits of leftover food in the corners of the town as Tayt walked him through the market that morning. Tayt had left Senna's house early, and it was still cool out.

It was strange how she felt that morning. She'd been in many cities, seen many markets. But this was the first time she could remember actually walking through a market with her head held up, not skulking in the shadows waiting to pilfer someone's purse. And it was the first time she didn't feel the blank, black eyes of Anica staring at her from behind every corner.

She took in a deep breath and watched as Rizzek scrabbled at a mound of dirt at the base of a tree, digging to dislodge a biscuit that had somehow been buried there the night before.

This certainly was a great feeling.

That feeling of freedom and cozy welcome lasted for several weeks. Since Anica was destroyed, there really wasn't any hurry to get to the last temple, and none of them felt particularly in any hurry to leave the warmth and joy of the kender village. Sindri, Wilden, Rizzek, and Tayt were bounced back and forth among the households of Sindri's relatives, where they shared their tales around fireplaces and stone mounds, none of which were in quite the same place when Tayt awoke the next morning.

Midyear Day with its firefly collecting and the raucous celebration that was Midsummer's Eve came and went. The end of summer neared, and Tayt found herself sleeping in a mound of down pillows next to a massive hearth in the center of Sindri's cousin Phadri's house. She opened her eyes and stared contentedly at the dying embers of last night's fires. Behind her, something rustled.

"Hey, Tayt, you up?"

Tayt stretched and rolled over to find Sindri standing over her, his pack hanging from his shoulders. He held his hoopak staff up like a walking stick.

"Sort of," she muttered. "You going somewhere?"

Sindri grinned. "We all are. We've stayed with every single one of my relatives, their friends, and their friends' friends, and now I think it's time we finally go find out more about my powers!"

Tayt moaned and scrunched her eyes closed. The pillows were so very comfortable.

Sindri nudged her gently with his boot. "Hey, c'mon, sleepyhead. Wilden's already up."

Tayt grunted and tugged a pillow over her head. "Five minutes," she mumbled.

"Don't make me call Rizzek," Sindri warned.

Tayt grinned under her pillow, but didn't move.

"You asked for it!" Sindri said. "Hey Rizzek!"

Something heavy landed on Tayt's chest and Rizzek's loud howling screamed in her ears.

"Hey!" Tayt called, and she sat up. Rizzek darted from her chest to the floor and ran around, his head tilted back as he continued to yowl at the top of his lungs.

She playfully tossed a pillow at him, which the little creature darted with ease. "All right, all right, I'm up!" she said.

Many hours later, after they'd all bathed and eaten and said their many farewells, Tayt, Sindri, Wilden, and Rizzek found themselves riding out of the northern edge of the Kenderwood, heading toward cliffs that overlooked the Blood Sea of Istar. They passed kender in little huts and on small farms, and an occasional human or two just traveling by as they went. But the farther north they went, the fewer homes they saw. They traveled over rocky ground covered with what little scraggy underbrush had managed to grow here.

Then, after almost a day of travel, they reached the cliffs.

Tayt couldn't help but take in a breath as she saw the ocean. The cliffs hung high above stormy surf that crashed against the jagged boulders below, exploding into waves of white. The sea beyond, though, seemed an endless, calm sheet of deep blue dotted with vessels that looked as small as toys, they were so far away. High above, white seagulls squawked as they soared low looking for food, and the crisp ocean breeze carried the smell of salt and fish to Tayt's nose.

"Oh, this is very, very . . . big," she said. Being so high up, she felt a bit woozy.

"Never seen the ocean before?" Sindri asked her.

Tayt shook her head. "I grew up in the desert, you know, and then I went west. I never made it as far as the ocean."

Sindri looked past her at Wilden. "You neither, Wilden?"

Wilden's gaze was fixed at something beyond the waves, and he shook his head at Sindri's question. "Oh, no," he said. "I mean, yes, of course I have, I'm from Palanthas. I've just never seen. . . ." He pointed.

So overwhelmed by the new sights, Tayt hadn't seen it at first, but the sea wasn't endless blue after all. No, the farther north she looked the more the ocean turned from blue to purple, and then to a deep red. The horizon had a crimson haze, as though the waters churned up flecks of rusty water droplets.

"The Blood Sea," Tayt said. "You don't suppose it's actually . . ." She shuddered.

Rizzek, who sat draped over Sindri's shoulders, yelped. "Blood?" Shaking, he dug his head beneath Sindri's cloak.

Wilden shook his head. "I don't know," he said. "There are stories, of course. Some say it is the blood of everyone killed when Istar was destroyed and overtaken by the ocean. Others say it's nothing more than red soil pulled up by the giant spinning whirlpool."

Tayt shuddered again. "I think I'm going to think it's that."

Sindri leaped forward. "Aw," he said. "That's not interesting at all. Blood of the Cataclysm's victims? Now *that's* the stuff of legends!"

Wilden laughed. "I suppose so."

Tayt shrugged it off, then looked around the cliffs. She saw nothing but a few bushes to their left, and lots of rock. "What do your notes say, Wilden? Do we need to head east or west from here, or what?" she asked. "We can't really go farther north than this."

"Oh," Sindri said, stiffening as he realized something. "Those temples . . . they *were* ancient. You don't suppose this last one might have been farther north and destroyed by the Cataclysm, do you?"

Wilden didn't answer as he pulled out his notes from his pack and looked them over with a grim face.

"Well?" Sindri asked as he bounced from foot to foot.

Wilden's brow furrowed as he looked up from his map and spun around. "Actually, according to this, the temple should be here."

Sindri spun around too. "Where?"

"*Here,*" Wilden repeated. "As in, right at this very spot."

They all looked down at their feet, expecting to see the traces of long faded tile, or perhaps the remains of broken pillars.

Nothing. All Tayt saw were a few pieces of grass and a line of determined ants.

"Hmm," Sindri said as he looked left and right, hands on his hips. "Well, maybe it's underground. The last one was inside a mountain."

Wilden nodded. "Could very well be. Which would mean we need to find a cave."

As one, they leaned over the cliff edge to look for any craggy opening that might be a cliff. Seeing nothing, Sindri leaned back and scanned the cliff. Perking up, he scurried away toward a pair of bushes that looked like the overused bristles of some giant's paintbrush.

"Sindri?" Tayt called. "See something?"

"I think so!" he called. He reached the bushes and attempted to push through them gently—only to find that they moved with ease. Beneath them was a wooden trapdoor.

"Oh neat," Sindri whispered as Wilden and Tayt came up behind him. Tayt clenched her jaw in uncertainty as he grabbed the trapdoor's handle and tugged. With a creak, the trapdoor opened and slammed against the cliff face. Air rushed up at Sindri, blowing back his hair. He blinked twice, then looked down into the darkness. Tayt followed his gaze and saw stairs cut from the stone, leading into darkness below.

Grinning, Sindri spun around toward his friends. "I think I—"

"YOU SHALL NOT PASS."

Tayt spun around and gasped. As she watched, a tornado of clouds and water descended from the sky, twisting and shifting together until it formed into the shape of a giant man. Lightning cracked within its torrential form.

Before anyone could say anything, the giant stormy creature raised a hand and water enveloped them all.

CHAPTER

7 SECURITY

Sindri sputtered as brackish water enveloped his eyes, his nose, his throat. He struggled to keep his head above the sudden torrent of water even as it pushed him backward on the smooth cliff. He flailed, searching for the surface, all thoughts of the temple abandoned in favor of a much more single-minded pursuit: *air.*

The water eased at last, leaving him lying in a puddle between two small boulders. Sindri gulped in a breath before wiping at his face with a soaked sleeve. He caught sight of Wilden farther along the cliff, blond hair straggled and tangled, hands already clasping the handles of his scythes. Above them, the humanoid mass of tremulous fog crackled with lightning.

Coughing, Sindri climbed to his feet. The storm creature raised its arms above its head and opened its mouth in a thunderous roar, lightning zipping to a sky that now roiled with gray clouds. Beyond it, Sindri saw Tayt and Rizzek, disoriented and trying to regain their balance. Before they could move, the storm giant lowered one of its swirling hands and blasted a bolt of lighting.

"No!" Sindri cried. With a stamp of his foot, magic power jolted **83** from the pit of his gut into the earth. Tayt raised her hands and clenched her eyes just as a wall of stone burst up to shield her. Lightning exploded against it, sending stone shrapnel flying.

"Ha!" Sindri cried with a pump of his fist.

With another booming bellow, the stormy creature turned to face Sindri. Water gushed from its fist with the force of a towering waterfall—and hit Sindri square in his chest.

"Sindri, I—" Wilden called behind him, but the words were quickly overtaken by the roar of the torrential, watery attack.

Sindri could hear nothing, feel nothing but water battering his skin and tugging at his cloak. He sputtered and struggled to stay standing, but it was too much. The water blast shoved him backward toward the cliff's edge, and before Sindri knew what happened, solid ground disappeared and he was falling through the air.

The world became a blur of blue and red ocean, of gray sky, of the rocky cliff as Sindri spun around and around, tumbling toward the jagged rocks below. Sindri's stomach jostled between his legs and his throat, and for a moment he wondered what it might be like to land full force against those rocks before plunging into the frigid white froth of the crashing waves.

Then Sindri saw Wilden spinning above him, his normally calm eyes filled with fear.

Even as the rocks below seemed to rise to impale him, Sindri raised his hands and said, *"Pfeatherfall."*

Air billowed beneath him, as soft and as comfortable as the pillows in Cousin Phadri's home back in Weavewillow. Wilden's ascent slowed as well, and as one they lowered slowly toward the rocks.

Wilden took in a breath, then grinned down at Sindri. "Fast thinking," he said.

Sindri grinned back. "Well, can't afford to think slow when I have a journey to complete."

Above, stone exploded as more lightning flashed. Tayt screamed in anger and Sindri saw a flare of orange light as she cast a fire spell.

"Wilden!" Sindri called as he continued his slow fall, "I'm going to try something. Hang on!" Wilden nodded and braced himself.

Eyes half closed, Sindri held his arms outstretched and willed his magic to leave his fingertips. Beneath them, the raging, crashing waves undulated, rising and falling in a rhythm that started calm but soon grew faster and faster until, in one giant burst, the water churned upward.

It caught Sindri and Wilden from underneath and threw them upward, a geyser of such strength it felt almost solid. Power lanced through Sindri's limbs, interacting with the water, and he felt almost giddy as he and Wilden flew back up over the edge of the cliff and onto solid rock.

"I'll need to do that again sometime," Sindri said as he spun around to take in the scene.

Scythes pulled free, Wilden nodded, his expression all business. "First things first, eh?"

There was no sign of the stormy beast that had appeared, and for a moment the cliff face was silent. Glancing about, Sindri caught sight of Tayt farther inland, where the cliffs met the grasslands and trees. Like Sindri and Wilden, she was soaked, and she hunched over on her knees as though just punched in the gut. A waterlogged Rizzek clung terrified to her pant leg.

Wilden raced toward her, and Sindri was about to do the same when the air charged with electricity and thunderclaps boomed between the sudden formation of dark clouds.

Hair standing on end, Sindri looked up. Wind tugged at his cloak and his soaked shirt, and he blinked as water droplets splashed in his eye. The gray clouds above swirled together faster and faster into a blur, then spiraled down to the cliff between Sindri and his companions. Clouds and water cycloned together, forming once again into the figure of a giant man.

Bright flashes of lightning leaped between the creature's ham-size fists as it swirled to reform, seeming even larger than before. "YOU SHALL NOT PASS," it boomed again, then spun to face Tayt, Wilden, and a cowering Rizzek. In a crackling and blinding white flash, lightning sprung from its fingertips.

The first enormous bolt struck the ground immediately in front of Tayt. She leaped backward, her narrow escape evidenced by the smell of singed grass. A sudden blow to her right side and Tayt cried out as she collided with the muddy earth. She turned to face Wilden, who had knocked her aside in time to avoid being struck by a second and third bolt of the storm giant's lightning.

"Rizzek!" Wilden cried, and the little lizard creature leaped into his arms just as Wilden finished muttering a few spell words. Rock exploded as another bolt of lightning struck. And when the dust settled, Sindri's friends were gone.

"Oh no," Sindri said, unable to look away from the singed grass and stone.

"By the gods, that felt really, really strange," Tayt said from behind him.

Sindri spun around and laughed with relief when he saw that Wilden, Tayt, and Rizzek had reappeared right behind him. Wilden's teleportation spell had come in handy yet again. They sat very near the cliff's edge, the churning sea dark and foreboding beyond them.

"Sindri!" Tayt cried, and he spun just in time to see a flash of lightning zipping toward his face. Then she shouted, *"Tak'kelihatan kendala!"*

The air shimmered in front of Sindri moments before lightning struck, sending up a cascade of sparks. The air cracked and the concussion of the impact sent Sindri sprawling backward, ears ringing.

"What *is* this thing!" Tayt shouted as the stormy creature prepared to throw another bolt of lightning.

"Something created by very powerful magic!" Wilden shouted back over the roar of the creature's surging body. "And something we need to find a way to shield ourselves from—quick!"

Sindri climbed to his feet and grinned. "Leave that up to me."

Again his strange power churned within him. Sindri focused the power into the stone beneath his feet, clenching his jaw and his fists as he willed the stone to move. It did, sending cracks snaking along the cliff top and, as another burst of lightning shot from the cloud creature's fists, a wall of stone rose up to envelope Sindri and his companions.

More explosions, more stones flying. But the wall held.

Sindri gasped from the effort of it, but the exhaustion was momentary. He spun back to his friends. "This won't last long. We need to get rid of that thing. How do you suppose we attack a creature made up of water?"

Another boom as lightning struck the stone wall. Rock crumbled around Sindri's feet as cracks formed in their shield.

"It's water," Wilden said as he absently pet a shivering, frightened Rizzek, whom he still clutched in his arms. "Maybe we can try and dissipate it with a wind spell."

"Oh, steam!" Tayt cried. At her companions' looks, she ran a hand through her water-soaked hair. "Fire, I mean. It's already partly wind. I tried casting a fire spell when you two fell, mainly because it's all that came to mind, but it did make the giant storm monster disappear for a few moments, as though it was frightened. Maybe that's how to get rid of it—we can burn it away."

Sindri grinned at her. "Tayt, you're a genius," he said.

Wilden slapped her on the back. "A genius who has a thing for fire spells, I think."

Another concussion as lightning cracked, and this time, Sindri's stone shield burst apart. Rizzek yowled in fear as Wilden and Tayt ducked.

Sindri only raised his hands and thought: Away.

As though caught in a terrific wind, the bits and pieces of the collapsing stone wall swirled away from the cowering companions to skitter harmlessly across the cliff.

The storm giant raised its swirling fists toward the sky and bellowed.

"Yes, yes, quiet down," Sindri said. Then, raising his hands, he thought: Burn.

The giant's bellow turned into a screech as what passed for its left foot disappeared in a cloud of billowing steam. Sindri willed the golden power within him to churn outward, and the fire continued to climb the giant's leg, producing satisfying steam clouds as it rose upward.

Sindri looked over his shoulder at Tayt and Wilden. "Great idea, Tayt. Got any other ones?"

"Sindri," Wilden said as he and Tayt got to their feet. He pointed at the storm giant.

Sindri followed Wilden's pointed finger. The giant had stopped screaming. Instead, it stood as still as a man-shaped hurricane could while tentacles of water spiraled from its body. They swirled in serpentine shapes toward the billowing flames—engulfing them and smothering them into nothingness. Sindri groaned as the water then coalesced at the giant's empty ankle and within seconds had reformed the missing foot.

"Well, that's just cheating," Tayt grumbled.

Wilden ran past Sindri, racing toward the storm giant while muttering magic words. His scythes glowed red, then white, with heat. As Sindri watched in awe, the renegade hunter leaped atop the nearest boulder, then vaulted into the air. As he ascended within reach of the giant, his scythe blades burst into blue flames.

The giant roared again as Wilden's burning scythes arced into its insubstantial body, leaving a trail of vapor and bursts of water wherever they entered. Turning, the giant leveled another blast of water at Wilden. Wilden landed, muttering more words of magic. Shadow enveloped him and he disappeared just as a burst of water cascaded into the spot where he'd been standing.

Reforming behind the giant's back, Wilden continued his merciless flurry of burning slashes, each bringing a cry of anguish from the storm giant. Sindri scowled—the cries weren't ones of pain, not exactly. They seemed *angry.*

Wilden ascended another boulder and leaped. With a scissoring dual-bladed sweep, he severed the storm giant's right arm from its body, then vaporized a wide gash into its side as he descended back to the ground.

Sindri raised his hands and again thought: Burn. The air around the giant's leg ignited, and white steam again flowed toward the sky.

"NO!" the creature roared, still seeming more angry than in pain. "YOU SHALL NOT PASS!"

Wilden fell back, gasping as he came to stand between Sindri and Tayt. He flipped back his hair, sending water flinging through the air. "Whoever created this thing really knew what they were doing," he said between breaths.

Again the storm giant doused Sindri's magic flames. Sindri noticed, however, that as it reformed the parts of it that had burned away, it grew smaller. Perhaps they—

The giant bellowed a roar that made the ground beneath them tremble. Two other roars echoed from behind them.

Sindri, Wilden, and Tayt spun. The trapdoor that was hidden beneath the false bushes still lay open, and Rizzek had found the wherewithal to scrabble down the steps. Unfortunately for the little creature, the underground entrance was the last place he wanted to be, for descending from the sky on either side of the cavern were another pair of stormy giants, each swirling mass identical to the first.

"Ha!" Sindri said, "Now it's three on three!"

Tayt shot him a look before readying herself next to Wilden for the renewed onslaught. Behind them, the first giant roared again, and the giants flanking the cavern raised their arms.

Sindri took in a deep breath and readied himself for the onslaught of water and lightning.

"Cease!"

The voice echoed from the depths beneath the trapdoor, and with a startled yelp Rizzek leaped from the steps and leaped back to Sindri. As he did, all three storm giants lowered their arms. Their swirling bodies slowed until they drifted away on salt-tinted ocean breezes. Above them, gray clouds dissipated to reveal the sparkling blue sky.

Soaked and confused, Sindri, Wilden, and Tayt lowered their arms and caught their breath.

Steady footsteps clicked from the darkness beneath the trapdoor. They grew steadier and louder as a figure ascended the stone stairs and stepped atop the cliffs.

The figure was that of a man, tall and slender and dressed in fine clothes of orange and yellow silk. His skin was tan, his hair a rich butter yellow, and between his coloring and clothing he appeared to glow golden in the daylight. There was something *off* about his clothes, Sindri realized, as though they were a style long out of date, but the man held himself as though he were a royal.

The man smiled, a wide smile that showed a row of glittering white teeth. "Hello," he said.

Bewildered, Wilden and Tayt said nothing, so Sindri stepped forward and bowed.

"Hello," he said. "And thank you. Were those your cloud monsters?"

The man chuckled, then nodded. "Indeed they were. They aren't actual storm giants, of course. Just my own version." His voice was deep, comforting, and strangely familiar. Sindri was certain he'd heard it before, but he wasn't sure where.

"I'm afraid they got a bit overzealous," the man went on. "But you understand, what lies beneath that trapdoor is not for prying eyes and I need it protected."

Tayt crossed her arms, finally regaining her composure. "Your guards might want to try a warning before they go blasting people off cliffs."

The man shrugged. "They do what they were made to do."

Clipping his scythes to his belt, Wilden stepped forward. "Well, thank you for sending them off," he said as he ran a hand through his sopping hair in a futile attempt to style it. "Might you tell us who you are?"

"Seeing as I live here, that question seems more appropriate coming from me." The man smiled gently. "But since I already know who you are, Wilden, you're spared answering me."

A sudden weight landed on Sindri's shoulder and tiny claws scrabbled at his cheek.

"The man," Rizzek rasped. "It's the man!"

Sindri tilted his head and tried to meet Rizzek's wide amber eyes. "The man? What man?"

"The man!" Rizzek cried, and he leaped from Sindri's shoulders. Darting in circles around the golden man's feet, Rizzek yowled happily. "He gave map and scale. He sent me to warn you!"

"The scale?" Sindri asked, removing the golden scale from the front of his robe. Its damp surface gave off a soft glint in the sunlight.

"Yes, yes, the scale and map!" Rizzek leaped familiarly into the slender man's chest. The man chuckled as he caught Rizzek and then gently placed the wet, furry thing back on the ground.

Sindri stared at the man before beginning his own excited speech. "It's you!" he cried. "You're the one who warned me about Anica, and who sent me to find the temples. But if it was you, then . . . is this the third temple? Who are you? Why did you bring me here?"

"I have many answers for you, Sindri," the man replied with a smile, "though most of them will have to wait for a moment. For now, however, know that my name is Auren." He bowed slightly, one orange-sleeved arm crossing behind his back.

"Nice to meet you, Auren," Sindri said and returned the bow with a flourish of his waterlogged cloak.

Wilden stepped back to gather his pack, which had fallen into a damp mess during the fight. "Well, it seems some of the pieces of this puzzle are finally falling into place," he said as he pulled the pack onto his shoulder.

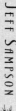

Auren chuckled. "That they are. What say we get you four below. We can speak there."

Tayt shivered and grabbed her own pack. "You wouldn't happen to have a fire for us to warm up by, would you?"

"Even better," Auren said. With a wave of his hand, a gust of hot wind swirled around Sindri, Wilden, Tayt, and Rizzek. Steam curled from their clothes and hair as water evaporated away. In moments, they were dry as though they'd just changed clothes.

Tayt nodded appreciatively. "You'll need to teach me how to do that one, Wilden."

Wilden laughed. "I'll have to learn it first."

Auren clapped his hands together. "Well, friends, come. I've been awaiting your arrival with no small measure of anticipation. I tried to lead you here as best I could without incident."

"I suppose almost getting killed a few dozen times doesn't count as an incident," Wilden said with a wry smile.

Auren sighed. "Well, I did say *try*. Things didn't quite work out the way . . . No, this is not the place. Below."

"As long as it's dry," Wilden said.

With a charming laugh, Auren nodded. "Definitely," he said. "And excellent for talking. Out here, there are a few too many nearby ears for me to be comfortable." He gestured with one arm to the innocuous trapdoor from which he had appeared.

Sindri stared into the darkness. Following strange men into underground caves usually wasn't the best of ideas. But there was something about Auren Sindri couldn't quite explain. He shrugged. "Shall we?" he asked, turning to Tayt and Wilden.

Wilden stepped forward in response. Tayt followed immediately after, and all three walked toward Auren and the cave entrance.

Still smiling, Auren turned and strode into the cavern before them, humming an unfamiliar tune as Rizzek darted excitedly around his feet. Despite the fight only moments earlier, Sindri couldn't help but feel excitement coursing throughout him.

This is it, he thought. Now I'll finally have answers.

He descended the stairs into the darkness, the trapdoor magically closing itself behind him. If Sindri had stayed outside a moment longer, he might have noticed the dark, feathered shape circling the skies above the cliff.

Instead, the misty bird watched the trapdoor close, then flew off to return to its master.

CHAPTER

8 AUREN

Auren led them down a flight of stairs carved from the stone. Darkness enveloped them as the trapdoor closed, but Auren waved one of his hands and a glowing orb appeared to hover in front of them, lighting their path.

It was cold here underground, and Rizzek shivered atop Sindri's shoulders where he'd promptly jumped once it was apparent how far down they would be walking. Pulling his cloak tight around himself, Sindri looked up at the ceiling as they spiraled even deeper into the cliffside. Stalactites dangled, resembling bumpy cones that looked a bit like dragon snouts. Sindri could still hear muffled waves crashing against the cliff face distantly, but otherwise the only sounds were the clomping of boots against stone stairs.

Finally, they reached an oak door. It was tall, twice as tall as Wilden, and wide enough so that they could all walk through it side by side if they wanted. It bore no decoration save for a simple brass door handle.

"We're here," Auren said in his strangely familiar deep voice. He smiled down at Sindri, his face shimmering as golden as the sun in the light from the hovering orb.

Sindri took in a breath, then smiled right back. This was it. He felt he'd been doing nothing but seeking answers for months, only to find out very little. Now, that would all change.

"Lead on," Wilden said. Beside him, Tayt shifted uncomfortably.

Auren nodded, then pushed through the door.

Inside was a place Sindri could only describe as a palace.

"Oh wow!" Sindri said. He couldn't help himself. He pushed past Auren and ran through the door, spinning to take everything in.

The ceiling appeared to be miles above his head, stretching out as far as the sky. Arches spanned its width, and the stone was painted with an endless mural of dragons and humans and elves reenacting their lives in vivid color.

The arches met pillars that spiraled down to meet a floor covered with golden tile. Fountains shaped like giant seashells twisted up from the golden floor, sparkling fresh water cascading down their sides. Golden benches were arranged around the fountains in a circle, their cushions shimmering with red and green silk.

Between the pillars and along the distant walls, marble statues stood proudly and life-size portraits showed off ancient artistry that only the finest of nobles could ever dream of affording. Among them, palm trees and cascading, viney plants sprouted from wide golden pots.

And it was only the beginning, for Sindri saw doors leading off to other areas of this underground palace, to secrets he just had to explore.

"Hold on there, Sindri," Auren said, and a gentle yet firm hand fell on the kender's shoulder. Startled, Rizzek yelped and leaped away, landing on the golden floor with a clack of his claws.

Sindri looked up at Auren, agape. "How?" he asked. "How could this have been here, beneath the cliffs, and no one ever knew?

How could you have built it? Who *are* you?"

Wilden and Tayt came into the massive great hall as well. Tayt's eyes opened wide at the rich sight of it all, but Wilden strode to look up at Auren purposefully.

"Something I'd like to know myself," Wilden said as he crossed his arms. "Creating something like this in secret, especially just north of a land full of curious kender, isn't really possible."

Auren chuckled, then walked to the closest fountain. Sindri followed and saw that, up close, the fountain shimmered pearly pink and blue, as though it actually were a giant shell.

Letting cool water cascade over his fingers, Auren responded, "This place has been here far longer than the kender have. In fact, it was with pleasant surprise that I found it still in good shape. I haven't had to repair much, though of course there was a bit of structural damage due to the Cataclysm shaking the foundation, and some of the paint needed a bit of touching up."

Flicking water playfully at Rizzek, who yelped and darted beneath a bench, Auren turned to look at Sindri, Wilden, and Tayt.

"But that's not important," he said. "What you are really here to learn are the answers to your questions. Down here, we will be safe from prying eyes and unfriendly ears." He spread his arms wide and bowed his head. "Ask away, friends."

Sindri sat down on a bench and sank into its plush cushion, setting his pack and hoopak beside him. "Well," he said, "I suppose the first thing I might want to know is how you got involved with this."

Auren nodded. "Of course." Looking to Wilden and Tayt, he motioned toward the benches surrounding the fountain. "Please, sit. This might take awhile and I'd like you to be comfortable."

Wary, Tayt crept to Sindri's side and sat down, arms hugging her chest. Wilden sat on a bench opposite Auren and crossed his legs.

Auren smiled his sparkling, perfect smile. "Very good." He took a breath and looked over at the nearest statue—one of several kender climbing over one another to be the first to grab a key flying on butterfly's wings. "It began several years ago, when I first returned to this place. I had to come in and out quite a bit back then, and I garnered some attention. That was how I met a kender woman named Moonbeam Suncatcher."

"Aunt Moonbeam!" Sindri said, then leaned forward eagerly. "I can't believe she never told me about this place."

Auren chuckled, then began to pace, the sound of his footsteps echoing in the painted ceiling. "I'm afraid I never got a chance to show Moonbeam down here, mainly because I didn't want it to be well known I was here, and also because of that bum knee of hers—wouldn't want her attempting the climb in and out."

Sindri felt at his legs and realized his calf muscles ached. He nodded in understanding.

"Anyway," Auren continued, "I found Moonbeam to be a most charming woman—rather bold and brash and loud, and she had quite a few interesting stories. I took her to the tavern in Flotsam a few times, and she often mentioned her nephew the kender wizard.

"Eventually we lost touch, as I became too busy in my work in restoring this place, and I'm sure she found someone more interesting than me to speak to. And I came to forget the kender wizard."

"Until . . ." Wilden prompted.

Auren met his eyes. "Until," he repeated, "I started hearing stories about a kender wizard from more people than just Moonbeam. More, ah, *reputable* people—no offense intended, Sindri."

Sindri shrugged. "None taken."

"It was little things at first," Auren continued. "Visitors to local taverns spreading tales of an evil dragon and the kender wizard who helped destroy her. Then came the stories from as close as Khur about the little wizard traveling and helping a group of elves. Most people laughed it off. But I knew there would be those who wouldn't. And so I began to do some research.

"I contacted others I knew who might have heard something, and that was when I learned I wasn't the only one who was out searching for this kender wizard—a Black Robe was on the lookout as well."

"Anica." Tayt scowled.

Auren stopped pacing, then nodded. "Yes, Anica. I was seeking Sindri mostly out of curiosity, but this woman was absolutely ruthless in her methods of searching. Following her contacts, I managed to discover where Sindri resided—Cairngorn Keep. And I knew that if I knew where Sindri was, then she surely did as well. I did not trust the intentions of this person."

"And then you sought *her* out," Sindri said, nodding thoughtfully. "So you *were* the man Rizzek always went on about."

"Yes," Rizzek rasped from beneath the bench. "Man give map, give scale."

"But how?" Tayt asked. "Anica doesn't trust anyone. How did you convince her to trust you?"

Auren leaned forward. As he did, his hair darkened from gold to black, and his blue eyes clouded to a stormy gray. "A little bit of trickery is how."

Wilden nodded. "So you're a wizard, then."

Auren leaned back and his golden hair and blue eyes returned. He considered a moment, then said, "I suppose you could say that."

"What did you do when you met Anica?" Sindri asked.

Auren nodded and resumed his pacing. "I found out as much information on Anica as I could before actually approaching her. I read old records of her exploits at magic school, spoke with those she had dealings with. Once ready, I posed as a fellow Black Robe and went to her keep. You had already left, Tayt, by the time I finagled my way into Anica's good graces."

Tayt nodded, a thoughtful look on her face. Sindri didn't know how much time she spent on the streets as a spellfilch, but he thought it had to have been at least a year or two.

"She wasn't expecting me, of course," Auren continued. "And yes, she was wary. But Anica does enjoy her games, and she does enjoy flattery. I seemed an attractive, upper-class wizard, and here I was flirting with her and allowing her to dangle her secrets in front of me. She let me stay with her for months, and we dined together, entertained one another, even shared a room for a time."

Tayt shuddered. "That sounds awful."

"It was," Auren said with a shudder of his own. "Oh believe me, it was. It took every ounce of strength I had not to take my leave of the situation altogether. But each day I stayed with her, the more she opened up to me, and the more she spoke of her latest project—the kender wizard, Sindri."

Sindri stiffened. "Her . . . project? Is that what she called me?"

Auren nodded. "She did, and I knew that I could not abandon this trickery, not yet, for it also became clear that she was working with someone else on this 'project.' Someone far more powerful than she or I. One day, after many months and when her plans were ready to begin, she asked me to stand by her side and help her complete them. And it was then that she told me who her master was."

Auren stopped pacing, his back to Sindri, Wilden, and Tayt.

They all leaned forward, waiting anxiously.

"The person behind this all," Auren said after a moment, "the power who sought to destroy Sindri these many months was . . . something more than I expected."

He turned and looked directly into Sindri's eyes.

"The one out to stop you and your magic, Sindri, is Nuitari himself."

Sindri stiffened, and beside him Tayt gasped. Rizzek whimpered, and Wilden was motionless. For a long moment, no one spoke. The only sound was that of the endless trickling of the fountains echoing between the high arches.

"Nuitari," Wilden said slowly. "The black moon god, he who oversees all Black Robes. *That* Nuitari? He has taken a personal interest in stopping Sindri?"

Sindri took in a breath. "Oh wow."

"That's one word for it," Tayt whispered.

Wilden stood and ran his hands through his hair. "This . . . this can't be. A god of magic seeking to destroy someone outright? Something like this . . . if Nuitari has done so. . . ." He stopped and took a step toward Auren, anxiousness written on his face. "Have you any proof?"

Auren bowed his head. "Think about what has occurred, what you have seen, and you will know this to be true."

Sindri thought back to when this all began. The massive cloud creature, the devouring dark beast that everyone said Anica could never create without some sort of extra power—extra power a moon good could give.

He remembered also Anica going against her unknown master's wishes, seeking to capture Sindri and use his power rather than destroy him as instructed. And as Tayt had told him, Anica had cursed the night sky as her powers seemed suddenly sapped from her, taken from her as though the moon she drew her power from had cut her off.

"No," Sindri shook his head, then leaped to his feet, startling both Rizzek and Tayt. "No! Why would the black moon god want to destroy *me*? I haven't done anything! I was studying with Maddoc, and he's a Black Robe. I did everything I was supposed to to become a wizard myself, didn't I?"

"No," Wilden said as he collapsed onto the bench, clearly overwhelmed by this information. "Sindri, remember what we've learned from the temples. You're not just a regular magic-user, even if you were training under a Black Robe. Nuitari would destroy you for the same reason the Wizards' Conclave wanted you captured—because you are not supposed to exist. You've brought back some sort of ancient wild magic to the world. As a gatekeeper of magic, Nuitari couldn't stand by and let that happen."

Sindri's whole body slackened as he realized the truth of the matter. It wasn't just the people of Krynn who thought he shouldn't be a wizard. Even the *gods* thought he shouldn't.

"Oh," Sindri whispered, and his shoulders slumped as he went to sit back down next to Tayt.

Tayt looked among Sindri, Wilden, and Auren, confused. "But . . . Nuitari's a god. A god! Surely if he was the one out to destroy Sindri he could just, I don't know, smite him from above. It has to be someone that was just messing with Anica, using her and claiming to be Nuitari."

Auren shook his head. "I was there when she consulted her master. Hidden, of course, for I could not reveal myself to not be an actual Black Robe. It was the god himself." Auren looked away. "But you are right. Thing is, just as with mortals, gods don't always agree. Should he take a straightforward course of action against Sindri, Nuitari would find himself facing off with Solinari and Lunitari."

"So he used a follower to do his dirty work," Wilden said. He looked down at his feet and nodded slowly. "He found one of the most vile Black Robes he could, someone out of the way, and whispered secret orders. And his plan might have worked—"

"If it wasn't for me," Auren finished. "Anica's initial plan was simple. Create a dark beast that's sole purpose would be to seek out and destroy the one person on Krynn who held onto the ancient sorcery. I was the one who convinced her to test out the beast before actually sending it after you, Sindri, which was easy enough to do as she'd decided to do something very stupid."

Auren turned back and looked them all in the eye one by one. "See, one of the reasons Anica was chosen by Nuitari was that she'd discovered a temple many years ago, one that she was unable to enter but which she knew contained magical secrets. She built her keep above it, and later captured gnome slaves to build a maze to guard it. She even locked it with a key that she made into an eye so that no one else would have access. Nuitari knew her obsession with this temple, and told her that should she destroy Sindri, he would give her the power to enter it and learn more.

"But Anica did her own research, and she learned that the key to reinvigorating the temple's power was Sindri himself. She figured—perhaps correctly—that if Nuitari wanted Sindri dead, he wasn't likely to grant her access to the secrets of his powers. And so, she decided to betray Nuitari and kidnap Sindri, figuring that with the wild magic Sindri possessed she'd have no use for the black moon god."

"So the test," Tayt said, "was as me and Sindri guessed it—to make sure the dark beast would capture Sindri without hurting him."

Auren nodded. "Exactly. I created a map that would lead you, Sindri, to the temples, with the golden scale to be used as a marker. I knew Rizzek was a kind soul and not loyal to his master, and so while I kept up my disguise as Anica's consort, I tasked him with bringing these items to you—which he did marvelously."

Rizzek ducked his head and hid farther beneath the bench.

"But what I didn't know was that Anica was able to see through Rizzek's eyes," Auren went on. "And though I cast a spell that made it so that she could not see or hear properly while I gave Rizzek my instructions, she still knew she could not trust me. She attacked me and wounded me badly, and so I had to flee. Before I did, I found a way to break the lock Anica had put in place and snuck into the temple beneath the keep. I adjusted the writings so that you would be led here, to me, once you found your own way past her defenses."

"How?" Wilden asked. "Only Sindri is able to access the temples' true powers, isn't he? And that still doesn't explain why you did all this—why would a man, even a White Robe, try to stop the wishes of a god?"

Auren tilted his head and smiled. "Well, I'm not exactly a man."

He backed away from them, his grin seeming to grow wider as he did. No, Sindri realized, not just seeming to grow wider—it *was* growing wider. As were Auren's shoulders, his legs, his arms. His back bulged and his neck elongated, and in two blinks of Sindri's eyes, Auren was no longer a man.

Auren had twisted, shifted, and grown to become an immense,

glittering gold dragon.

No one could move.

"This," Auren's voice boomed from high above, "would be the last secret I have to share."

"Oh wow," Sindri breathed.

Tayt nudged him and said, "You keep saying that."

Sindri nudged her back. "For good reason!"

Wings tight against his massive back, Auren the gold dragon walked delicately forward, rounding the fountains and pillars with practiced ease.

Lowering his massive head to look Sindri, Wilden, and Tayt in the face, Auren grinned a wide, lizardy smile. "I suppose it is in my nature to stop injustice when I discover it. I've done it my entire life, and I'm afraid it's gotten me in more than just a few scrapes. I learned to pick my battles long ago. I know how important Sindri is—and so his was the battle I picked."

Wilden blinked and looked back and forth. "This place," he said. "This *lair*, it's been here a very long time, hasn't it?"

Auren nodded, and the motion made the air stir, sending water from the fountain splashing against Sindri's skin.

"I left this place long ago," he said. "*We* did. But even after the centuries that passed, I still call it home."

"A real live gold dragon lair!" Sindri cried, and he couldn't help but clap in glee. "I've always wanted to see one! Oh, you'll have to show me all the rooms."

Auren chuckled, and the sound rumbled deep like distant thunder in his long neck. "In time, Sindri, in time," he said. "But know this: Though you have defeated Anica, Nuitari hasn't given up, I'm sure of it. He still cannot destroy you directly, but he will find other wizards to do his bidding. You must be prepared."

Sindri nodded. "The last temple," he said. "That's where I need to go. It still exists, right?"

"It does, and I've been there," Auren said, and he pulled his long neck back so that his head was dozens of feet above. "And there are things there that you must see." The dragon blinked his wide blue eyes and looked between Wilden and Tayt. "You two have been a great help to Sindri. I only wish I had been able to be there to help through your trials as well, as I'd planned. For now, you two will need to stay here. This final step is for Sindri alone."

Tayt nodded. "I understand."

Wilden nodded as well, though he still appeared to Sindri to be overwhelmed. "Nuitari . . ." he said. "I don't know what we can do. Sindri's power . . . Nuitari is a moon god, and the moon gods control all magic. Auren . . ."

Auren flapped his wings in two great strokes. "Yes," he said, "and we are but a renegade hunter, a spell-filch, a magically created pet, and a dragon. But we also have with us a powerful kender magic-user. And I know deep in my old bones that he will know what to do once he finishes his journey, because he was meant to know. You must know it too."

Sindri leaped from his bench and scrambled to Wilden's side. Grabbing the man's hand, he nodded solemnly. "I've faced some bad things before, Wilden," he said. "Maybe not a god, but . . . we'll figure it out. We have to."

Wilden looked into Sindri's eyes, face grim. "You know," he whispered, "I should try to stop you. I am of the conclave. If a moon god wants you destroyed, I cannot stand in his way."

Sindri smiled. "But you would never do that, Wilden."

Wilden laughed sadly. "No, I would never do that. But, as soon as you leave, and I've tried nothing to stop you, that's it, Sindri.

There's no going back for me."

Sindri stepped back. "You can make a go of stopping me if you want."

Wilden didn't move. He thought for a moment, then smiled. "Have a good trip, Sindri. We'll be here when you get back."

Sindri nodded and shook Wilden's hand. With a quick hug for Tayt, he grabbed his pack and hoopak and raced toward the giant creature that was Auren.

With a yowl, something heavy landed on Sindri's shoulders.

"Rizzek." Sindri pat him gently.

"It's all right, Sindri," Auren said. "He can come too."

With a wave farewell to his friends, Sindri scrambled up Auren's lowered neck and clung to the crook between his shoulder blades.

Auren looked down at Wilden and Tayt, the two of them shivering. The dragon's voice left his scaly lips in soothing, comforting waves.

"Please, make yourself at home," he said. "There are many rooms. Rest and eat. We will be back soon, and then this will all be over."

Sindri knew the words to be true, just as he knew that this moment, his meeting Auren, this flight to the temple, had been fated for a very, very long time.

"See you soon," Sindri said with a wave.

Auren left them, turning toward the back of the massive great hall to a door that opened of its own accord. With a flap of his wings, Auren shot through the doorway and down a tunnel, wind overtaking Sindri as he clung to the dragon's scales, the golden walls and arches a blur around him.

And then, before Sindri knew it, they burst out of the cliffside and into the sky. His heart racing with elation, Sindri soared off with Rizzek and the gold dragon toward the horizon, off to the final temple and the end of Sindri's journey.

CHAPTER

9   FATHERS AND SONS

T his would be it." Garin looked down at his notes. "And no temple."

Davyn stepped to Garin's side and shaded his eyes. There was nothing around them but cliffs overlooking the ocean, scattered bits of stone lying about as though there had been a rain of rocks. For a moment Davyn thought he saw a flash of gold zip toward the horizon, but it was likely just daylight glinting off the ocean waves.

Rina and Marten came to either side of Davyn. Rina bit her lip.

"Maybe we made a wrong turn," she said. "Following ancient directions, it would be easy to—"

"I made no such error," Garin interrupted, his tone abrupt. Davyn put his arm around Rina protectively, and she tried not to scowl.

Garin paced atop the cliff, the ocean breeze rustling his robe and wispy hair. He waved one hand in the air as though divining for secrets, while the other hand scratched at his stubble. "No, we're here," he grumbled after a moment, so low that Davyn almost couldn't hear. "There is magic close by, I can feel it. But not the same magic as the temple."

Davyn, Rina, Garin, and the renegade hunter Marten had been on the road for weeks, heading east from the destroyed oasis keep. Eyeless Anica and beastly Arvin disappeared after their brief scuffle near the underground temple, and Davyn and his companions made haste with the knowledge that the deformed duo would be hot on Sindri's trail.

They'd found a few fallen sheaves of unused parchment in the temple, and that was how they realized that Sindri and his companions had made rubbings of the markings on the wall. It didn't take long for Garin and his silent renegade hunter to decipher the markings and figure out a trail to the location of the next temple.

Now they were here—exactly where Garin's notes told them to go. And as far as Davyn could see, there was nothing.

"Garin," Davyn said, "those etchings were old. Perhaps they could have been misread."

Garin did not stop pacing as he said, "I assure you, Davyn, I did no such thing. There must be a secret entrance around here somewhere, some—".

"Master." Davyn was surprised to find that Marten had spoken. Silently, the black-clad renegade hunter slipped past Davyn and Rina and went to stand at Garin's side. He pointed toward a pair of tall, scrubby bushes nearby. Something glinted silver beneath them.

Garin grinned and slapped Marten on the back. Before they could investigate, however, someone coughed.

"I expected to see many things when I came here," a dangerously familiar voice said. "But I can say with much certainty that the last person I ever expected to see was my son."

For a moment, the world stilled. Davyn's heart beat against the inside of his chest, flushing blood into his face. Despite himself, despite everything that had happened, old, angry thoughts came to mind.

"Maddoc," he whispered.

Davyn turned to find Maddoc standing inland where the grass met the cliffs. The old wizard had seen better days. His regal robes were tattered at the edges, and dark circles lined his blue eyes. His hair had long since gone from salt-and-pepper to pure silver, and curiously he now wore leather gloves.

Maddoc smiled his unreadable smile. "Davyn. Rina. It has been a long time."

Beside Davyn, Rina stiffened. With everything that her brother Elidor had gone through, she had her own reasons for mixed feelings about the old wizard. Despite this, she said, "We have been well. Are you here with Sindri?"

"Who is this man?"

Garin burst between Davyn and Rina, Marten slinking behind. The White Robe tightened his lips as he gave Maddoc a once over. He turned away and met Davyn's eye. "Well?"

Davyn cleared his throat and steeled his features. "This is Maddoc," he said.

Garin raised his eyebrows in realization, then turned back to Maddoc. "You're the one who was teaching the kender. And also the one who disregarded my missives and made it necessary for us to send Wilden to collect the kender."

Maddoc nodded, his face revealing no emotion. "An action I much regret, considering the consequences that have been consistent and many."

Garin crossed his arms. "And where is the kender now?"

Davyn watched Maddoc's eyes carefully, and he could tell the wizard was fighting not to roll them.

Maddoc walked forward and brushed past Garin. Meeting Davyn's eyes, he said, "Sindri is here. Well, below here anyway. The temple is not here, but something else is hidden beneath these cliffs. There is a doorway beneath those bushes." He extended a finger near Davyn's face and pointed. Davyn crinkled his nose as the stench of death wafted from Maddoc's glove.

Garin cleared his throat and tapped Maddoc none too gently on his shoulder. Near him, Marten hovered protectively. "I am leading this expedition, Maddoc, and so you can address your answers to me."

Maddoc looked over his shoulder and raised a bushy eyebrow. "Davyn, son, is he always like this?"

Davyn looked down. He wasn't exactly Garin's biggest fan, especially considering that the wizard was out to capture Sindri, but he wasn't exactly sure how he felt toward Maddoc either.

At Davyn's silence, Rina stepped forward and answered. "Maddoc, a lot has happened," she said. "We have traveled far to find out what became of Sindri, and of you. We are of course glad to hear all of you are well, but there are two wizards on the loose after all of you, and we need to warn Sindri. For now, I think we should all play nice."

Maddoc smiled at her, cool and stiff. "Rina, you seem older than when we last traveled together."

Rina shrugged. "Time will do that."

Garin stomped his foot and came to stand between Maddoc and Davyn. "Yes, well, I still think it's only proper to answer the person who asked you the question. I can understand your anger over the harsh measures that had to be taken, but with the power the kender possesses, you can understand that—"

Maddoc grunted and stepped over to the edge of the cliff. He looked out over the dark sea, and Davyn followed his gaze.

"Yes," he grumbled after a moment. "I'm sure we'll have many discussions about this very soon. Those wizards . . . they are Anica and Arvin, aren't they?"

"Yes," Davyn said. "And there's something changed about them. They have a lot of power."

"Then we must warn Sindri."

Garin took a few deep breaths, then turned to Marten. "Let's explore the bushes and find the kender, then."

Marten nodded and ran swiftly. He gripped the scrubby brushes hard, only to discover they came free easily. Beneath them was a hatch door.

While Garin went to Marten's side to investigate, Davyn took a breath and stepped next to Maddoc. Far beneath their feet, the ocean crashed against the cliff.

"Maddoc," Davyn whispered. "Why are you up here and not already below with Sindri? Something isn't right about all this, and I don't believe we can trust Garin to help us despite those other wizards. Do I have to worry about trusting you as well?"

Maddoc did not turn away from the ocean. After a long moment he opened his lips to speak.

At that moment, thunder echoed between the clouds and a sudden wind tugged at Davyn's hair. Rina shouted, and Davyn turned to see a cyclone crackling with electricity spiraling down from above.

"I forgot to mention," Maddoc said behind him. "The trapdoor has a security system."

Tayt could not look away from the fish. It was bright green and the size of a dinner plate. It darted between waving strands of seaweed just outside a tall, round window in the side of Auren's library wall that showed the ocean outside.

"This is a bit strange," she said, then closed her eyes for just a moment to orient herself. She had a sinking feeling that the ocean couldn't possibly be held up by a single pane of glass, and she expected any moment for the water to punch through and envelop her. The ocean had seemed such a massive, dark, dangerous thing, and she'd heard tales of what lay in its depths—sea elves and serpentine monsters and the ghosts of those destroyed during the Cataclysm.

Tayt shuddered, and a gentle hand fell on her shoulder.

"It's lovely," Wilden whispered beside her, and Tayt opened her eyes just in time to see a school of the large green fish come to collect their friend from in front of the window before darting off.

Tayt turned away and looked back into the library. She rubbed her arms as she came close to the fire—a fire that had been lit in a fireplace that filled one entire wall. Orange light filled the relatively small room, washing over plush chairs and around bookcases bursting with tomes written in languages she couldn't understand.

"So," she said, staring into the dancing flames. "Nuitari, huh?"

Wilden said nothing as he continued to stare at the dark water beyond the window.

Tayt turned to him, frowning with concern. "Wilden," she said. "Hey, it's going to be all right."

Back to her, Wilden lowered his head and took a shaky breath. Tayt had never seen the young man so unsettled. It scared her, knowing that he was frightened.

"I can only hope," Wilden whispered. "I never imagined that we'd be up against a god . . . that I would turn away from. . . . We can only hope Sindri finds his answers."

Tayt crept toward Wilden, the fire casting a long shadow before her that draped Wilden in darkness.

"You do think he can do it, though, right? Find a way to end this? The gold dragon thought so. And gods, a dragon! Surely. . . ." She trailed off as Wilden stood motionless, unresponsive.

A moment of silence fell, punctuated only by the popping of logs in the fireplace. Finally, Wilden muttered, "We can only hope."

A chime filled the air, startling Tayt. She jumped and spun around as a voice she didn't recognize spoke out.

"Pardon my intrusion, master and madam, but we appear to have visitors upstairs."

Wilden turned away from the window and joined Tayt, his arm placed protectively in front of her. Tayt ran her hand through her hair, her eyes narrowing as she scanned the room—until they came to rest on a small, golden statue set on a table next to one of the reading chairs. It was a metal-molded dragon, Tayt was certain, but the thing was *moving*.

The dragon statue tilted its head. "Master and madam, there is apparently a large group of individuals at the top of the cliff above. Do you think this might be a situation you want to look into?"

Wilden narrowed his eyes. "What are you?" he asked.

The dragon flashed a long, toothy grin. "I am Master Auren's personal sentry, and now that you are his valued guest, your sentry as well. Currently the stormy apparition that you met earlier is attacking an older gentleman in white wizard's robe, another old gentleman in tattered black robes, a tall man dressed all in black, a young man in green armor, and an elf girl with a particularly attractive bow that Master Auren might be interested in obtaining for his personal horde."

Tayt looked up at Wilden to see that his face had tightened in recognition. "Yes," he said. "We will go meet them. How do we call off the storm giant?"

The dragon statue bowed its head. "You must merely command it, good master. As a valued guest of Master Auren, it wouldn't do to have you harmed by his magically manifested guards."

Wilden nodded to the statue, then met Tayt's eyes. "Let's go."

They ran out of the fire-lit library and into the massive main hall, rounding the fountains to race toward the door that led to the stairway. They bounded up the calcified stone steps until they could make out lines of the trapdoor that led to the top of the cliff.

Tayt reached the trapdoor first and pushed into it with her shoulders. The wooden door swung up and open easily, and a gust of salty ocean air slapped her face, making her blink.

She looked around the scene to find the figures the dragon statue had told them about. They were casting magic and slinging arrows and swinging swords, valiantly fighting off the stormy giant that had caused her, Wilden, and Sindri so much trouble only an hour earlier. Thunder cracked and lightning's electricity made Tayt's skin bristle.

As Wilden leaped out of the trapdoor beside her, Tayt saw the only person she recognized—Maddoc, face grim and stern as ever as he stood beside a boy dressed in green armor.

"Stop!" Wilden shouted over the thundering of the storm giant's attacks, the wind whipping his long hair across his face. "Cease your attack!"

Incredulous, Tayt watched as the storm giant did just that. It spiraled into the clouds above, leaving behind a group of wet, bedraggled men and one elf girl. They all stared at Wilden and Tayt, as though unable to comprehend what had just happened.

"Well," Tayt whispered as she climbed out of the hatch and came to Wilden's side, "that worked pretty well."

Wilden ignored her—his focus was instead on the old man in the white robes.

The old man stepped forward, face stern for a moment as he looked between Tayt and Wilden. "Who—" Tayt started to ask.

"Wilden," the old man said, and smiled. "Ah, Wilden, I have been looking for you."

"Garin."

Though Wilden stood motionless, the old, grizzled wizard ran forward and pulled him into an embrace. Holding Wilden out at arm's length, Garin regarded him with a bemused smile. "Ah, my boy, it's so good to find you. All of this business with following this kender. We certainly have much to discuss, eh?"

Wilden swallowed, his face blank. "Yes," he said. "Yes we do."

Tayt saw Garin's smile fall, if only briefly. She'd learned about dishonest smiles, living with someone like her old master, Anica. Garin wasn't as happy about seeing Wilden as he pretended.

"Wilden, Tayt." Tayt looked past Garin to see Maddoc standing behind him, his eyebrows arched and his hands behind his back.

Tayt nodded, wary. "Maddoc," she said. "Sorry we didn't say anything before we parted ways, but Sindri—"

Maddoc waved a dismissive hand. "Sindri and I went over things. I understand."

Tayt tilted her head. "Then why are you here?"

Maddoc's lip curled ever so slightly into a sneer, but he did not respond.

Clearing his throat, the boy in green armor stepped forward and offered Tayt his hand. "Hello," he offered. "I'm Davyn, a friend of Sindri's."

"Davyn," Tayt repeated, recognizing the name. "Yes, I know you. Well, not personally, but Sindri tells stories about his adventures all the time. I wasn't actually sure you were real. Aren't you Maddoc's—"

"Son?" Maddoc finished, his voice low. "Long ago, perhaps."

Davyn did not look back, though his stern, angry expression almost perfectly mimicked the Black Robe's.

"And this is my . . . my friend Rina," Davyn said as a lithe, absolutely beautiful elf girl came to Davyn's side. "She traveled with Sindri for a time as well."

Tayt shook the elf girl's slender hand and found herself unable to speak. Elves were known for their eternal, ethereal beauty, but Tayt had never seen one up close before. Despite the disheveled look of the others after their battle with the storm giant, Rina looked as though she'd just spent hours being made up. Long, golden curls fell over her shoulders, and Tayt noticed a blue pendant hanging around her neck.

Davyn reached out and shook Wilden's hand as well. "So you're Wilden."

Wilden nodded. "And this is Tayt. We're friends of Sindri's as well."

Davyn smiled and shook his shaggy hair out of his eyes. "Yeah, Sindri tends to make those wherever he goes. Rina and I, we were going to visit him at Cairngorn, but we came upon its ruins instead. That's where we ran into Garin and Marten."

Only then did Tayt realize that a fifth figure had been standing there the whole time. The man was clad entirely in black, clearly a renegade hunter like Wilden, and was exceptionally silent.

Garin cleared his throat. "Yes, wonderful, introductions all around. As lovely as our reunion has been, and we do thank you for getting rid of that tornado creature, we're here to see Sindri. The conclave would have words with him."

Tayt stiffened. "He's not here," she said, her voice a bit more shaky with nerves than she would have liked. Knowing what they knew about Nuitari, someone from the conclave was the last person she wanted to talk to. "He's off to the last temple. He's going to figure out his destiny."

Garin smiled at her, tight-lipped. "Yes, so I've heard." Turning to Wilden, he said, "And Wilden, you'll lead us to him?"

Wilden lowered his head. "No."

Garin narrowed his brow. "No?"

"I can't, I—"

Someone nearby laughed, the sound like someone walking over dead leaves.

Tayt turned and immediately gasped.

"No," she said, her whole body shaking. "No! We destroyed you!"

"Not quite."

The laugh, the voice belonged to someone Tayt had hoped to never see again: Anica. The woman's dried apple face was creased into her sickeningly false smile, her eye sockets as empty as Tayt had left them. Beside her stood Tayt's old traveling companion—the creepy, stout old wizard, Arvin, the Goblin Man.

Anica stepped forward, her grin widening, creasing her face with a maze of wrinkles. The old woman faced Tayt, her dry, hollow eye sockets aimed directly into Tayt's eyes though surely they couldn't see.

"We have come for Sindri, my dear," Anica said. "And this time, there is nothing you can do to stop us."

CHAPTER

10   An Abundance of Goblins

Arvin stepped forward and grinned, his drooping ears shifting and lengthening into ragged red points. With a manic giggle, he regarded the assembled group.

"Oh Anica, look," he said. "I would have sworn I was leading us astray, but it would appear by the presence of all these fine people that we followed our master's directions to the letter."

Regarding Davyn and his companions with her empty eyes, Anica tightened her lips into a withered smile and patted Arvin on his back. "I see, dear. Good show."

Davyn glanced briefly at the pair, then turned his attention to the grasses beyond them. Not seeing anyone else creeping from the sparse trees, he unsheathed his sword. "You're not going to touch Sindri," he said.

Arvin giggled again. "Ah yes, Sindri. Now where could he be? I thought he'd come out to greet us, but I imagine Maddoc might have him squirreled away."

Davyn dared a glance to his left. Maddoc stood tall and stoic, hands behind his back as he regarded his old friend the Goblin Man. He arched a bushy eyebrow.

"Arvin. Anica. Fancy seeing you here."

Davyn stood his ground as Anica stepped forward. The rotund little woman looked nothing so much as someone's ailing grandmother, but there was no mistaking the evil that lay in the abyss that were her eye sockets.

"I can't say we're too pleased with you, Maddoc," she said. "One *wonders* what a Black Robe such as yourself expects to be able to do against a wizard like my dear Arvin. Surely you must know by now who our master is."

"Oh no."

Davyn turned his head at the whisper and saw the short, dark-skinned girl he'd just met—Tayt. She grabbed the arm of the renegade hunter at her side, Wilden, and whispered frantically in his ear.

Maddoc didn't seem to notice their whispers. Instead, he raised his other eyebrow. "I don't particularly care, Anica. Surely anyone who would choose you and Arvin as his lackeys can't be much of a threat."

A slender hand gripped Davyn's sleeve, and Rina's sweet breath lanced against his cheek. "I can hear the other two," she whispered. "Their master, it's—"

Booming laughter echoed across the cliffs, drowning out even the noise of the ocean below. Rina recoiled and readied her bow and Davyn turned his attention back to Arvin. The squat little man had tilted his head back, his arms outstretched at his sides to reveal curved, crimson claws.

Beside Davyn, Garin readied his staff, and Wilden unsheathed his scythes. Next to them, the silent renegade hunter brought out a nearly identical looking pair from their holsters. Maddoc and Tayt stayed back.

Anica did not move from her spot, nor did her hideous smile fade as behind her, Arvin's laughter turned into high-pitched, animalistic howls. With a gasp, the old man arched his back and his entire body shuddered.

Davyn couldn't help but want to retch as he watched the old man's skin turn a deep red. Dozens of goblin faces emerged from beneath his robes. Arvin screamed as the goblins churned against each other, tugging at his skin as though trying to claw their way out.

With a sickening wet pop, the first goblin did exactly that.

Davyn's grip on his sword slacked as he looked on, horrified, as goblin after goblin tore itself free from Arvin's body. They fell to the stony earth in slimy, naked bundles, shivering as they opened their jaws wide to wail in anger. Arvin's screams met theirs as more of the disgusting creatures piled up at his feet, disoriented.

That is, until Anica turned, waved her hands, and muttered a few quick phrases. Their black eyes glimmered with awareness and they ceased their howling, choosing instead to slowly stand, seeming frail and defenseless despite their sharp claws and mouths full of jagged teeth.

And then, with one last shudder, Arvin's screams ended and he collapsed to the stony ground, lost in his sea of goblins. At least two dozen had torn their way free from Arvin's old body.

Anica turned back to the companions and met Maddoc's eyes. "I suppose our master wasn't such a fool after all."

Before anyone could speak, the goblins shrieked in unison and charged.

Rina stepped backward, unleashing a flurry of arrows. One met a goblin square in its forehead and it fell back, dead. The goblins surged over its body, uncaring of their fallen companion.

Davyn looked over his shoulder at the wizards behind him. "Kill them!" he cried, and charged into the fray. He knocked two goblins aside with the flat of his blade as he kicked another in the side of the head, sending it sprawling. He quickly turned and swung his powerful sword, slicing through the goblins that rushed him.

He turned to see the two renegade hunters expertly dodging slashing claws as they swiped with their blades. Rina stood back near Tayt, loosing volley after volley from her ornate bow.

Davyn gutted a goblin that leaped for his throat just as he saw Tayt withdraw a deep blue stone from a belt pouch and hold it up to her lips. She whispered some word of magic then blew on the stone. It disintegrated into a cloud of dust that surrounded the goblins closing in on her and Rina. The beasts shrieked and clawed at their own faces, collapsing to the stony ground. Tayt then drew a knife from her boot and raced past them to where more goblins lay waiting.

Davyn grunted as he dodged more shredding claws, looking above the sea of red and orange flesh to find Maddoc standing at the cliff's edge, the distant ocean maelstrom raging behind him.

Maddoc bared his teeth and stretched out his gloved hands, not at the goblins but past them, where Anica watched on with an amused expression. *"Dran'tikala,"* he intoned, and a creeping wave of darkness emanated from his body like heavy, oily smoke. It advanced quickly, weaving past the spinning renegade hunters and through the screeching goblins until it swirled around the feet of the convulsing Goblin Man.

The oily darkness slithered up Arvin's shuddering legs, enveloping him. Then, as suddenly as the spell started, it drifted away as though it were nothing more than smoke caught in the wind. Davyn ducked a wild swing from a goblin then looked back over at Maddoc. The old man's features twisted in confusion.

"Oh, did we mention?" Anica called in her slick, vile voice. "Our master, Maddoc, is your god—*Nuitari*."

So stunned was he by what she'd just said, Davyn missed blocking a blow and sharp claws raked at his neck, drawing blood. Unable to spare a thought for what a god would want with Sindri, Davyn turned back to the fray, bellowed a war cry, and brought down his sword.

Wilden parried a clawed swing at his head and struck the goblin in the ribs. Beside him, Garin's silent renegade hunter mirrored Wilden's movements, his twin crescent scythes leaving dozens of cuts etched into goblin bodies.

There was something terribly familiar about the way this man moved—the forms he employed in quick succession, the spells he cast to shield himself. Wilden was certain he'd seen the style before, but then, many of the conclave's renegade hunters were trained by the same masters.

He didn't have time to think about it for long. He scissored the neck of one of the deformed, scowling goblins with his scythes. As he did, he saw Tayt valiantly guarding Rina while the elf girl did her best to shoot the goblins.

Tayt's look was determined, but Wilden had seen the flash of resigned horror that had gone through her eyes when Anica had made her presence known.

Tayt had just escaped that vile witch. He would make sure she wouldn't have to face her again.

With a yell, Wilden leaped over a rampaging goblin to stand back to back with the other renegade hunter.

"Keep them distracted," he whispered. The two of them held

their weapons ready, goblins stalking slowly about them. "I'm going for the old woman."

The renegade hunter nodded.

Wilden closed his eyes, spread his arms wide, and whispered his spell: *"Cepat tanda, perubahan ayun."* His surroundings disintegrated around him in a flash of shadow.

As the world reappeared, he found himself exactly where he wanted to be: directly behind Anica, farther in the grass. From here he could see the battle scene clearly: There were still at least a dozen goblins leaping at the group, dangerously close to the edge of the cliff. The shaggy haired boy Davyn swung his sword expertly at the rear of the rampaging creatures as the other renegade hunter kept them busy from the front. Rina kept up a steady stream of arrows—the quiver curiously never went empty—and Tayt fought with fist and dagger to protect the elf. Maddoc stood dumbfounded while Garin chose to whack away with his staff rather than take the time to cast a spell.

Anica watched it all, cackling. Features still, Wilden raised his scythes high above the poof of white that was the woman's hair.

Something hit him full force from behind and Wilden flew forward to land at the old woman's feet. He spun, flinging off the stubby, saggy body of the crazed Goblin Man.

The Goblin Man loomed above him, beady eyes narrowed with hate. "Now now," he growled, "mustn't be doing that." Then, he raised his hands and began to cast a spell.

"Behind you!"

Davyn swiveled and brought his sword up just in time to parry a particularly vicious blow. He riposted, sending the goblin flying backward. Rina ran to join him, firing volleys of arrows as she moved.

"Davyn!" Rina pointed past him to where Anica stood with her back to the fight. At her feet, Davyn could make out a collapsed form on the ground, the Goblin Man hovering over him. Laughing maniacally, he raised his clawed hands to cast a deadly spell. Black roots had grown from the ground and bound Wilden around his chest and his waist, strapping him helplessly against the craggy stone ground.

"Rina, do it, *now!*"

In one fluid motion, Rina drew and nocked an arrow from her quiver, readying it against her face. The pendant around her neck glowed blue, and she let go of the bowstring.

Her arrow arced through the fray, narrowly missing several goblins. As it spun, the shaft glistened in the light and the arrow grew translucent until it was an arrow no longer, but a shard of solid ice.

Arvin howled as it struck his upraised hand.

The frozen arrow shattered instantly, encasing the man's hand in ice. The ice spread until it surrounded his entire arm, freezing it in its upright position. Arvin turned away from Wilden, naked hatred in his small black eyes.

"*Kill her!*" he shouted, and the goblins closest to him turned their goo-slickened heads toward Rina.

"We need to act now!" Davyn shouted to the others as the remaining goblins began a loping charge toward Rina. He glanced at Maddoc, who still stood doing nothing at the cliff's edge.

"Maddoc!" he shouted. "Cast a spell!"

Scowling, Maddoc met Davyn's eyes, and for a moment Davyn could swear he saw years of impotent rage in that one gaze.

"Their master is blocking my spells," he growled.

Davyn growled himself as he swiped his sword through the midsection of the nearest goblin. A few feet away, he saw the White Robe Garin doing what Maddoc was not—fighting the goblins despite not having time for magic.

Two goblins had torn off from the fray swarming toward Rina. Garin managed to block the repeated swipes of their claws with his staff, but he was slowly but surely being driven to the cliff's edge. Sweat beaded on his brow as he sought a free moment with which to begin casting.

Davyn's heavy sword arced downward, severing the goblins' arms. Garin looked him in the eye and gave a curt nod. Breathing heavily, Davyn nodded back. "We need to get to Wilden. Can you protect him until I think of something?"

Garin's features knotted. "Of course," he said. "I can shield him from harm until you can reach him, but be quick about it. I wasn't built to swing this staff like a bloody sword!"

Davyn nodded, and Garin began chanting magic words. A sphere of golden light surrounded Wilden just as Anica leaped to attack.

Davyn turned back to the screaming goblins and resumed his attack. Among his hacking, the practiced fighting of the renegade hunter, Tayt's street fighting, and Rina's arrows, the remaining goblins fell in moments.

Just as Davyn's last blow struck and the lone remaining goblin fell dead, the shield protecting Wilden fell free.

Wilden struggled against the vines that clung to him, but he couldn't move to cast a spell or slice himself free.

Arvin loomed over him. His breath hit Wilden's face in putrid waves.

"Where is Sindri?" he asked with a tilt of his head. "Tell me quickly and I might consider not killing you."

Wilden looked the old man directly in his beady eyes. They were as black as Anica's false stone eyes had been, and he knew then that it was true, all of it—the power of Nuitari lay behind the hideous wizard's gaze. Going against Arvin would be going against a god.

Wilden spat directly in Arvin's eyes. "Go to the Abyss, Arvin."

Arvin leaned back. He flicked away the spittle with clawed hands.

"I'll ask you again," Arvin said, "because I do so often make errors when asking questions, and it's likely you misheard me: *Where is Sindri Suncatcher?*"

Someone chuckled, the sound full of bitter amusement. Wilden tilted his head to see Maddoc standing at the edge of the cliff with his hands behind his back. Near him, the rest of the group stood warily among the bodies of the fallen goblins, waiting for their moment to strike.

Arvin's jowls drooped as his brow furrowed in confusion. "Whyever are you laughing, Maddoc?"

Maddoc shook his head. "You pathetic fool," he spat. "If Sindri's all you're here for, you're much too late. He's gone, and so you've toiled here for nothing."

"You're lying!" Anica said as she came to Arvin's side. "We were told he—"

"Well you were told wrong, you eyeless hag," Tayt called. "Sindri's long gone from here, and soon he'll find out all he needs to know to destroy you."

Silence fell, and nothing could be heard except the crashing of the waves against the cliffside and the distant calls of gulls. Arvin glanced from one wary defender to the next. A moment passed, and he sighed.

"Oh dear," he said, shoulders slumped. "All this effort and no kender to show for it. But I guess not much could be expected of—"

Anica came up behind him and thumped him on the head. "Now, none of that. You did just fine for a first try, dear." She tilted her head toward Wilden and smiled. "And if we kill this annoying man before we go, then this could hardly be called a failure."

"Wilden!" Tayt and Garin cried in unison.

Wilden braced himself, not taking his eyes away from Anica as she raised her withered hands to cast a killing spell. As she did, a wall of flame appeared before her. She screeched and Wilden smelled burning hair.

"This won't keep me away for long, Wilden!" Anica screamed over the wall of flames. "We will see you again in Kendermore. And neither you nor Tayt will escape my wrath!"

"Kendermore," Wilden whispered. If they couldn't kill Sindri, Wilden realized, then the natural conclusion for villains like Arvin and Anica would be to go and kill his friends and family until Sindri came home.

Wilden ignored Anica's continued ranting as he struggled to escape his bonds. In moments, Davyn and the renegade hunter were at his side, slicing through the magically created vines. The wall of flame raged on.

"We have to stop them," Wilden said as he was dragged backward to his feet. "They're going to hurt Sindri's family." He pulled his scythe free and stood side by side with Davyn and the other renegade hunter just as the magical wall of flame fell away.

When it did, Arvin and Anica were gone.

THE STOLEN SUN

CHAPTER

11   SECRETS OF THE PAST

The sea boiled with blood.

Sindri leaned over Auren's side and stared down at the ocean in awe. The crimson waves of the Blood Sea roiled below as black clouds swirled above in the endless, raging storm. Lightning sparked distantly on the darkened horizon, followed by thunder that rumbled behind the constant whooshing of the wind.

Sindri brushed his soaked hair out of his face and blinked rain out of his eyes. "Oh wow."

"Keep back." Auren's voice seemed to rumble up from beneath the gold scales of his neck. "Can't have you falling off. The ocean below is haunted, you know. No telling what might happen should you fall in."

Sindri sat back, eyes wide.

"Haunted! How interesting."

Auren rumbled deep in his throat in response. The dragon fought against the storm, his massive head held low as his wings rose and fell in a steady rhythm. Auren caught the brunt of the storm head on, but rain soaked Sindri's hair and the harsh wind tore at his cloak.

Rizzek, curled in Sindri's lap, whimpered. Clutching Auren's neck tighter with his thighs, Sindri scratched behind Rizzek's ears.

"It'll be all right," he whispered. "We're almost there."

Rizzek whined and dug his head farther into Sindri's lap.

Auren tilted his head to look back at Sindri. "You're right," he shouted over another burst of thunder. "The island is up ahead! Hang on tight!"

With Rizzek safe between his legs, Sindri leaned forward and gripped the dragon tightly around his neck. Soon after that, Auren tilted forward into a dive.

Sindri kept his eyes wide open, smiling in glee as they rushed down toward the angry red ocean, even as Rizzek yelped in fear. Wind blew Sindri's hair and cloak straight back and rain stabbed his face like icy daggers. Under him, Auren's muscles twitched as the dragon struggled to keep his wings spread.

And then, just as Sindri felt as weightless as air, Auren leveled off. There, on the edge of the red ocean, was the island.

It was more of a rock, really. A very large rock that seemed to Sindri to be shaped a bit like a bowl. Jagged cliffs rose high from the ocean, the waves cresting against their edges and leaving behind frothy pink foam. But the cliffs were a bit like a wall that surrounded the island, for they sloped inward to form a deep, protected valley. From what Sindri could tell, even if anyone managed to make it through the Maelstrom of the Blood Sea, they wouldn't be able to scale the cliffs anyway. There was no way to get to the temple that lay hidden at the island's center.

Unless, of course, you could fly.

The storm died down as Auren tilted slightly to his side to circle over the island's cliffs. Sindri let go of the dragon's neck and looked down at the island below. Trees and vines grew untamed, shrouding the island's valley in overgrown darkness. But as Sindri narrowed his eyes, he just barely made out stone pillars and tiled floors of a temple—his temple!

Sindri held his breath, his whole body shaking with anticipation as Auren soared down toward the temple. As they grew near, Sindri felt a warmth against his chest as the golden dragon scale around his neck began to glow. The temple's pillars and arches, its fountains and the tiled floor, shimmered with golden magic. It spread in a wave, the temple's glow cutting through the harsh darkness of the untamed valley forest.

Near the temple, a large area of trees and bushes had been crushed flat. Auren landed there gently, then folded his wings to his side.

"And we're here," the dragon rumbled.

Sindri found he couldn't move or speak, not even when Rizzek darted free from his arms and ran down to hug the ground. Instead, Sindri looked over the sprawling temple with a feeling of such wonder and joy he could hardly stand it. Unlike the other temples, it was completely intact, unmolested by outside hands. Here, in this most hidden of places, the secrets Sindri desired most to know would surely be revealed.

"Do you need help down?" Auren asked.

Sindri shook his head, startled from his thoughts, and then smiled at Auren's tilted head.

"Oh no," he said. "Sorry about that. It's just . . . this place. I'm finally here."

Auren nodded and slowly blinked his plate-sized blue eyes. "Yes, you are."

Shaken from his silence, Sindri clapped his hands in glee and slid down Auren's side. He was racing through the long grass of the island's ground and toward the glowing golden temple before he

JEFF SAMPSON

even thought about doing so. Realizing he wouldn't be able to read anything without Auren's help, he skidded to a stop and turned to find the gold dragon.

Standing among the broken trees wasn't Auren the gold dragon, but Auren in his human form. His orange and yellow silk clothes were as fine as before, his golden hair and tanned skin unmarred by their journey. Auren came to Sindri's side, hands behind his back. Behind him, Rizzek continued to roll in the grass and purr-click in contentment.

Sindri jumped from foot to foot as he looked up at the strange man. "So where should we start?"

Auren spread his hands wide. "Anywhere that you like, Sindri. Go ahead, step inside."

Sindri didn't have to be told twice. He turned to look at the temple. Marble steps led to its entrance, a wide archway guarded by two golden statues. The statues were of a small man and a small woman dressed in old-fashioned robes. They looked a bit like tall dwarves, with the same stubby bodies and grim expressions Sindri had seen on several of the dwarves he'd known in his time, but there was a sharpness to their features Sindri had only ever seen in humans.

Sindri stood toe to toe with the golden male statue and looked into his empty eyes with curiosity. "Were these the Wizards of the Sun?" he asked.

Auren came to his side. "They were, though history knows them as the scions. These two depicted here, from what the inscriptions at their feet say, were two of the leaders behind the Order of the Sun and their project to build the three temples. This being the last temple, statues were raised in their honor."

Sindri tilted his head. "They look so serious," he said.

Auren looked down at Sindri, solemn. "They were the last of their kind, and soon after this place was built, a battle was held and they were destroyed. They didn't have much reason to smile."

Sindri looked down at his wet trousers and shifted his feet. "Oh."

Slithery, magic words left Auren's lips and Sindri's clothes grew lighter, his body warmer. Touching his now dry hair, he realized that Auren had cast a spell.

Taking a breath, Sindri stepped back from the statues of the scions. "Well, come on! Let's see what else we can find."

Sindri darted through the archway and into the temple, Auren walking steadily behind. Like the other temples, the floor was covered with tiles that depicted ancient magic, only these also showed golden-robed scions forcing back a tide of darkness with the help of a gold dragon. Long-dry fountains stood like marble blooms atop the tile, and surrounding everything were flowery pillars and walls etched with ancient writing.

"Here," Sindri said, pointing to the nearest wall. "Let's start here!"

Quietly, Auren came up behind Sindri. "All right. Place your hands against the wall, Sindri."

Sindri looked up at the golden-skinned man. "What for?"

Auren's somber expression did not change. "You will see."

With a shrug, Sindri did as instructed. As soon as his palms touched the cool, glowing stone of the temple, the constant power whirring in his stomach jumped.

And with it, images flashed through his mind.

It was night, but the stars were not in the correct places. Small men and women with skin that glowed golden huddled together near a meager fire. They spoke words in a language Sindri couldn't understand, their faces grim, their tones low and rushed.

Sindri recognized the man and the woman—their statues now stood in front of the final temple. The woman's look was distant as the man spoke in harsh tones, his hands moving about in quick, commanding motions.

"This is when your journey began."

Sindri looked to his side but saw nothing except darkened trees. He sensed, however, that Auren was close by.

"What is this?" he asked.

"This," Auren said, "is the first meeting of what would become the Order of the Sun. The woman you saw as the statue, she is the one who foresaw the future of the scions. She was the one who had the vision of their downfall . . . and of the eventual resurgence of wild magic to Krynn."

Sindri looked back and studied the woman carefully. While her skin glowed a pale gold, her eyes were a deep red that swirled with magic. Sindri had a strange feeling that she wasn't looking distantly away from the group, as he originally thought—she was looking at *him*.

Firm hands gripped Sindri's wrists and lowered his hands from the wall. Sindri blinked as the golden temple reappeared around them, Auren at Sindri's side.

Sindri looked up and met Auren's blue eyes. "I have to see more."

Auren stepped back and spread his hands. "Then continue."

Sindri spun and found another wall. He ran to it and pressed his palms firmly against its surface.

Another vision came.

This one was erratic and shifted constantly. One moment, Sindri was in a port town, standing on the docks as a young human man with a dangerous grin on his face commanded the ocean to rise up and flood the streets, even as merchants pleaded with him and offered him their wares.

The next moment, Sindri was deep inside a cave, watching a group of dwarves cower before a dwarf woman with a black skull tattooed over her face. With a clench of her fist, she commanded the walls to grow together to crush the cowering dwarves, and they screamed in pain and terror—

At another moment in time, a small man lay back against a hill with his feet propped atop a tree stump, casually commanding the ground before him to reform with a flick of his fingers, not noticing that his lethargic use of magic was uprooting trees nearby and causing upheavals in soil of a neighboring farm. Sindri spun around and . . .

. . . found himself before a wall of flames as a farmhouse burned. Nearby a woman wailed as tears made paths down her soot-stained cheeks. Inside the nearby barn, animals brayed as they burned, incapable of escaping the inferno that consumed their pens. Several people with faces painted red exited the farmhouse, their arms full of what they could carry. One red-faced thief snorted at the wailing woman and flicked his fingers, setting the woman ablaze.

Sindri started and pulled his hands away from the wall, not believing what he'd just seen. Even though he was back in the temple, he could still smell horrible fire, and tears welled in his eyes.

"They . . ." Sindri said. "They were *evil*." He spun around to face Auren and indignantly stomped his foot. "They were murderous, thieving, uncaring monsters! What were these scions? What were they?"

Auren stood still next to one of the empty fountains, hands behind his back. "They were people, Sindri," he said softly. "They were changed and granted access to the magic that still lives in the bones of the world. Granted access to *all* of the magic. Very few people have the capability of dealing with such power without abusing it. And not everyone who was granted the power deserved it."

Even as Sindri clenched his jaw in anger, the tears over what he'd just seen coursed down his cheeks. "I don't understand!" he said. "What does this mean? That my magic is *evil?* That the people whose power I share deserved to be destroyed?"

Auren lowered his head. "What it means is what you feel in your heart it means, Sindri. Is that what you feel? Do you believe that what you possess is inherently evil?"

Sindri slumped down to the tiled floor and hugged his knees to his chest. He didn't have any idea what he felt. His power was amazing and wonderful and all he'd ever hoped for. But he'd just seen what others with that same power had done in the past. And he knew that whatever had happened to them, they'd had coming.

With a deep breath, Sindri leaped to his feet. "I need another wall," he said. Not waiting for Auren to respond, he raced through an archway and skidded to a stop before another one. He placed his hands upon its cool surface and let the vision come.

He was here, in the temple, but many years ago. Torches burned on the distant cliff faces as an army surged down into the valley. Scions ran frantically about him, the golden robes shimmering bright in the light of the red and silver moons that shone full above.

There was a dragon here, a large gold dragon standing just outside the temple that seemed instantly familiar to Sindri. In a strange, ancient language that Sindri didn't understand, the dragon spoke with the woman and the man depicted in the statues.

The army and their torches grew closer, and as one the scions laid their hands against the dragon's side. They lowered their heads, closed their eyes, and shimmering magic light surrounded the dragon.

It was over in an instant and the dragon leaped into the sky just as the army attacked. There were men and women in armor and bearing swords, but there were others too, wearing robes of red, black, and white, casting magic tentatively.

The scions fought back, raising the land and letting forth bursts of flame, showing such power that Sindri instinctively thought it shouldn't exist, but knew from the constant rumbling within himself that it was very possible.

But the scions were outnumbered and they began to fall. From a distance, Sindri saw the gold dragon ensnared, captured by the new wizards that had come to destroy the dangerous sorcerers of old.

Sindri let his hands fall from the wall.

"The dragon," Auren whispered from behind him, "was an ancestor of mine. His name was Theoran."

Sindri did not look away from the glowing marble wall and its ancient, unreadable carvings.

"I know," he whispered back.

Auren came to Sindri's side and continued. "It took years to discover what happened to him," the dragon went on. "I was told the wizards who captured him took him to what is now known as Solamnia. They locked him up and drained his blood, using its power as their own despite terrible consequences."

Sindri swallowed and looked down at his boots. "And then he died, and his soul was trapped for a long, long time." Brushing his hair out of his eyes, he turned and met Auren's bright blue eyes. "Until I freed him. And until he gave me that power I saw the scions putting into him."

Auren nodded, a slight smile playing at his lips. "He must have had quite a sense of humor to have decided you would be the chosen one," he said. "Someone no one would expect would be granted the power the scions lost so long ago."

Sindri looked back to the wall, fighting back the tears that threatened to come. "But they deserved to have it taken away," he said. "I saw what they did. Their power was untamed and dangerous. What I have . . . I think I know why Nuitari wants me dead. If I exist, and if I bring back this magic to the world, all because of one dead dragon's sense of humor . . . bad things could happen, couldn't they?"

Auren said nothing.

Sindri stomped his foot and turned to storm out of the temple. He ran through the archway and down the steps, back to the broken trees, and plopped down on the ground.

"It's not fair!" he cried out, startling Rizzek nearby.

Auren appeared as stoic as ever at the temple's steps. "No," he said. "It's not. But it is the way things are."

Sindri's shoulders slumped and he looked down at the grass. "So what do I do, Auren?" he asked. "I have my magic, and it's all I ever wanted. But if I was chosen to bring it back to the world, and there's a *god* out to stop me . . ." He looked up at the gray sky. "What am I supposed to do?"

Auren stood above him, breathing in deep the piney valley air. "Whatever it is, I trust it will be the right decision," he said. "But perhaps it would be best if you thought on it."

Sindri sighed. He peered over and saw Rizzek cowering beneath a fallen tree trunk, then beckoned the little lizard creature over with his hands.

"Yeah," he said as Rizzek curled into his lap. "I suppose it is."

"I'll be back, Sindri."

Auren's voice boomed, echoing between the valley's walls, and Sindri turned to find that he was once again the immense gold dragon. Wings outstretched, he lowered his head to look Sindri in the eye.

"Whatever you decide, it is your choice. Remember: Just because some people misused magic in the past doesn't mean everyone will in the future. It also doesn't mean that they won't."

Sindri swallowed and nodded. "Thank you," he whispered. "I'll remember."

With a lizardy smile, Auren leaned back on his haunches, spread his wings wide, and leaped into the air. When the gust of air left in the dragon's wake settled down, Sindri blinked his eyes and looked toward the afternoon sky.

Somewhere behind those clouds, waiting to rear his head once night fell, was Nuitari.

Sindri had stolen the power of the sun. Soon, he'd have to face the wrath of a god.

CHAPTER

12   BEHIND THE MASK

After Arvin and Anica's sudden disappearance, Wilden had relayed to the gathered group what Anica had said about Kendermore, and they knew immediately they had to take action lest Sindri's family be harmed.

While Maddoc, Davyn, and Rina stayed behind at the dragon's lair to await Sindri's return, Wilden and the others saddled up Garin's horses and began the trek back to the Kenderwood to prepare.

It wasn't exactly the companions Wilden had hoped to travel with. While Tayt provided a sisterly sort of companionship, his discomfort with his former master and the renegade hunter hadn't gone away. Though Tayt attempted to make conversation to break the awkward silence, both Garin and the renegade hunter remained quiet as they rode through the forest.

Wilden knew Garin, and he knew the man was incredibly fond of hearing himself speak. The look Garin cast between Tayt and Wilden made it apparent that he didn't want to speak in front of her.

Wilden didn't know what to make of Marten either. He remained stoic, even during battle. As they traveled, the hunter would sometimes catch Wilden's eyes and stare. Although Marten would break eye contact as soon as possible, Wilden couldn't help feeling somewhat unnerved.

An hour into their travel, Tayt finally gave up attempting conversation. She, too, silently plodded on as night overtook them. The silence only lengthened their journey as the hours passed. It seemed to take forever for the horses to take each step. The woods appeared endless and just as quiet as Wilden and his companions.

"So, is anyone else famished?"

Tayt's voice broke the silence of the evening. Wilden's stomach growled, as if in response to Tayt's question.

"That's not a bad idea," said Garin as he halted his horse. "There seems to be a small clearing over there as well. Let's make camp for a while before we continue our journey."

They stopped in a clearing and tethered their horses to the trees. Delegating tasks, Garin set Tayt to look for water and Marten to hunt for a small supper. Wilden and Garin started a fire and prepared camp. Continuing to remain silent toward one another, they gathered wood, cleared out brush and, with a quick spell, set up a blazing fire.

"Wilden," Garin finally said, breaking the silence between them.

Wilden turned to find Garin facing him from the other side of the fire. The shadows cast by the fire's flames deepened the older man's wrinkles, making him appear much older. He regarded Wilden with hurt eyes.

Wilden swallowed and bowed his head. "Master."

Garin put his hands behind his back and rounded the flames.

He glanced to his side, as though looking to see if Tayt or Marten were about, then sighed.

"I do not know what to say," Garin said. "I do not understand what has happened here. You have forsaken your duty, Wilden. You have betrayed the conclave and the gods."

Raising his head, Wilden dared to look into his mentor's shadowed eyes.

"I know," Wilden whispered. He licked his lips, which suddenly felt much too dry, and ran his hand through his long hair. "I know."

Garin stepped back and splayed his hands at his side in exasperation. "Then what are you doing out here?" he demanded. "You were sent on the mission to catch the kender because I trusted you. None of the other wizards saw the threat that we did, and you vowed to capture the renegade. Now you help him? Now you go against the wishes of the gods? For what, Wilden?"

Wilden shook his head and backed away from the flame. Bark cut into his back as he hit a tree, and he let himself lean against it. Again he swallowed.

"Sindri," he said after a moment. "I do it for Sindri—because he's important."

"The will of a god of magic must be done!" Garin shouted. Startled birds cawed and burst from the trees and Garin yelped despite himself. Ducking, the man dared to peer up into the night sky, where the moon gods watched the goings-on below.

Straightening, Garin again came to stand before Wilden. Wilden met his eyes.

"The revelation back at the dragon's lair has not left my mind, Wilden," Garin said in a hushed voice. "If Nuitari is indeed behind the attempts to capture or destroy Sindri Suncatcher, then we must not stand in the way. You understand that, do you not?"

Wilden stood tall and defiant, and did not look away. "I understand perfectly. And I choose to stand by Sindri rather than get out of the way of a god of black magic."

Garin scowled. "It does not matter what magic he oversees," he said. "He is still one of the three gods that oversees our order." Garin lowered his head and sighed. "Wilden, my boy, do not do this. Think of what you are giving up." He looked up and met Wilden's eyes. "There is still so much you need to learn. You have great potential, but despite your foresight, your magic skills are lacking. Even Master Zobel thinks that there are a few kinks in your fighting style that need to be worked out. Please, Wilden, help me turn over the kender and the spellfilch, and I can see to it that your punishment for all of this is small, and we can resume your training—make you great."

Wilden looked over the flames. Tayt had returned to continue setting up camp, trying her hardest not to intrude on Garin and Wilden. She worked quietly, her expression thoughtful, before heading back into the woods to escape the tense situation near the fire.

Tayt had just escaped imprisonment. Wilden couldn't bear to see her imprisoned again.

"I can't," Wilden whispered as he watched Tayt disappear into the trees. "I won't betray my . . . my friends."

Garin clenched his fists, and his voice shook when he spoke. "Wilden, it is not a betrayal to turn them over to the conclave. It will do nothing but help them. We can solve their problems, teach them to properly use their powers. We can control—"

"Control." Wilden shook his head and looked back at Garin. "That's what this is all about, isn't it? The conclave, the moon gods, they want to take Sindri and Tayt and control their every move, make sure they fit inside the little boxes that have been set aside for all of us. You coming here, this had nothing to do with me."

"It has everything to do with you, Wilden." Garin's voice began to rise. "You are one of us. The kender and the girl, they are just small players in this vast game. They may be what matters now, but you have to think of what matters in your future—the conclave's future. We are your family, Wilden. How can you turn your back on us like this?"

Wilden stiffened and stepped back. "Family? You know nothing of my family."

Garin stepped with him. "I knew your mother and father once. They would have wanted you to come back. Your brother would have wanted you to come back."

Anger rushed through Wilden, a rage foreign to him. But the weeks that had passed, what they'd shown him had confused everything he'd ever been taught. And this man, this wizard, had been the one who had told Wilden the lies that befuddled him in the first place.

Clenching his fists and narrowing his eyes, Wilden stood face to face with his former master. The flame's shadows cast the old man's eyes in darkness.

"My mother and father," Wilden said, enunciating each word slowly, "would have wanted me to follow what I thought was right. Just like I thought you once wanted me to do. And as for my brother, how would you know what he wanted? You never paid attention to him, you delegated him away. He failed his Test of High Sorcery and he died, and you never seemed to care."

Wilden's voice caught in his throat, old and forgotten emotions rising like bile. "Sindri and Tayt, they're my family now. We struggled these past few months together, for what? For me to betray them right when they need me most? I could never do that. I could never abandon what I feel for them, and nothing you say will change my mind."

"Wilden—" Garin's eyes softened.

"And after this adventure is done, I will follow them to the next."

Wilden glared at Garin. The two were at an impasse. Garin would never give up trying to woo Wilden back to the conclave, no matter if he'd already done much to go against the will of a god of magic. And nothing Garin could say would convince Wilden to leave behind the friends he'd come to care for.

Branches crackled to Wilden's left. Marten appeared in the clearing, carrying a few dead rabbits.

"Excellent, Marten, just in time." Garin took the rabbits and said a quick spell under his breath. The fur flew off them to a pile on the side. Garin handed back the rabbits to Marten to skewer and place on the fire.

"I was just explaining to Wilden here why he should come back to the conclave again. Don't you agree?"

Marten's icy blue eyes met Wilden's. For the first time, Wilden stared back. His anger had not yet subsided, and he was sure that Marten would stop looking once he saw his rage. But they did not break eye contact. And for the first time, a long forgotten memory sparked in Wilden's mind.

"Those eyes," he said, not daring to tear away from the renegade hunter's gaze. "I know those eyes."

Garin came to stand between Wilden and Marten, a devious smile across his stubbled, lined face.

Wilden shook his head and glared into the old face of his mentor.

"Garin . . ."

Garin nodded, his smile growing. "Marten," he said faintly. "It's time."

Wilden looked over Garin's shoulder to see Marten close his eyes, nodding slowly. With a breath, Marten reached up and lifted up the black mask that had shrouded his face this entire time.

Wilden couldn't help but stare in disbelief. The features hidden behind the black mask were decidedly similar to his. As Wilden saw the shaggy blond hair coming out from underneath the mask, he knew what about Marten had seemed so familiar. Wilden's training, his composure, every last bit of himself that seemed strong and confident gave way at that moment, and Wilden felt his legs go slack.

"By the gods," he said, his hands shaking. "*Maro?*"

The blond renegade hunter's face, rugged and scarred, showed no emotion. He nodded slightly.

"Yes, Wilden," Garin said, gently pulling the young man out of the dirt. "It is your brother."

Wilden's head snapped to look at Garin. "But he's dead," he whispered. "He's been dead for years. He failed his test, he—"

"No, Wilden," his brother said as he approached Wilden. "I am alive. I have been this whole time."

Wilden swallowed. "But how?"

Garin heaved a deep sigh. "Maro—Marten, as he is now called—is powerful. We knew that from a young age. He has much more power than we could have ever hoped for. And as his strength grew, we knew that with him in your presence, all hope for you would be lost. You would look upon your brother with contempt and frustration as he progressed much faster than you ever could. And with those feelings, you would never become the soldier you are meant to be. And Marten realized this as he trained and watched you fall behind the work he was doing.

"So, upon his insisting, we took him away, faked his death, and hoped that your strength would flourish without him being there. And as you know, it did. Spectacularly. We were hoping to reintroduce you to him when you had reached your full potential. But now I realize that without your knowledge of Marten's existence, you will never become the soldier which you are capable of becoming. This is why you need to come back to the conclave, why you must give up this misguided quest to help a kender, of all people, use magic."

Garin's face suddenly looked much older and tired. Wilden looked back and forth between his former master and his brother. Wilden finally locked eyes with Marten once more.

"Maro," he said. "I don't know what to say."

The young man smiled. "You don't need to say anything," he said as he began to wrap his face back up. "You are conflicted of late, I can tell. You always get sullen when your mind is heavy." His smile disappeared behind the layers of black cloth.

Suddenly Tayt reappeared with the water, running from between the trees with a look of terror smeared across her face.

"Hey, guys," she said frantically. "I don't want you to panic but—"

Right from where Tayt had just reappeared, a goblin shot past them, running at breakneck speed. He hesitated as he hit their campsite, but decided to ignore them and kept moving. Then another goblin, running equally as fast, blew by the travelers. And then another. And another. The horses whinnied in fear and bucked as a multitude of goblins ran past where the group was standing.

"What is this?" Wilden exclaimed, shouting over the noise of the goblins passing through. "Why are there so many?"

"More important," Tayt shouted, "why aren't they stopping to fight?"

Garin reached into his bag and pulled out a handful of powder. "*Capik,*" he intoned as he threw the powder into the air. One of the goblins halted in its tracks.

"Grab him!" Garin yelled. "Before the spell wears off!"

Tayt tackled the goblin. Wilden grabbed his scythe and held it to the goblin's throat as Marten stepped on the goblin's hands and lowered his own blade onto the goblin's skull.

"Don't move, or we'll kill you," Wilden said, glaring at the dirty beast. "What is your purpose? Where are you headed?"

"That is not mine to say," the goblin groaned as it tried to twist out of Tayt's grasp.

Wilden pressed his blade harder on the goblin's neck. "I will ask once more. What is your purpose? Where are you headed?"

"Kendermore," the goblin cracked. "Kendermore."

"And what for? Why are you going there?" Tayt yelled as she wrestled a goblin foot that has slipped out from underneath her.

The goblin shrugged. "I don't know," it said. Blood dripped from the spot where Wilden's scythe began to pierce its throat. "A dark day is coming," it growled in Wilden's ear, "and we must be there."

A vision entered Wilden's mind of another place, where a man— no, not quite a man—cast spells. Goblins crawled over upturned earth, climbing over one another in their haste to obey the man—the Goblin Man.

"*Kill the kender,*" the Goblin Man wheezed, then giggled in his high-pitched, manic way. "*Kill them all.*"

Wilden's vision caused his grip to slacken, and he released his hold on the goblin. With a quick kick at Tayt, it shook itself free and ran between Garin and Marten to head southward—toward Kendermore.

"What was that about?" Tayt asked, as she stood up from where the goblin had shook her off.

Wilden quickly grabbed the reins of the nearest horse and untethered it from the tree.

"It means we have to get to Kendermore and Weavewillow," he said, mounting the horse. "And we have to get there *now*."

"I'm not going with you," Garin said, unmoving. "Not until you agree to come back to the conclave."

All that had just occurred with Garin and Marten rushed over Wilden. For a brief, glorious moment he'd forgotten the confusion, the anger, but now . . .

Wilden met his brother's eyes, and his hands trembled. He felt betrayed, felt overjoyed, felt . . .

No, Wilden told himself. Now is not the time.

"Garin," Wilden said, struggling to keep his voice steady. "The kender will die if we don't leave now."

"I stand my ground," Garin said. "This is more important than you know. And Marten will stand with me too. Isn't that right, Marten?"

Marten hesitated. "This is an unreasonable request," he said, glaring fiercely at his master. "People's lives are in danger."

"Kender," Garin spat. "Kender!" He rounded on Wilden, jabbing a knobby finger up at him to punctuate his words. "This must be resolved now. This betrayal, this bastardization of our magic, cannot continue. Make your choice, Wilden."

Wilden sat motionless. It was Marten, only his eyes showing through his mask, who spoke.

"Master, I cannot agree with you that this is more important than other lives."

"Well then," Garin said, unmistakable rage on his face. "I am betrayed by you both. I thought you to be renegade hunters, trained at my hand to stop those using magic without the consent of the gods and the conclave. Go, then. I and the conclave will see you soon. And then you will understand the consequences of your actions." With that, the old man turned his back on his two apprentices and walked away.

As Marten mounted his horse, he turned to Wilden. "Brother, this is what you truly believe then, isn't it?"

Wilden blinked, then looked up at the renegade hunter—his brother.

"It is," he whispered.

"Good. Then let us go quickly. We may be able to head the goblins off." Looking over his shoulder, he waved for Tayt to follow. "Tayt, we need to move out." Wilden kicked his heels into his horse's sides in unison with Marten, and the two of them then started to gallop south toward Kendermore.

Tayt looked upon the scene curiously as she hopped on her horse to follow. "Wait!" she called out as the two galloped ahead of her. "'Brother'? And since when does he talk?"

Wilden did not respond. He couldn't think about this now, couldn't think about how his whole world had completely changed.

Instead, he focused on the task at hand and rode forward as fast as his horse could carry him.

CHAPTER

13 MADDOC, ALONE

The gold dragon's lair was vast and beautiful, an ancient structure unlike anything Davyn had imagined.

But despite the towering fountains, the marble statues, the rooms of mystical devices, Davyn's mind lingered only on Sindri's fate—and on Maddoc's intentions.

Davyn sat next to Rina in a library they'd found just off the main hall of the dragon's lair. Like all the rooms, it was wide and tall. Shelves overflowing with crumbling scrolls and books with yellowed pages lined the walls. A window seemed to peer directly into the ocean, but it had grown dark and Davyn could see nothing but inky black. They'd lit a fire in the wide fireplace that took up one of the walls, the flames' light casting long shadows.

Maddoc paced in front of the shelves, silent and stoic, his eyes studying the spine of every book carefully as he passed. Davyn watched the old wizard's expression warily. Davyn was sure Maddoc was up to no good—that was, after all, his specialty.

The warmth from the hearth of the fire relaxed Davyn somewhat as the time passed. Rina closed her eyes and put her head on

Davyn's shoulder, her long blonde hair grazing his hand as she did so. Davyn put his head atop Rina's, but he was not in the mood to sleep. He was too worried about Sindri and too suspicious of what Maddoc was doing.

Maddoc kept walking around the library. Davyn continued to watch his "father" as he walked past each of the shelves in the room, studying them carefully. Even though they had just fought alongside one another, Davyn had addressed Maddoc directly only one or two times. He was torn between speaking with Maddoc to find out what had happened to Sindri in his care and keeping quiet in his deep resentment.

He didn't have to choose which path to take, for as Maddoc edged toward the fireplace, the Black Robe chose to speak.

"Davyn." Maddoc kept his back to him, arms behind himself as he continued to study the shelves. "We have much to catch up on, I'm sure. What brings you back to the kender's side this time?"

"Stroke of luck," Davyn said, shifting uncomfortably on the hearth. Rina adjusted her head on his shoulder as he moved. "Speaking of Sindri, why aren't you with him? I thought you were his mentor."

It was Maddoc's turn to shift uncomfortably. "I have my reasons."

Davyn had his suspicions. Maddoc had mostly never tried to intentionally harm anyone, but more often than not, he didn't mind stepping on others on his way to the top.

Maddoc reached out a gloved hand and caressed a shimmering orb. Davyn remembered the smell of death that had wafted from that hand and wondered what it meant.

"Ah, you are in luck, masters and madam! Master Auren has returned!"

Davyn blinked and looked around the room, trying to find the source of the voice. He could have sworn a small golden dragon statue on a nearby table had just moved. Large, deep footsteps echoed from the main hall, and Davyn shook his head. Disregarding Rina on his shoulder, Davyn jumped up off the hearth and ran toward the hallway. Maddoc followed, robes swishing behind him.

"Hey!" Rina protested, slipping down on the cushions after Davyn leaped up. After recovering from the shock of being woken, she followed the other two.

A man wearing silks stood near the towering marble fountain. A sense of awe washed over Davyn unlike anything he'd felt before—this person appeared to be a tan-skinned man, but there was an air of ancient dignity that was unmistakable. It had to be the dragon Tayt and Wilden had told them of.

"You must be Auren," Davyn said, taking a deep, respectful bow.

"Not quite the same visitors I'd left here," Auren said with a smile. "But I assume that they let you in. Yes, I am Auren. And you are Davyn, correct?"

Davyn looked up at the magnificent man. "How did you—"

"Dragons have their ways," Auren said with a wink. "Ah, and the dark wizard Maddoc and Lady Rinalasha. How pleased I am to meet you all!"

Maddoc raised an eyebrow, his face unreadable. Rina curtsied somewhat awkwardly, though her elven grace carried it off.

"Now, to what do I owe the pleasure?" Auren's teeth sparkled in the shimmering light from the sconces high above. "And where are the rest of my guests?"

Davyn gave another short bow. "They apologize for their quick disappearance, but the need was urgent. Anica and Arvin were here, master. They tried to capture Sindri but when they realized he was not here, they headed south. They have a new plan of action."

Auren's vast smile quickly disappeared from his face. "They went to Kendermore."

"Yes," Davyn said with another bow. He could not help himself in the dragon's presence. Davyn had known only one good dragon in the past, and he was a much more informal copper dragon, not nearly as regal as Auren. This, perhaps, was compounded by the fact that he was in the dragon's home, which was more awe inspiring than any other home he'd ever been in.

Auren's easy, regal nature disappeared, replaced instead with a fierce resolve. "Sindri is not with me, but I can retrieve him in a matter of moments."

Maddoc bristled. "Take Sindri to Kendermore? Right into the arms of Anica and Arvin? Are you a madman?"

Auren raised an eyebrow. "I'm not quite a man."

"Maddoc does have a point," Rina said. "Sindri's all that those two want. Shouldn't we just fight the battle for him and make sure he's safe?"

Auren shook his head. "If I am correct, Sindri will be the only one who can stop Anica and Arvin. We must take him. Besides, how do you think Sindri would feel if he knew we had left him behind on the biggest adventure of them all?"

Davyn gave a smile. "This is true."

Maddoc scowled. "Preposterous is what this is. I have done nothing these past several months except try to keep Sindri from the hands of Nuitari's lackeys, and now we would fall into their trap and hand deliver him."

Maddoc glared at Auren. "I have enough power to stop Anica and Arvin. Why bother pulling Sindri into this? He's too innocent to be bothered with all of this foolishness. Let me do it myself. Let me handle Sindri's problems. Sindri would not mind missing the action if he knew it was his mentor who had helped him."

Auren's blue eyes flashed gray as he locked onto Maddoc's. "Drop the act, wizard," Auren said. "Your false show of concern grows tiresome. I know why you are here." Auren strode forward, seeming to grow larger with each step. Auren stood face to face with Maddoc, looking him squarely in the eye.

"After all you've done, all the lies you've told and people you've treated like experiments, know this, wizard: You will never steal Sindri's power."

Maddoc opened his mouth as if to say something. Instead, he snapped it shut and glowered at Auren.

Davyn glanced at his adoptive father's face. He had been a fierce man, a man who claimed to seek knowledge. He seemed old now, decrepit and beaten. But Davyn knew at that moment, knew even stronger than when the history of his true father had been revealed, that Maddoc was dangerous. Maddoc could never be trusted.

Rina stepped forward and laid a tentative hand on Auren's shoulder. "Sindri," she said. "We need to get him."

Auren nodded and turned away from Maddoc. "Quickly," Auren said as he headed toward the door. "We haven't much time."

As the three travelers followed Auren, he began to transform into his true form. Golden scales appeared on his tanned skin as his limbs elongated, his face stretching into a dragon's pointed snout. Stopping suddenly, he turned toward the three humans.

"Not you, wizard," Auren said with a mouth that was half-human, half-dragon. "They don't allow dark wizards where we are going. You can let yourself out."

Nearly full dragon now, Auren turned to face the door, which sprung open on its own to accommodate the dragon's new size.

"Hop on," he said to Davyn and Rina. The two of them climbed onto Auren's back. And as they began to rise up the staircase, Davyn looked back. He couldn't help but notice a malicious look on Maddoc's face that spoke of years of deep, unsettling anger.

Maddoc sneered as the dragon Auren took Davyn and Rina away up the staircase. He stared up at the grandiose ceiling as he raised his hands and uttered a few words under his breath. An unearthly screech came from above as what appeared at first to be a chunk of rock from the ceiling fell toward him. As it did, the rock transformed, twisting into the shadowy, wispy form of a falcon with glowing red eyes.

"Shaera," Maddoc said as the undead creature landed on his shoulder. "Your master isn't happy." He absentmindedly stroked the creature's bony beak as he turned back toward the library. Shaera took wing and followed him.

As Maddoc looked around the vast room again, the musty smell of old parchment pierced his nose. He gestured toward the highest shelves.

"I think I know what's in here," he said as his familiar took off to where Maddoc had pointed. "But I can't find it on my own. Help me look, will you?"

The bird flapped around the room, circling the higher shelves Maddoc had not yet inspected. Maddoc watched intently as the bird circled the high ceilings.

"I know this dragon," Maddoc muttered to himself. "I know this dragon and I know what I can get from him. Clearly he thinks me not a threat." Maddoc smiled.

He fingered the old scrolls which scattered the lone desk in the room. "A desk," he said aloud. "What does a dragon need with a desk?"

Shaera landed atop a lamp and tilted her head curiously, watching as Maddoc pulled open the drawers to inspect them further. Each drawer contained nothing but quills, parchment, seals, and other mundane writing equipment.

After opening a third drawer, he found a scroll which at first glance seemed to glow slightly gold. He opened it to reveal a map, similar to the one that Sindri had been presented by Rizzek months ago. It was covered with strange symbols that Maddoc could not make out.

"Old magic," he muttered, brow furrowed.

He turned the map counterclockwise several times as Shaera took wing and resumed her search of the shelves.

"There must be a landmark here, something I recognize." Maddoc knew if he studied it long enough, something would jump out at him. After the fourth or fifth turn he saw it—a miniscule golden triangle that remained pointed in the same direction, whichever way he turned the map.

"The lair," Maddoc said. "But where are the others?"

A shrill squawk came from the bird above. Maddoc looked up and saw a small metallic object fall from where Shaera was flying.

Maddoc reached out just in time to catch what Shaera had dropped to him. When he opened his palm, his normally emotionless face broke out into a large grin. Enclosed in his hand was a plain silver orb. As Maddoc rolled it in the palm of his hand, the colors of the orb changed from silver, to red, to black, then back to silver again.

"So this is the connection," Maddoc said as he rolled the orb around in his hand. He placed the orb on the map and put his eye up to it. The orb became translucent and through it, he could see more miniscule triangles, all metallic, which were similar to the golden one he had seen earlier.

"I will never know what Sindri's power is, eh, Auren?" Maddoc turned to Shaera as she once again landed on his shoulder. "If this is what I believe it is, I will know a power thousands of times greater than anything Sindri could comprehend."

From his pack, he procured a small piece of dried meat and handed it to Shaera. The undead falcon tore it to shreds, not seeming to notice that the bits of meat fell into an empty rib cage. "You've done well." Maddoc gave her another piece of meat. "But before I dismiss you, I have one more job for you: Follow the dragon. Follow the kender. Tell me everything."

The falcon dug her claws into Maddoc's shoulder, then leaped to take wing. Maddoc took one last look at his prizes before he pocketed them.

"The only thing more powerful than untamed wild magic," Maddoc said to himself, "is the magic of a dragon." He climbed the stairs to the surface, smiling to himself triumphantly as he abandoned all thought of Sindri and new plans formed in his mind.

CHAPTER

14   Preparing for Battle

It was late in the evening when Wilden, Tayt, and Marten rode into the clearing that marked the boundaries of Weavewillow. The town's sparse buildings appeared almost lonely, with only the occasional laugh of a kender child disturbing the otherwise tranquil night air.

Wilden wondered how many of these buildings and their inhabitants would survive the coming invasion.

In the corner of town they found the hut built under a hill that acted as the city's back corner—the home of Sindri's aunt Moonbeam. She'd struck Wilden as a scrappy, capable woman, and she certainly knew how to spread word quickly through the Kenderwood, so Wilden figured she'd be as good a kender to meet with as any.

Moonbeam opened the door as they approached her house, and called out in greeting. "Well now, you folks look positively morose! A frown isn't any way to greet an old friend!" At this, Wilden and Tayt grinned slightly. The kender woman's bold, easy manner was infectious and soon the three were busily recounting the past few days.

"I see," Moonbeam said as they finished their narration, "and now it comes to this. So a great goblin army is heading this way?"

They nodded.

"I suppose, then, that we kender will need to be doing something about protecting our land." Moonbeam clapped her hands. "How exciting! I know a thing or two about fortifications, military tactics, the usual stuff."

Wilden sat forward and clutched Moonbeam's shoulder. "No, Moonbeam, it isn't safe. We should wake everyone, have them head to Kendermore to take refuge. With the walls keeping the goblins out, maybe—"

Moonbeam shook her head fiercely. "Oh, my good boy, you don't know a thing about kender, do you? Do you really think if we tell everyone that we're going to go hide under our beds while a bunch of filthy goblins ransack our town, they'll just agree and miss out on all the adventure? No, no, you kids should start coming up with plans for how we're going to stop those brutes while I get supper finished. If you need any help, you just let ol' Moonbeam know." She winked and hurried into the kitchen to check on supper.

Marten glanced at Wilden, but said nothing. Wilden grinned at him in response, still unsure of what the reappearance of his brother meant, but still trying not to worry.

Supper was delicious, if hurried, as they hastened to get defensive proceedings underway. Moonbeam produced a map from a wall covered with cubby holes filled to the brim with them and spread it over the dining table.

"You know the village far better than we do, Moonbeam," Wilden said, "and your input would be appreciated. From a strategic standpoint, this village is a nightmare. It's approachable from every side, has an ineffective defensive enclosure, no natural terrain advantages. Our only consolation—"

"Now wait a minute," Moonbeam interjected. "You're forgetting that we're surrounded by woods—woods the kender of this village know better than anyone else alive! We may not be ready to withstand an army, but we keep an eye on ourselves. I probably knew you were headed here before you did! How do you think I had that roast served up only half an hour after you arrived?"

Tayt smiled. "It was delicious, Moonbeam—"

"Call me Aunt Moonbeam, dear. You're family now, of course," Moonbeam interrupted. "And don't you worry your pretty little head over it. It's rare we have guests, and repeat visitors as well!" She smiled broadly and returned her attention to the map. "Now, if we have small watches stationed here, here, here and here," she said, gesturing, "and three scouting parties filling in the gaps, we'll know of anything amiss with enough time to concentrate our forces there. The kids can handle that. Just tell them it's a game and they'll work hard at having fun. The rest of the village can split into four flying companies, each headed by one of us, so we can respond quickly to any breaches."

Wilden nodded, clearly impressed with the kender woman's grasp of war strategy and terminology. He had been taught the basics of warfare, his expertise was pretty much just hand to hand, himself against however many attacked him.

"Moonbeam," he said, "the army approaching is likely to be several hundred goblins, and they'll be here by morning if not sooner. How many villagers are there?"

"There are maybe two hundred of us here," she said, "and of those, maybe a hundred and twenty can fight. Not too many kender stay home for too long. Most who have settled here are old and past their wandering days, children not yet old enough to catch the bug, and those just passing through on their way to their next adventure."

Marten said, "Then we'll need a plan for withdrawing from the village toward Kendermore." Off Moonbeam's scowl, he added, "Just to be safe, Moonbeam. If there are too many we can only hold them off for so long."

Moonbeam nodded. "There's no easy way through the woods, but if we centralize any logging we do for fortification and weapon production toward the northeast portion, we'll end up building ourselves part of a path. As it's the side nearest Kendermore, we're unlikely to face an assault there."

"Let's not forget we're facing Arvin," Wilden added, "who, despite his recently augmented powers, I don't think has a particularly good grasp of military strategy. I don't think we'll be facing anything but a head-on assault, likely from here." He pointed to the village's northern border. "I won't rule out the possibility that they'll approach from another side, since Anica's with him and Solinari knows she's a sneaky old hag, but we should focus on this border. Our biggest problem is avoiding being overwhelmed too quickly."

"I think we can suss up a few traps before morning, tricks and the like," said Moonbeam, "and a few of them might even surprise you young conclave types."

At this, Marten spoke up. "We'll need to begin preparations immediately. Can you rally the village?"

Moonbeam nodded vigorously. "Not a problem. By now, even the mayor is used to listening to me. And I know everyone here will be keen to join in on a rousing good fight!" She smiled, stood, and began clearing the table.

Marten, Wilden, and Tayt rose as well, wishing they shared her enthusiasm.

"Preposterous!" Hephdeezee sputtered, gesturing toward Moonbeam with his cane. "I was there too, you know, and that's simply *not* how it was done!"

It was past midnight and Wilden, Tayt, Marten, Hephdeezee, and Moonbeam sat in Hephdeezee's hut, making plans while kender ran around outside, rousing the whole town from its sleep.

Moonbeam had been recounting the defense of a battle some twenty years ago. "I'm telling you, Father, that's what happened! With so much flammable shrubbery about, it was impossible to use fire magic on the prairie. Volatile combinations of bizarre spell reagents, that's all I remember! Don't ask me how, but that crazy Red Robe melted the golems without starting a fire!"

"Everyone, please!" Wilden said impatiently. "This isn't helping us. Moonbeam, that would be some trick—we can't use fire here without risking burning your village to the ground—but unless you remember how it was done, we're wasting our time." Moonbeam looked indignant, but ceased her anecdote.

Wilden continued. "Now then," he said, "we don't have time to build any defensive structures, so our best bet is to build small, mobile barricades." He continued on, going back and forth with Marten, Moonbeam, and Hephdeezee about the best course of action.

Tayt stayed silent, choosing instead to look forlornly outside. Wilden followed her gaze. Outside the kender assembled in the darkened streets, and he shook his head. The only ones in the village were those unafflicted with the inexorable kender wanderlust. Those in prime physical condition were all out exploring the world. Messengers had been sent to Kendermore to prepare them for the onslaught of kender and goblins come morning, but they'd be too busy with their own preparations to send anymore than a few out to help the Weavewillow citizens. He hoped for the hundredth time that they would be enough.

Wilden was shaken from his thoughts by Marten and Hephdeezee heading toward a back room. He took in a breath and tried to focus.

"Moonbeam." He leaned over the table and clutched her hand. "You alone both understand our requirements and know the people here intimately well, so I'd like you to organize the manpower." Moonbeam nodded and Wilden continued, pointing at the map. "Set everyone you can to gathering logs, but set aside the craftiest kender you know. We need to start building those traps."

Moonbeam nodded again and set off to get the village's defense underway.

Tayt sidled up to Wilden, hugging herself to ward off cool night air that breezed through Hephdeezee's missing front wall. "Do we really have time for all of this?" she asked. "The goblins, if they attack too soon—"

Wilden closed his eyes. "Then we'll make do."

"Wilden—" Tayt said.

She was interrupted by Hephdeezee and Marten barreling out of the back, the former moving as fast as a jackrabbit despite his cane. "Your brother wants to see the weapons we have."

Wilden stood and turned his back on Tayt. "Yes, good, we should make sure they're ready to go. What do you have?"

Hephdeezee shrugged. "The usual: spare hoopaks, of course, and some chappaks and whippaks. Also, some swords and staffs that sometimes just appeared there."

"Show me."

Hephdeezee pointed out his open wall and gestured for Wilden to follow.

"What should I do?" Tayt asked behind him as he followed Hephdeezee, Marten at his side.

Wilden looked over his shoulder and met her worried eyes. She was right, of course. The vision he'd had in the woods showed the Goblin Man well underway. An attack could happen any moment, and all of this planning could be for naught.

"Find Moonbeam," he said. "She'll need your help."

Clenching her jaw so as to still her trembling, Tayt nodded and ran off through the darkened village, winding past the kender who milled about in their nightclothes.

Hephdeezee hobbled quickly down an alley that ran between the market stalls, leading Wilden and Marten to a small building hidden beneath a tree. As Hephdeezee made haste to pick the lock—this being the only building with four walls and a closed door—Wilden listened to the voices of the kender fill the night air, their tone filled with a mix of anger at being attacked and unbridled excitement at the thought of the forthcoming adventure.

"Here you go," Hephdeezee grumbled as the lock fell easily from his nimble, gnarled fingers. "Have at 'er. I'd best go help Moonbeam rally the troops!" With that, the stout, gruff old kender waddled out of the alley, leaving Wilden and Marten to inspect the hoopaks and axelike chappaks inside the small building. The whippaks, whiplike as their name suggested, looked useful for close-range fighting, allowing a small kender to stay back from an enemy.

"How much time do you think we have?" Marten asked.

Wilden turned at the sound of his brother's voice. "I don't know," he admitted. He set down one of the hoopaks and picked up a chappak, inspecting to make sure its edges had been sufficiently sharpened. "I've been hoping for a vision, but . . . nothing. It could be in the morning, the afternoon, perhaps a few hours for all I know.

What I do know is that they appear to be gathering forces north before they head down here to. . . ." He let his voice trail off.

Marten came to Wilden's side and picked up an axe. "The visions, your foresight. Garin always thought they'd be your greatest asset if you could control them."

Wilden swallowed. "That would likely be true."

The two fell silent. Wilden wasn't sure what to say. Ever since Garin stayed behind and the brothers had raced to Kendermore, the night had been a blur of frenzied, last-minute preparation for the coming onslaught. Wilden hadn't allowed himself a moment to think about all that had happened, choosing instead to distract himself with talk of warfare even though he was quite certain he was making most of his ideas up.

Now, with a few moments to breathe while they inspected the weapons, questions about Marten, about his "death" and reappearance, flooded Wilden's mind.

"Why?" Wilden asked as he set down an axe.

Marten turned to him and raised his eyebrows questioningly. He had stopped wearing his mask ever since they had arrived in Weavewillow. "Why what?"

Wilden rolled his eyes and punched his brother's shoulder, for just a moment remembering what it was like when they were young boys training next to each other in magic school and, later, on the conclave's elite renegade hunter training grounds.

"You know what I mean," he said. "Why fake your death to become part of the conclave's order only to abandon them now?"

Marten's face grew as motionless as stone. "I . . . I don't actually know. I didn't intend to. I was meant to stand by Garin's side." He turned his head and met Wilden's eyes. "But then I saw you again and I remembered the type of boy you were, and the type of man they'd said you'd become. You're my family, my only family, and if this has proven this important to you . . . then I must help."

Marten turned back to the weapon rack. "Besides, the conclave may think we are merely their puppets, but no amount of training can ever beat out of me—out of us—what is right. And letting goblins slaughter a bunch of kender, well, that isn't right."

Wilden nodded. "Thank you," he said. "I . . . there's a lot we will need to talk about once this is over. Garin will bring the whole conclave down upon me, and perhaps you as well—for good reason."

Marten placed a reassuring hand on Wilden's shoulder. "Well, we'll deal with that when the time comes, brother."

Wilden nodded and picked up the next weapon that needed inspecting. "Yes, we will."

The night air was filled with the constant noises of cutting, hammering, and shouting as the kender neared finishing their combat preparations.

Wilden was surprised by how much the kender had managed to put together in just a few short hours. Rows of small wooden barricades had been constructed, each designed to provide two adult kender with protection while allowing them to sling rocks with impunity at any approaching foes. A smaller number of one-kender barricades had been constructed, to allow an even more fluid response to enemy attacks.

Wilden's entire plan centered around this tiny kender force being able to defend against any intrusions into the village while taking out as many goblins as possible. Despite Moonbeam's confidence, he had a sinking feeling that successfully defending the village was beyond hope, and that their last stand would be at Kendermore.

With any luck, less than half the army would arrive unharmed at the gates of Kendermore.

Wilden and Marten rode out into the forest surrounding the village's northern border. Here, several kender were busy digging holes and sharpening rough wooden dowels for simple pit traps. Others were constructing a score of other inventive tricks and traps Moonbeam had devised. Overseeing them was Tayt, who looked nothing so much as terrified of being in a position of authority.

Moonbeam led Wilden and Marten to the smallest kender—the children who would be key to their defense. With the excited tiny boys and girls sitting at their feet cross-legged, Marten explained their jobs.

"You'll be hiding in the trees there and there," Marten said to the gathered children. The smallest, most nimble of the kender were tasked with springing triggered traps throughout the forest along the anticipated path of the enemy's approach.

Though dangerous, Marten and his brother hoped to minimize casualties by providing the kender with safe routes for withdrawal. And, as Moonbeam had pointed out to them, nobody knew the intricacies of the woods surrounding Weavewillow better than the kender who had grown up there.

"We've given you guidelines for when you're to spring these traps," Marten continued, "but we're counting on your judgment in determining the best time to use them. Remember, you only have one shot, and that's it. We can't rig anymore traps once the first ones are released."

The kender nodded, looking anxiously at the various contraptions cleverly hidden amongst the trees. Hidden caches of rocks, swinging log rams, even small ballistae were perched in locations deemed ideal by Wilden, Marten, and Moonbeam. With no opportunity to practice, and with strict instructions not to release the traps early, the young kender of the village practically writhed with anticipation of getting to try them out.

But they nodded obediently and went back to the village, knowing that their village's best chance of survival lay in everything going according to plan.

Tayt came to stand beside Wilden, eyeing Marten warily. Wilden looked north into the dark trees of the Kenderwood, imagining the goblins converging there, the Goblin Man's vicious face laughing endlessly in his mind as he screamed, "Kill them all!"

"Do you think we've done enough?" Tayt asked.

A stray breeze blew a dried leaf into her hair and Wilden picked it out. "We've done more than I ever expected," he said. "And the kender seem more than capable."

Tayt swallowed. "So I guess what we do now is wait?"

Wilden grinned and looked over at his brother. "Maro—Marten, do we renegade hunters just sit around and wait for our foes to ambush us?"

Marten met Wilden's smile with one of his own. "Not a chance. Want to go to the front lines and take a look?"

"Definitely."

Tayt shivered and hugged her arms. "I think I've decided that the conclave picks their renegade hunters by how absolutely crazy and fearless they are. It's a wonder they don't hire a legion of kender."

Wilden raised an eyebrow. "Does that mean you don't want to come?"

"Not a chance. Let's go see what Arvin is up to." Jaw clenched and looking stronger than Wilden had ever seen her, Tayt ran forward into the darkened trees.

Smiling despite himself, Wilden followed, Marten close behind.

CHAPTER

15   THE STOLEN SUN

It was almost dawn, and the sky was at its blackest.

Sindri sat in the center of the temple, wide awake despite the long night surrounded by towering arches and stoic statues that shimmered gold.

And a long night it had been. Sindri had stumbled into more visions, seen more images of the past. Not all of the scions misused their power, of course, but many had.

So Sindri had stared at the night sky, watched as crimson Lunitari and silver Solinari crossed the sky, coloring the stormy clouds above the distant maelstrom in hazy pink.

Deep in that sky, though, was an empty space—a hole torn into the field of stars, an empty, terrible thing: the black moon, Nuitari.

Sindri had seen that moon many times as his powers had grown. He'd seen it when the evil sorceress Asvoria had cast dark magic into him. He'd seen it in his dreams.

And here the moon was again, full, bursting with dark rage even as it seemed to fall in on itself and absorb the light around it. The 171 moon did not move from its position.

The first rays of the rising sun peeked over the eastern cliffs that surrounded the island valley, and before the sky could lighten, Sindri looked up at the moon, still watching from above.

"I know what you want," Sindri said. "And maybe . . ."

Sindri ceased speaking, not wanting to say the words. He'd thought long and hard about this situation, and he felt deep inside that there was only one way to end all of this. But he didn't dare say the words he thought. He didn't want his realizations to be true. Not yet.

"Kender man!"

Claws clacked against tile as Rizzek raced out of the trees and into the temple. The little creature had been rolling in the grass, and dew matted his fur. Bounding with his powerful back legs, Rizzek landed heavily in Sindri's lap.

"Hey there," Sindri said softly and scratched behind Rizzek's pointed ears.

Rizzek closed his eyes and purr-clicked in contentment. Then, as though remembering something, he blinked open his wide amber eyes and stood on his back legs in front of Sindri's chest.

"Kender man," Rizzek rasped, "dragon comes back. I see him."

Sindri nodded. "All right, then. We should go to meet him. I think I have a lot to talk to him about."

Rizzek leaped from his lap and Sindri stood, his eyes lingering on the etchings on the walls. Shaking his head, he headed out the front of the temple, past the statues of the two scions that had led the so-called Order of the Sun. Sindri looked up at the sky, which was gray now. The dark moon that was Nuitari was no longer visible.

Over the edge of the cliffs, Sindri caught a glimpse of something glinting gold. It grew larger as it came closer, and Sindri grinned despite himself. A real live gold dragon! With all that had happened, it had been hard to remember how amazing this was—not many people got to meet gold dragons, let alone get shown around their lairs.

As Auren grew closer, his massive wings raising up a wind that shook the tree tops, Sindri noticed two shadowy figures clinging to his back. A boy and a girl—Wilden and Tayt? But no, the girl's hair flowed long and curly behind her. Who, then?

Sindri's cloak and hair whipped about from the force of the wind from Auren's wings, and he stood back as the dragon landed gracefully, despite his size. Shielding his eyes, Sindri ran forward to meet the dragon and his visitors.

And Sindri stopped in shock and wonderment when he saw a friend he didn't think he'd see again for a long time.

"Davyn!"

The young warrior grinned as he leaped from Auren's back to land on the ground. He was taller, Sindri noticed, musclier and his hair was messier than ever. He had scarcely hit the ground before Sindri bounded forward to hug him around the waist.

"Davyn!" he cried again, and he leaped back to look his old friend in the face. "What are you doing here? Oh Davyn, so much has happened, and I'm sure so much has happened with you too. And wow! You look like a real live warrior! I really like your new armor."

Davyn laughed, then turned around to provide a hand to the girl as she, too, leaped down from Auren's back. Her hair was longer and she had new armor—plus a really neat new bow that glowed with magic—but it was definitely Sindri's old friend Rina.

"Rina!" Sindri cried, drowning out Davyn as he began to speak. As Davyn smiled to himself and shook his head, Sindri hugged Rina around the waist as well.

"Good to see you again too, Sindri," she said. "It feels like ages since I've seen you."

Sindri looked up at her. "Did you get my letters?"

Rina nodded. "I did, thank you. I'm not sure how that courier found me in Icereach, but I was really glad to hear that everything worked out with Elidor. Made it easier to take a vacation."

Davyn came to Rina's side and put his hand absentmindedly behind her back. Sindri raised an eyebrow at that—whatever happened to Nearra? Those two had always been making moon eyes at one another, after all. They certainly did have a good bit to catch up on.

Hot breath lashed against Sindri's back, and he spun to find that Auren had curled his long neck around so that Sindri stood face to snout with the massive creature.

"I am so glad to reunite you with your friends, Sindri," Auren said, his voice rumbling deep from within his massive body. "They traveled far to make sure you were all right. But we have come with urgent news."

The elation that had come over Sindri upon seeing his old friends immediately drifted away, and a hollow feeling settled into his stomach.

"Something's wrong," he said, and he knew from the sullen expressions that settled onto Davyn and Rina's faces that he was right.

Davyn rested his hand on Sindri's shoulder and kneeled to come face to face. "I wish this were a good visit. It was supposed to be, but when we got to Cairngorn . . ."

Sindri shrugged. "Yeah. A monster did that. But hurry, tell me, what is it?"

174

"It's the Goblin Man," Davyn went on. "Arvin. And some old

witch named Anica. They followed you to Auren's lair, sent by Nuitari to kill you. When you weren't there, they decided to draw you out . . . by attacking your family."

Sindri leaped back, eyes narrowed. "What? They're going to Weavewillow?"

Rina nodded. "They are. And the Goblin Man, he's not how he was when we first met him. He's . . . changed."

"Like how?" Sindri asked.

"Like goblins-leaping-off-of-his-body-to-form-little-armies changed."

Sindri blinked. "Well, that sounds like something to see!" He shook his head. "We have to leave right away. We need to stop them."

Not waiting for anyone to respond, Sindri raced back up the marble steps to the temple, skidding over tile as he searched for his pack and his hoopak. Rina followed him, her steps graceful and silent as she ran slender fingers over the etchings on the golden walls.

"This place is amazing," she whispered as Sindri crouched down to shove his papers and leftover bits of bread into his pack. "The temple at that woman's keep was dark and sort of half destroyed, but this . . ." Tucking curly locks behind her pointed ear, she looked down to meet Sindri's gaze, and concern fell over her face.

"Hey, don't look so sad, Sindri," she said, and she fell to her knees in front of him. She placed a gentle hand on his shoulder. "You're the greatest kender wizard I've ever met. You'll be able to help your family. And I'll be there to help, just like you were when my town was attacked."

Sindri hefted his pack onto his shoulder and scuffed his toe against the tile. "Well, let's hope this battle goes better than that one."

Rina sighed and leaned back. "Yeah."

Sindri's things gathered, they ran out of the temple. Sindri looked over his shoulder as he ran to climb atop Auren's back, taking in the temple for what might be the last time.

He hadn't been thinking about his family when Rina had seen the sadness in his eyes. Sure, he was worried, but he'd faced a lot of villains in his time, and he was certain they could work it out.

He'd been thinking about his visions once more. And what had to happen for Nuitari to leave him be.

Shaking his head, Sindri whistled for Rizzek and scrambled up Auren's scaled side. With Davyn behind him and Rina behind Davyn, Sindri clung to Rizzek and patted Auren's side. "Let's go!" he shouted.

With a rumble of assent, Auren spread his wings, bunched up his back legs, and with a giant leap, they were soaring above the trees. Sindri couldn't help but whoop for joy as wind tugged at his hair. No matter the situation, flying on the back of a dragon would always be thrilling.

With morning fully upon them, the companions atop the gold dragon's back looked down over the tumultuous red sea beneath them, the island and its temple disappearing on the horizon as they flew south to Kendermore.

Midmorning daylight streamed down between the leaves of the late summer trees. Wilden clung to the branches of the tallest tree at the edge of their makeshift perimeter, shading his eyes as he looked deep into the woods.

There, just north and on the horizon, lines of shadowy figures waited. Wilden could make out small tents, and smoke from fires drifted up to meet the clouds. Distant, gurgling voices filled the air.

Arvin's army waited. The kender scouts had reported more goblins racing through the trees, meeting up with the Goblin Man and Anica. His call for supporters had gone far and wide, no doubt influenced by Nuitari's power.

Wilden leaned back against the tree, eyes scanning the branches around him. Kender men and women hid silently between the leaves, fidgeting in their anxiousness. Below, traps waited to be sprung.

A finger tapped on Wilden's shoulder, and he shouted in surprise.

Turning, he found Tayt grinning at him. She'd climbed up the tree, a basket filled with breads and meats hanging over her shoulder.

"You never look behind you, you know that?" she said as she ducked a knotted bough and came to sit on the branch beside him.

He grinned. "Yeah, I still have the bruise on the back of my head from the last time you exploited my little weakness."

Tayt punched at his arm and grinned sheepishly, thinking of the time she and Sindri had evaded his capture. "You do not." Pulling free the basket, she set it between them. "Senna Suncatcher sent me with some food. She said you didn't eat much this morning."

Swallowing, Wilden ran his hand through his hair, shaking it as he found bits of crumbled leaves stuck between the strands. "I don't have much of an appetite."

Tayt's face fell solemn, and she looked down at her dangling feet. "Yeah."

They sat there in silence for a moment. Kender whispers filled

Wilden's ears, as did the distant sound of Arvin's goblin army chanting some guttural, vicious song of war.

"We didn't get to speak much last night," Tayt said after a moment. "Ever since we left Auren's lair and you met up again with Garin. It's all been kind of a whirlwind, I guess, with the dragon and Nuitari and the Goblin Man . . . but it kind of feels like you're avoiding me."

"No!" Wilden said, much too quickly. Gently grabbing her shoulder, he looked her in her gray eyes. "No," he said again, softly. "Not at all. It's just, much has happened. I had a lot to take in."

Tayt nodded. "I understand, even if it's not all entirely clear. I mean, you have a brother again. If I'd just found out that my mother and father were alive, I don't know how I'd react. And, you know, I remember how you were when we first met, how devoted you were to the conclave. Trusting me, trusting Sindri, it had to be hard."

Wilden looked away. "Not just hard, Tayt. A violation of everything I was ever taught."

"Then why are you still helping us?" she asked, her voice soft. "You could have gone back with Garin, helped him capture Sindri like he wanted. Maybe that would have calmed down Nuitari, for all we know."

Wilden looked at Tayt again, studying her face. Gone was the distrust, the hardness that had been there when they'd first met. She wasn't a spellfilch, nor was she a slave or a street rat. She wasn't a renegade deserving of punishment. She was just a girl, a girl who'd been faced with some harsh choices, a girl who wanted to be a wizard, just like him.

"I don't know," Wilden admitted. "I feel things, but I can't give them words." He grinned. "I guess that's why I'm a fighter, not a scribe. All I know is, no matter who from the past shows up, you and Sindri, you're my family. And I won't let anything hurt either of you ever again."

Tayt's jaw clenched, as it often did when she tried to hide emotion. But still her lip quivered, her eyes shimmered.

Coughing and rubbing at her eyes, she looked away. "Well, that's just sappy is what it is."

Wilden laughed and slapped her on the back. "Yeah, I guess it is. So, hey, how about let's eat? The battle will soon be upon us and—"

He didn't get to finish. At that moment, far north where Arvin and his monstrous army convened, a piercing howl cut into the bright blue sky. Robins darted from the trees at the unearthly sound, turning to fluttering shadows as they disappeared into the sky.

Wilden leaned forward, straining his eyes to see. The shadowy forms of the goblins writhed as though they stomped about, and their chanting grew from a low murmur to a deafening roar. The piercing howl did not cease, its sound slicing into Wilden's ears.

"Wilden, look!"

Tayt tugged at Wilden's tunic, and he looked over at her. She pointed at the sky, and Wilden looked up.

The sun had risen almost to midsky as noon came upon them. But now a shadow grew along its edges. Darkness enveloped the sun, tendrils of black pulling it into a gaping maw of nothingness, like some horrifying deep sea creature devouring its prey.

The shrieks and hoots of the goblins grew to a crescendo as the sun was completely eclipsed, stolen from the daytime sky by the black moon god himself, Nuitari.

Night fell early over the Kenderwood, turning bright clearings into shadowy groves and sending terrified woodland creatures running to hide in their burrows for fear of night predators. Kender voices rose from all around Wilden and Tayt, murmuring their surprise and excitement over this most unexpected event.

"Wilden!" a voice shouted from below. "Tayt!"

At the base of the tree, the now familiar face of Wilden's brother looked up at them. He gestured frantically north. "They are approaching."

North, at the goblin camp, torches had been lit. Dots of orange flame cast terrifying shadows as slowly but surely the goblin army began its advance.

"It's time," Wilden whispered. Closing his eyes, he pictured Sindri and Tayt, reminding himself what all of this was for.

"Oh gods," Tayt whispered next to him. "Wilden, I'm . . . I . . ."

Wilden clutched her arm. "I am too. But we've faced monsters like this before. We can do this, Tayt." He turned her face towards his and looked into her eyes resolutely. "We can do this."

Steeling her features, Tayt nodded. "For Sindri, and for his family," she said.

"For Sindri," Wilden agreed, and they both leaped down to join Marten below and put their plans into action.

CHAPTER

16   TRICKS AND TRAPS

Wilden, Marten, and Tayt raced through the trees, stepping carefully to avoid their traps as they headed back towards the village of Weavewillow. "Be ready, everyone!" Wilden called as he ran past, and the flurry of motion in the trees told him the kender heard him well.

"Here's where we find out if all our plans will work," he said as they continued through the forest. Marten only nodded, and Tayt seemed lost in her thoughts, unaware of Wilden's words as she plunged ahead.

Wilden glanced over his shoulder and saw a wall of torches burning brightly in the distance. He judged they had less than half an hour until the goblin army, headed by Arvin and Anica, found its way to the beginning of their defenses.

"Marten, you stay here and make sure that the kender execute these traps properly." Marten nodded, and Wilden added as he ran off, "And make sure they get out alive!"

"Don't worry, brother," Marten called out after him.

Wilden grinned in spite of himself as he and Tayt continued running. Minutes later they reached the edge of the clearing that **181** marked the southwestern edge of Weavewillow.

Every kender in the village not busy preparing to trigger traps was waiting, weapon in hand, behind the shields they'd constructed. Though some shifted uncomfortably at the weight, none showed the slightest sign of fear. Moonbeam saw the pair approach and called out to them.

"Wilden! Tayt! We're all ready here!" she said with an excited smile. "Everyone's had a nice, early lunch and is just ready to bash some goblin heads!"

Wilden nodded and clasped her shoulder as they stopped before her. "Glad to hear it. We have about half an hour before the goblins hit the first series of traps. Marten's there overseeing things, and I know he'll make life difficult for them. In the meantime, get everyone here toward the barricades. We want the goblins to be able to come at us as few at a time as possible."

He turned to address the assembled kender. "The moment is here, my friends," he said, his voice ringing out across the quiet town. "The goblin army approaches, and we must defend your homes with our lives. Fight bravely and well, but do not try to be heroes! Heroes rarely get home in time for supper." At this the kender laughed, and Wilden smiled.

"When I sound the signal," he said, indicating the hunting horn at his belt, "you must drop everything and make for Kendermore! Do not hesitate, and do not worry, for I and a few others will remain here, stemming the advance to allow as many of you to escape as possible. Now take your positions, and let's give the goblins a fight they won't soon forget!" The kender cheered, an uproarious cheer lasting a full minute before they scrambled to their predesignated places.

"And you," Wilden said, turning to Tayt.

"Yes?"

"Stay alive." He smiled at her, then strode to where Moonbeam was waiting.

Tayt stood a moment, thinking quietly, then followed after.

The power was intoxicating.

Through the heady haze of overpowering black magic, it was hard for Arvin to remember what it had been like before—before he did his experiments with shapeshifting and goblins, before he reunited with Anica, before Nuitari descended from the heavens and gave Arvin the magic he had longed for his whole life.

It was everything he'd ever hoped for.

Above, the midday sky was overtaken by darkness. Arvin cast his eyes skyward as around him, his goblin horde hooted and hollered. Nuitari had blocked the sun, tendrils of his dark power enveloping the sky. The god had made it clear that this would be the last stand. If Arvin failed, as he was apt to do, then . . .

Arvin giggled maniacally to himself. Oh, but he wouldn't fail. Not this time.

Arvin and his army stormed forward. The red-skinned creatures had come, summoned by the Goblin Man's god-granted power, entranced and ready to do his bidding. They were disgusting little things, but he needed them for . . . he smiled. He could hardly wait for Sindri to appear.

"Arvin, dear," Anica said.

Arvin turned to her and smiled, feeling his cheeks grow taut as they spread wide into a sharp-toothed, gobliny grin. "Yes?"

The woman faced him, the reflection of torchlight in her hollow eye sockets reminders of her failure. Her wrinkled face creased into a smile. "Shall you give the order?"

Arvin had been so distracted he'd hardly noticed that they'd made their way through the trees of the Kenderwood, and that Sindri's oh-so-quaint little village lay ahead with nary a kender in sight.

Clenching hands that had lenghtened into claws, Arvin felt the constant dark power flow from above and seep into his pores. He giggled maniacally in pleasure.

"Oh yes," he whispered. "Oh yes I shall."

He raised a hand and the sea of goblins, with their scarred faces and broken armor, ceased their useless hollering and stood still.

"We are here!" Arvin cried, spreading his arms wide, his black robes flapping in the breeze. "And now the kender shall fall! Kill them all!"

Arvin looked again to the sky, his arms still raised as the goblins let out their terrible war cries and surged forward.

The Goblin Man locked his eyes onto Nuitari's dark form. And he laughed, long and loud.

"They're here!" a kender cried out.

He hardly needed to shout. The gravelly, bloodthirsty goblin calls echoed between the darkened trees.

Wilden took in a breath as the red-skinned creatures burst through the trees. He glanced to his left, where farther down, Marten kept watch over other kender and their traps. "Here we go," Wilden whispered, readying himself to command those who'd been stuck with him.

Wilden's eyes widened as he gauged the size of the advancing goblin force. They easily numbered over four hundred, perhaps as many as six. His heart sank as he realized Arvin had been able to summon even more of the creatures than any of them had predicted.

JEFF SAMPSON

When the first wave of goblins burst into the clearing and began passing through it, Wilden gave the signal. Instantly, two enormous boulders tied to ropes fell from the trees, crushing several dozen goblins each.

At the same time, the boulders acted as counterweights and began pulling up an enormous rope net concealed by foliage from beneath the feet of the goblins. Many shrieked and let their weapons clatter to the ground as they were suspended helplessly several dozen feet off the ground. The kender who had pushed the boulders quickly scrambled backward through the trees.

The rest of the goblins didn't even slow.

A goblin stepped onto a leaf-covered tarp concealing a spike-lined pit. As others followed, the additional weight snapped the thin supporting ropes and the tarp tumbled downward, taking many goblins with it. Their screams ceased abruptly as they were impaled on the sharpened wooden stakes at the pit's bottom.

The more prudent goblins slowed their advance as they saw their comrades disappear into the ground, but in vain—the surging goblin mass behind them slowed for nothing, and it continued pushing them into the holes. Those that didn't die from the spikes or the sheer height of the fall suffered broken bones or were crushed as more goblins, writhing and kicking, piled atop them.

The goblins continued to fall into the hole until it was filled. Then the rest simply walked over them.

Wilden shuddered at the utter lack of compassion amongst his monstrous foes, but was glad to see them expending their lives so readily. If a trap as simple as the pit had slowed their foes this much, the odds were more in their favor than the sheer number of enemies had made it seem.

Two kender released a cache of bundled logs that dropped from

THE STOLEN SUN

185

the leafy canopy directly into the middle of the goblin swarm. Screams filled the air—many quickly silenced—as goblins were crushed. Those behind the carnage were forced to climb over or go around, stemming the flow of attackers somewhat. Wilden nodded in satisfaction as the traps continued working as intended.

More log- and rope-based traps further slowed the advance. A series of five particularly large logs swung horizontally from high in the trees, sweeping several goblins off their feet and sending them flying into trees in the distance. The same logs then arced back and took out many more goblins as they swung in the opposite direction. Each of the five logs repeated this sweeping motion several times before settling directly in the path of the attackers.

The forest air filled with groans and cries of pain as the number of injured goblins grew. Many were struggling vainly to continue marching forward with broken or missing limbs. Others had abandoned the attack and were seeking instead to flee.

But the majority of the goblins were unharmed and continued to rush through the forest, not caring if they tread on the dead and injured. Many stopped only to pick up the weapons of the fallen, then continued advancing, now wielding swords, axes, and clubs in both hands.

"Go!" Wilden shouted, and he and the young kender next to him cut their own ropes, sending a shower of fist-sized rocks into the goblins. Then Wilden and the kender children raced through the trees toward Weavewillow. Years of hunter training served Wilden well—he had little problem coordinating his rapid movement amidst the branches and leaves. The young kender, having played in these very woods for years as children, were doing similarly well.

They passed several other kender, and as they ran by, Wilden said quickly, "Once you spring your traps, be ready to run. Rendezvous at the village." The kender nodded solemnly and returned to watching the enemy, waiting for the perfect moment to activate their traps.

More logs went flying, more boulders came crashing down, more hidden pits were revealed, and more goblins continued dying by the scores.

Wilden reached the clearing and raced toward the relative safety of the first real defensive positions. They had done all they could. Arvin's goblin swarm was blunted, by his best estimate, by at least two hundred.

A kender shouted, "They're coming through the trees!" Wilden looked back to see the last of the forward squad—those kender who had volunteered to trigger the traps—running back toward the defensive line, Marten in the lead.

Immediately, Wilden removed his crescent blades from his belt and stood waiting behind the barrier of kender-borne shields. "Be ready!" he called out. "Stay alive, and remember: We can win!"

The kender cheered loud and long.

They were still cheering as the first wave of goblins broke free of the traps and trees and began charging at the wall of shielded kender, weapons of iron and steel glinting in the torchlight. Wilden nodded in satisfaction at seeing the utter lack of creative strategy behind the goblins' attacks— they were attacking where they saw enemies, seeking to overwhelm them with force alone.

He knew Arvin and Anica might be another matter.

"Be ready to attack on my signal!" Wilden shouted, and other kender echoed his command down the line. The kender readied their hoopaks, loading stones and building a swinging momentum with which to launch the rocks toward the goblins.

As the goblins neared the edge of hoopak range, Wilden raised his hand. The kender raised their swinging hoopaks, needing only a moment to fire.

Wilden lowered his hand and shouted, *"Attack!"*

More than a hundred fist-sized stones went hurling through the air and into the mass of goblins. Where they struck, bones shattered and goblins cried out in pain and agony before collapsing helplessly to the ground. As before, goblins ignored the injured, preferring instead to step on and over their fallen comrades as they continued their unceasing advance toward Weavewillow.

"Quickly reload!" Wilden shouted. The kender pairings behind the defensive shields paid off, as one held the shield in place while the other reloaded both slings. Within moments, the hoopaks were ready to fire once again, and Wilden gave the order.

The second volley of stones crashed into the goblins with similar effect.

Then the first of the uninjured goblins reached the wall of shields and began attacking. Wood splintered and chips went flying as swords and axes hacked into the kender defense.

Kender defenders quickly countered with thrusts between their shields with the spear end of their hoopaks, attempting to stab the goblins before their shields were taken apart completely. Goblin blood began to flow as the first row of goblins suffered numerous wounds.

Wilden was about to leap into the fray, but paused as he noticed goblin heads appearing over the shield wall. With creeping horror, he realized what was happening and immediately called out orders.

"Everyone, *full retreat!*" He pulled the hunting horn from his belt and blew as hard as he could. He quickly blew another sustained blast, then dropped the horn to ready himself.

The goblins were climbing over each other, then over the shields.

As the attackers spilled over the shields, the swords of two different goblins pierced a kender woman's body. She cried out fiercely before collapsing to the ground and dying.

The rest of the kender continued retreating. As the last of the shield bearers dropped back safely from the goblin masses, Wilden removed a handful of sand from his belt pouch. *"Cepat belit,"* he intoned, then threw the sand into the air.

Then he turned and ran.

The sand flew upward in a small cloud but did not fall. Each grain hung suspended in midair. Then they began to move horizontally—slowly at first, then with increasing speed until the particles whipped through the air in a frenzy, pulling dirt off the ground.

The goblins screamed as the sandstorm engulfed them. The coarse particles stung their skin and invaded their open mouths and eyes. Wilden spared a glance over his shoulder to see if his spell was effective, then continued forward with satisfaction. He might not have halted the advance outside the village, but he hadn't expected to. Their strategy was one of delay and attrition, and it was working far better than he'd expected.

Abruptly, the sounds of his sandstorm ceased, and Wilden skidded to a halt. He watched as Anica and Arvin stepped past the writhing goblin bodies and looked his way.

"Why, hello there!" Arvin said. "If it isn't my old friend Wilden. I'm sorry I didn't properly kill you back at the cliffs. I do so often tend to bungle even the easiest of tasks." He giggled, and Wilden noticed the insane tones had completely overwritten the natural sound of his voice.

"Prepare to die, boy," Anica hissed.

Wilden glared at them, then threw back his head and laughed

uproariously. Both Arvin and Anica stared at him for several seconds.

Finally, irritated at being dismissed so, Anica shrieked, "What *is* so funny, boy? Do you think us incapable of ending you? I'd be *overjoyed* to prove you wrong."

"You worthless hag," Wilden spat. "We've won. More than a third of your petty little goblin army is dead or dying, and we've taken almost no casualties. We may be retreating, but behind us lies the full might of Kendermore. The conclave is likely on its way," he added, choosing not to bring up the fact that if the conclave was coming at all, it was likely to arrest him and his brother.

"You don't have any more tricks up your sleeve, Arvin," Wilden continued. "If you were still able to produce goblins, by now you'd have created replacements for all the ones we've killed. You've reached the limits of your powers. Besides, Sindri isn't even here. You've wasted your time and energy." Wilden grinned wickedly. "Why not just turn around and head on home while you still have enough of your goblin lackeys to carry you?"

Arvin stood speechless, and Anica looked like she was ready to explode. "So," she hissed through tightly clenched teeth, "the little puppy has fangs."

Arvin let out a loud, hysterical cackle.

"You're right, boy, you're right," the Goblin Man said in his thin, rasping voice. "I'm all out of little goblins, and you've certainly managed to butcher more than I'd anticipated. You've cut me to the quick! And yet, I wonder."

He raised both arms above his head and began twitching as his body began glowing. Strands of pure magical energy danced along his body, glowing bright white, then deepening to a dark purple hue. Wilden took a step backward.

Then the wounded goblins began to lift off the ground. They started spinning wildly in the air, their screams coming in bursts as they rotated. Wilden watched with increasing horror as they flew, weapons and all, directly at Arvin.

And into him.

They passed into Arvin's glowing body like stones breaking the surface of a lake. As the goblins returned to Arvin's body, their faces, warped and twisted, appeared in the surface of his skin.

Then Arvin began to increase in size.

At first he grew unevenly, with sudden spurts and bulges, goblin eyes and teeth protruding from the landscape of his skin. Before long, however, his body had begun bloating outward exponentially. Wilden watched as wounded goblins flew from where they lay dying in the Kenderwood and into Arvin's bubbling form.

The Goblin Man was now thirty feet tall, a misshapen mass of goblin parts with weapons and chunks of flesh bristling from his skin. He was growing still larger when Wilden turned and ran.

CHAPTER

17 HOMEWARD BOUND

S indri clung to Auren's side, his eyes focused straight ahead. It felt like they'd been flying for days—probably because after only a few hours of daylight the sky had darkened once again to blackness.

Straining to keep his eyes open despite the onslaught of rain and wind, Sindri looked up at the dark sky. Through the writhing ocean clouds he could very clearly make out the black moon, Nuitari, eclipsing the sun. Sindri's skin tingled with the god's dark gaze.

Narrowing his eyes, he looked back ahead. The ride on Auren's back had been thrilling for only a few moments. Now all he cared about was getting home to help his family.

"We're almost to shore," Auren's voice rumbled beneath Sindri's legs. "My lair is just ahead."

Rina and Davyn said something behind Sindri, but he couldn't hear them. In Sindri's lap, Rizzek whimpered and curled up tighter. Sindri scratched behind the little creature's ear and leaned over Auren's side to see the shore for himself. Though the flapping of Auren's vast wings blew Sindri's hair into his face, he could still make out the cliffs where he, Wilden, and Tayt had fought Auren's stormy guards. Waves crashed against the rocks below, the dusky water cresting into white foam.

"Hurry," Sindri whispered to himself, fidgeting atop Auren's scaly back. He kept picturing his poor mother being poked by goblin spears, Wilden and Tayt drowned in a sea of goblin flesh, and other ghastly images.

So focused was he on the darkened spires of the trees of the Kenderwood beyond the cliffs, Sindri barely noticed the shadowy figures clinging to the cliff face as Auren flew above his hidden home. Only when the figures leaped to their feet and began caterwauling at the top of their lungs did Sindri realize what they were.

"Goblins!" Sindri shouted, but his voice was lost to the wind.

Spears flew through the air, slicing past Sindri's face. He raised his arm to protect his face.

"We're being attacked!" Davyn shouted behind Sindri.

"Good!" Sindri shouted back. "That means Arvin and Anica are here instead of at Wea—"

A thunderous roar burst up from beneath Sindri. Auren's entire body shuddered and quite suddenly the world began to spin.

The scenery whirled around Sindri, a blur, and for three terrifyingly thrilling seconds all he could hear was the echo of Auren's roar and the sound of Rizzek's fearful yowling. They landed against the cliff with a massive thump, and Sindri bounced into the air.

Oh, he thought, I'm flying.

For the brief moments he was weightless, Sindri looked down to see Auren cradling a wing on the cliff, Rina and Davyn still clinging to his back. A small group of goblins, their shriveled red and orange bodies covered in the remnants of armor they found on old battlefields, surrounded them. The goblins shook their fists and screamed war cries in their harsh, guttural voices.

"Kender man!" Rizzek shouted.

Blinking, Sindri looked up and saw that not only he had been tossed into the sky—so had a terrified Rizzek. With the ground rapidly rushing up toward them, Sindri wiggled his fingers and said, *"Pfeatherfall."*

A cushion of air billowed beneath Sindri's feet, slowing his fall. Gently, Rizzek floated down and hovered in front of Sindri's face. The little creature trembled all over and gasped for air.

"K-kender man, I—"

Sindri smiled and patted Rizzek on his head. "It's all right. We'll handle this."

Nodding his long head, Rizzek gripped Sindri's sleeve and quickly scrambled up his arm to his shoulders. As Rizzek hid his head beneath Sindri's cloak, they landed softly against the ground.

Sindri spun around to take in the scene. Rina still sat upon Auren's back, but she'd unhooked her bow and was shooting a flurry of arrows. Davyn had bounded to the ground and was swinging his sword in wide arcs. He handled his sword much more expertly than when Sindri had last seen him. The goblins that didn't meet the end of Davyn's blade or the sharp tips of Rina's arrows leaped back, growling and stabbing forward with their spears.

Auren's lizardy face was pained. On the ground now, Sindri could see what the problem was—several spears had pierced his wings, ripping the tender flesh.

"Oh, these goblins are going to pay," Sindri said. Looking back up at black moon floating in the dark sky, Sindri scowled. "You hear that, Nuitari?"

The floodgates that held back Sindri's magic fell free, and power filled his insides. As Davyn and Rina took out several of the vicious creatures that clawed at Auren's side, Sindri closed his eyes and let the wild magic swell within him.

Fly, he thought.

The ground beneath Sindri's feet rumbled. Stones jumped and a crack snaked from Sindri's boots to the shouting goblins ahead. A chunk of earth burst from the ground at their feet, tossing a dozen of the creatures into the air. Shrieking, they flew over the cliff's edge to plummet to the rocks below.

As one, the remaining few dozen goblins spun to face Sindri. For a moment, they eyed him silently, their scarred, fanged mouths open in surprise.

Then, completely ignoring Rina, Davyn, and Auren, they raised their spears and raced toward Sindri.

Sindri grinned. "Oh, goblins," he said, shaking his head. Then, looking at the spears stuck in Auren's injured wing, he thought: Goblin-kabob.

The spears ripped free from Auren's wing, and the dragon raised his head and let out another thunderous roar that shook the trees behind Sindri. The spears whistled as they sliced through the air, and in a moment, six goblins fell to the ground, impaled.

Auren stomped a massive foot in pain and Sindri winced. "Sorry, Auren!" Sindri called, only realizing then how much it must have hurt Auren to have the spears torn from his wounds.

"Aargh!" Davyn cried as he appeared at Sindri's side just as the remaining goblins reached him. The young warrior's blade swung forward, cleaving a head from its shoulders.

"You got really good at that!" Sindri grinned.

Davyn kept his back to Sindri as he made two more jabs, and two more goblins fell. "And you got *really* good at magic," Davyn shouted over the roar of the rampaging goblins.

Beyond the goblins, Rina leaped from Auren's back. She landed in a crouch, nocked an arrow, and let it fly. It was followed by another and another. Several goblins fell to her barrage.

With his power swirling inside him, Sindri wiggled his fingers and prepared to cast another spell. Before he could, Auren leaped back onto his back legs, aimed his massive head toward the sky, and spread his wings wide. He opened his jaws and bellowed to the night sky.

The remaining goblins again ceased their attacks. They turned just as Auren let himself fall back down to his front legs. The ground shook from the impact and Auren stalked forward, the massive gold dragon seeming far larger than ever before.

Auren narrowed his blue eyes and raised his lizardy lips in a sneer. "If you value your lives," he grumbled from deep within his gut, *"run."*

A feeling washed over Sindri, one of such awe he'd never experienced before. Auren was doing something, he realized, casting something like the dragonfear that evil dragons cast over Sindri's non-kender friends. Only this time, it was the bad guys—the goblins—that trembled in fear.

In a flash, Auren's head shot forward, dwarfing the shaking goblins. The dragon's nostrils flared and he said, "I warned you."

From deep within Auren's body, Sindri heard a low rumble. Auren took in a long breath, as if his lungs were bottomless, and when he exhaled, flame burst forth.

All but two of the remaining goblins were consumed by the fire. Their pained screams filled the air as they ran toward the cliffs, leaping from its edge to the water below. The two goblins that had escaped incineration yelped and turned to run toward the woods behind Sindri.

"Not so fast," Auren rumbled, and with one quick swat from his front leg, the two fell.

Arching his back and lowering his giant head, Auren looked down at the cowering goblins. "You have explaining to do." Before they could move, his head shot forward, head butting the two into unconsciousness.

That done, Auren grimaced, took two great steps backward, and fell to his side.

Sindri pumped his fist into the air and let out a whoop. "That was amazing!"

Auren only groaned in response.

Slinging her bow over her shoulder, Rina ran to Auren's side and ran her hands gently over his scales. "Auren," she said, "you're hurt. Is there anything we can do?"

Blinking his eyes slowly, Auren raised his lips into his version of a smile. "Thank you for your concern, Lady Rinalasha. Yes, yes, down below I have some enchanted salve that will help mend the wounds in my wing enough so that we can fly. Sindri, Davyn, can you fetch it? My sentry in the library will know where it is. Rina, please stay here with me, I will need help questioning these two goblins once they awaken."

Davyn sheathed his sword and came to Sindri's side. "Question them?"

Auren nodded his massive head. "Yes. They were left here to attack us, but Arvin and Anica are nowhere near here. We need to know their plans."

Sindri swallowed. Yes—the attack against Weavewillow. They needed to focus.

"Come on, let's go!" Sindri cried. He grabbed Davyn's arm and dragged the boy toward the hidden entrance to Auren's lair. Rizzek whimpered on Sindri's shoulder, shifted his back legs, and dug his head deeper beneath Sindri's cloak.

Sindri and Davyn raced down the stone steps and into Auren's lair. Sindri hardly had time to marvel once again at the wonder of it all as they ran through the great hall toward what Davyn told Sindri was Auren's library.

"There," Davyn said, pointing to a small gold dragon statue on a table as Sindri ran through the door and into the library. "That thing spoke when Auren came back earlier. It's probably the sentry."

The golden figure came to life, twisting its neck to look up at Sindri. "Right you are, Masters Davyn and Sindri."

"Oh neat," Sindri whispered. The entire room was wonderful, with the endless trinkets and the ocean window and—no, he needed to pay attention!

Sindri crouched to his knees so as to be eye to eye with the sentry. "Auren said you could tell us where he kept a salve that could heal his wing."

The sentry blinked its blank gold eyes, then nodded. "Of course, Master Sindri. If you would exit the library, take a right at the first fountain, and enter the medicine pantry, you'll find it there. It is a silver vial labeled, 'For Emergencies Only.' "

Sindri grinned. "Thanks."

The sentry bowed its head. "My pleasure, Master Sindri, and I do so hope you come visit us again."

Sindri raced out of the room, Davyn at his heels. The pantry was right where the sentry had said—it was a small room lined with wooden shelves. Bottles, vials, and bags of medicines sat there, and Sindri dug through them with a frenzy.

"Strange," Davyn muttered.

Sindri peered at the label of one bottle, then cast it aside when it wasn't what he was looking for. "What's that?"

Davyn shook his head and helped Sindri look. "Oh, nothing, Sindri. It's just, Maddoc was here earlier. He's gone now."

Sindri stopped and narrowed his eyes. "Maddoc? What? I told him I didn't want to see him again."

"You did?" Davyn narrowed his eyes as well.

"Yes. He's up to no good . . ." Something caught Sindri's eye, and he read aloud. " 'For Emergencies Only'! I found it!"

Davyn nodded and the two of them bounded to their feet to race up out of the lair.

"The goblins that were here waiting for us," Davyn said between breaths as they bounded up the stone steps toward the wooden door. "Maddoc knew we'd be coming this way. Do you think . . ."

Sindri shook his head. "No," he said vehemently. "Maddoc would never go help Arvin and Anica, not after what they did. But we can't worry about him now, Davyn, my family—"

Davyn met Sindri's eyes as they reached the trapdoor leading to the cliff face. "I know, Sindri. We'll talk about him later."

Sindri nodded. "Later."

Darkness overwhelmed them as they leaped outside. Jumping over fallen goblin bodies and running round the jagged piece of stone he'd magically made burst from the ground, Sindri came to Auren's side and held the bottle high. "Got it!"

Auren grunted and nodded his head. "Good. Rina, be a dear and rub that on my wing."

Rina took the bottle from Sindri and said, "Of course."

Sindri stomped to the sides of the two goblins that lay unconscious in front of Auren. "These two wake up yet?"

Auren shook his head, and Sindri kneeled. He raised a hand

and slapped one of them hard across the face. "Hey!" he said, then slapped again. "Wake up!"

The creature slowly blinked open its eyes. As it caught sight of Sindri's face, it began to open its jagged-toothed mouth to scream a war cry, then stopped as its eyes focused on Auren.

Sindri grinned. "Yeah, you remember what happened, huh? So unless you want to get all toasty like your friends, tell me why you're here."

The creature spat, missing Sindri's face by inches. "Never," it grunted. "Our master—"

"Isn't here now, is he?" Davyn said, crossing his arms as he came to Sindri's side. "So how about telling us where he is?"

The goblin growled.

Lowering his massive head, Auren put his snout right in front of the goblin's head, bared his teeth, and growled as well.

The goblin gulped. "The attack is happening now," it said. "Our master and his mistress are attacking the Kenderwood to draw out . . ." The goblin narrowed its yellow eyes and looked at Sindri. "*You.*"

Sindri scowled. "They're attacking now?"

The goblin laughed. "Yes, you wretched kender. They left us all along the cliffs to wait for you, and we are supposed to alert our master when you arrive. He's going to tear the kender apart until you show yourself and he kills you dead."

Davyn kneeled and jabbed his finger into the goblin's chest. "And you thought you could all become your master's heroes by killing the kender wizard first, eh?"

"Oh yes." The goblin grinned, showing off its pointed, dirty teeth. "And we figured the longer it took for you to show up, the more kender we'd get to kill."

Clenching his fists, Sindri stood. So much anger roared within him. Above, he felt that Nuitari was looking down and laughing.

"There," Rina said and she raced back from Auren's side. "Auren, is it better?"

Auren closed his eyes, his expression content. "Yes," he said. "Oh yes, that's much better." Flapping his wings, he stood and opened his eyes. "Let's go, Sindri."

Sindri's chest heaved in anger at the goblin's words. He kicked a pile of pebbles at it and its unconscious friend. "You're lucky I don't have any time to waste on you. Go."

The goblin didn't move, choosing instead to sneer in contempt.

Sindri stepped forward, magic power crackling around his fists in little shots of lightning. "I said go!" he roared.

With a yelp, the goblin jumped to its feet and ran off into the trees.

"You've grown really powerful," Davyn said to Sindri as Rina climbed atop Auren's back.

"Yeah," Sindri whispered as he waited his turn to ascend Auren's side. "I guess I have."

With the friends atop Auren's back, the gold dragon leaped into the darkened sky and raced toward the battle raging in the once peaceful Kenderwood.

CHAPTER

18   To Kendermore

Wilden ran as fast as his body would
allow through the partly cleared path
away from Weavewillow, through the Kenderwood and toward
Kendermore. He was afraid.

Arvin continued to display new levels of power he had never
previously possessed. The rate of growth, as Wilden understood
magic, should be impossible. Arvin had summoned a horde of
goblins from across the countryside, and he now appeared able
to augment his own powers with theirs at will.

The traps the kender had designed so carefully along this
escape route would have no perceptible effect on Arvin's huge,
empowered form. The defenses had been based on hordes of
normal-sized creatures, and had worked beautifully in taking
a huge chunk out of the goblin army's viability. Now all Arvin
needed to do was lead the charge, and every trap the kender had
left would be sprung before the remaining goblins ever reached
them.

Wilden had no choice but to continue running. As he caught
up with the last of the retreating kender, he caught sight of his

brother. "Marten!" he called out. "Arvin's gone and changed the rules on us!"

"Tell me about it when we stop!" Marten shouted back, and the two continued running. The wall of Kendermore was in sight beyond the increasingly sparse trees of the Kenderwood.

Wilden risked a backward glance and saw that Arvin's newly expanded form seemed incapable of moving as quickly as the retreating band of defenders. With that minimal comfort in mind, he sped onward, pausing only to pick up a kender child who was falling behind.

As they reached the clearing before the wall of Kendermore, Wilden silently hoped they would survive the coming fight.

Tayt and Moonbeam had reached the clearing in front of Kendermore's walls first, and both quickly began the rudimentary defenses they had planned the night before. Several spare weapons—kender hoopaks and a small complement of swords, daggers, and maces—were stored under waterproof oiled skins.

The principal portion of this final defense, however, centered around the three swaths of ground they had carefully soaked in pitch. In the tall grass surrounding Kendermore, the substance was largely unnoticeable unless one knew where to look. Wilden and Moonbeam had been confident the attackers would be too busy focusing on staying alive to notice.

As more kender joined them in the clearing, Moonbeam began getting everyone organized. "Quickly!" she shouted. "We don't have much time. Two of you go to the gates and let the guards know we're here in Kendermore. They know what to expect. The rest of you, grab a weapon if you need it. If anyone's hurt, we have bandages over this way." She pointed to several skins of water and an uncovered crate full of cloth for bandages.

The kender quickly got to work, replacing broken or misplaced weapons and generally discussing the way the fight was going thus far. Many were upset at the thought of their village being overrun by the goblin army in spite of their excitement at the grand adventure that was this battle, but most were simply angry at Arvin and his goblin army, and ready to exact punishment.

Tayt glanced up from strapping a second dagger to her left thigh in time to see Wilden and Marten approaching. With an inward sigh of relief, she moved to greet them. "Everything here is going as planned," she said to Wilden, indicating the kender busily preparing. "I checked the pitch lines, and they're fine. The rest—"

"None of that matters now," said Wilden, and Tayt noticed he was breathing unevenly, a wild, uncertain look in his eyes. "Neither of you were there, but I saw Arvin. He's found a way to increase his own power by absorbing the goblins that died. I watched him do it with all of the wounded, and then he started in on those still healthy." He closed his eyes and poured water from a skin over his head and neck. "Last I saw, he was thirty feet tall and still growing."

Tayt's eyes widened, and Marten shook his head in disbelief.

"I'm not sure what we can do," Wilden continued. "We didn't plan for this. I'm not sure what powers the Goblin Man's growth has brought with it, but you can bet he's got more than size in his favor."

Marten nodded. "What do you think we should do?"

"The three of us are the only ones who really stand a chance against Arvin," Wilden said. "Anica also poses a threat, but we'll have to count on the kender handling themselves against the goblins."

As if on cue, the goblin army burst into the clearing, completely unscathed, as Wilden had predicted. At the head, crashing through the trees, was a thirty-foot tall monster that may once have been Arvin, but Tayt couldn't tell. It didn't have a clearly defined face or limbs, but seemed to be a shifting mass of eyes and claws punctuated with teeth and steel weapons jutting outward, threatening to perforate anyone who wandered too close.

The kender paused as the sounds of the goblin army cut through the air, intruding on their preparations. "Be ready!" Wilden called. "Slingers, get ready. We only have one shot at getting this right!"

The creature that had once been Arvin slowed to allow the goblin horde to charge past. Their eyes were filled with bloodlust and their weapons glinted in the torchlight. Wilden watched with satisfaction as they raced over the first strip of pitch-soaked earth without notice and continued toward the second. Wilden raised his hand high above his head, his scythe acting as a signal flag. The kender behind him began lighting the projectiles in their hoopaks, oil-soaked rag bundles tied tightly.

As the goblins passed the second strip of pitch, Wilden swept his scythe downward, shouting, "Now!"

Immediately, dozens of flaming projectiles arced overhead as the kender swung their hoopaks. The goblins didn't even pause their charge until the first of the projectiles hit the oily ground and ignited.

The resulting flames spread brutally, forming an immense wall of fire rising eight feet into the air. The goblins caught in the flames screamed as they burned.

Within moments, three walls of fire were burning, with most

of the goblin army caught in or between the flames. Those who were not consumed directly in the fire found themselves dying of the heat or of suffocation as plumes of smoke made the air around them unbreathable.

As those goblins still able attempted to escape the burning massacre, the kender charged, spear-tipped hoopaks at the ready. Wilden, Marten, and Tayt stood by and watched, waiting for the monstrous Arvin to make his first move.

As kender and goblin met, weapons clashed, and the fight began in earnest. Wilden watched as one kender skewered a goblin through the nose with the pointy end of his hoopak, then swung the other end into a neighboring goblin's temple, knocking it unconscious.

Two teenage kender were particularly vicious as they each took turns cutting down goblins with the other at his back. They swung whippaks—kender staffs with leather straps attached to the ends— like whips. The leather straps lashed outward in wide arcs, catching entire clusters of goblins with the heavy, sharpened edges. They laughed with each other as they cut down goblin after goblin.

They were still laughing as the goblins overwhelmed them.

"Wilden!" Tayt cried as she stabbed a goblin in the chest with her dagger. "We need help!" She quickly thrust her dagger again, felling another goblin as it threatened to bludgeon a kender woman from behind. The goblin fell to the ground, squirming and shrieking as Tayt hurried off to help others before the situation began to grow desperate.

Wilden made deadly use of his weapons, lacerating goblins and leaving a steady trail of monstrous bodies behind him. He darted in and out of the fray, attempting to assist those kender who were struggling to repel goblin attacks. Seeing a young kender boy collapse to the ground, one arm upraised in a futile attempt at parrying the coming blows, Wilden sprung upward over the heads of several dozen goblins and neatly sliced the offending goblin's head from its shoulders.

He didn't see the blow, only felt it whistle past his forehead as he instinctively sprang backward. The next goblin's sword missed him, and Wilden struck the goblin a mortal blow. He turned to check on the kender boy, only to find the life fading from the boy's eyes, the goblin's sword lodged deeply in his stomach.

Wilden's eyes narrowed as he began furiously incanting phrases of magic. His weapons glowed red.

He threw a scythe at a goblin in the distance, and the scythe sailed through the air as though shot from a bow. The scythe passed all the way through the goblin's body, and the creature looked down at the hole in its chest, surprised.

The scythe stopped in midair, then soared back toward Wilden, as though fastened to his right wrist by an invisible chain. He caught it deftly, then tossed both scythes at new targets with deadly accuracy. Two more goblins fell, and again the scythes whipped back into his hands.

Wilden began letting the scythes swing away from his hands in gradual outward spirals, the sharp sounds of the blades cutting through the air drawing attention from the surrounding goblins. Some glared at him viciously, while others prudently began backing away in fear.

Wilden's eyes narrowed and the scythes picked up speed, whirring faster and faster until they became steel gray blurs in the air. Palms outraised, Wilden shouted, *"Meraka derah!"* and the spinning blades arced outward toward the goblin masses.

From a distance, the goblins seemed to disappear in a shower of blood.

Wilden continued incanting his spell, satisfied at the destruction he was wreaking on the goblin army, when he heard Marten shout.

"Arvin's attacking!"

Anica perched atop Arvin's coagulating mass. "Arvin, you clown," she hissed. "Hurry up and end this. These foolish kender are no match for us, and I have a score to settle with that pitiful little pawn of the conclave and my betrayer of a slave."

Arvin's massive body shuddered, and his voice could be heard emanating from somewhere deep within. "My poor goblins seem to be making a mess of things. So many of them dead—how pitiful! I suppose you expected this, and I can't say I'm surprised, but I really thought they might do a bit more. I suppose it's time to finish up."

The goblin mass, with Anica atop, lurched forward across the battlefield, absorbing more fallen goblins as it did so. With each shuddering step, the ground shook and Arvin grew larger, goblin corpses contributing to his mass until he was easily seventy feet tall. With sweeping steps, he brushed aside goblin and kender alike, the screams barely penetrating his conscious mind.

Anica continued to scan the landscape, searching for the faces of the two people who had destroyed her at her keep—Tayt and Wilden.

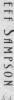
Wilden watched in horror as Arvin's enormous step crushed several goblins and kender. One second they were standing there, locked in combat, and the next, they were gone. He hadn't even heard their cries.

"Everyone, fall back!" Wilden commanded. "Get into Kendermore if you can, but get away now! There's nothing we can do against that!" He watched as the kender turned and fled the battlefield, dragging the wounded with them.

"Don't let the maggots get away!" he heard Anica scream.

Arvin's body pulsated and warped, and Wilden watched as the assortment of embedded weapons disappeared beneath the seemingly fluid surface of Arvin's skin.

Moments later, the weapons reappeared, emerging as deadly clusters of jagged steel from the palms of Arvin's huge misshapen hands. Wordlessly, Arvin hurled each of the giant orbs of weaponry at the retreating kender. Wilden could only watch as the balls landed, each crushing and stabbing several kender to death.

Shaking with rage, he quickly began intoning a spell.

"Kendala api, api cepat!" The walls of flames on the ground, slowly dying, sprang to life again and towered higher and higher, flames licking cruelly at Arvin's massive goblin body. The goblin eyeballs rolled as they burned, randomly distributed mouths screamed tiny shrieks of pain as Arvin continued his slow approach, ignoring the flames.

Wilden shouted a word of power that echoed off the battlefield, and the flames rose higher. They met and joined, solidifying into a net of solid fire fifty feet high, trapping Arvin within.

Then Wilden's eyes widened as Arvin's body shuddered and swelled. Suddenly the fiery cage containing him burst apart, the magical fragments slowly trailing to the ground like leaves from an autumn tree. The wall of flame continued burning, but it no longer touched Arvin.

High on Arvin's lumpy shoulder, Anica turned her empty gaze upon Wilden. He shivered involuntarily.

Anica called out to him, "There you are, you little nuisance. You keep refusing to die, so we have some unfinished business!"

"Sorry, Anica," Wilden shouted back, "but I don't plan on dying yet. If you want me, you'll have to come find me." With that, he turned and sprinted away from Arvin's massive form.

He wove deftly between corpses and living goblins, scythes lashing out dangerously as he passed. He heard Anica shrieking behind him, urging Arvin forward, eager to finish the killing that had been so rudely interrupted for her.

The kender were finally reaching the walls of Kendermore, shoving through the open gates.

"Moonbeam," Wilden called, spotting Sindri's aunt. "Is everyone all right?"

"We're fine here, Wilden!" she called back. "We're hurting, but all right! If it wasn't for that *big* one, we'd still be fighting those dirty goblin goons!"

"How many didn't make it?"

"Only a few, but that's a few too many," Moonbeam replied with a sigh. "I'd forgotten what bloody business war is. Your friend, the cute one, she was leading some of the older villagers back here. I haven't seen her yet," Moonbeam said, glancing around, "but I expect she'll be checking in sometime soon."

"I expect so," Wilden said. "Get the others inside. I'll be dealing with our big friend over there," he said with a glance over his shoulder. "Somehow, I don't expect we'll be able to convince him to turn around and leave." Moonbeam laughed and nodded, then returned to barking orders at the other kender.

A cry pierced the air, and Wilden's hair stood on end as he realized the voice was Tayt's.

Wilden immediately sprinted farther along the wall in the

direction of Tayt's cry. He stumbled when he saw her: She was lying on the ground, blood flowing freely from wounds on her forehead and ribs. She held her dagger poised defensively above her. Several elderly kender were running back toward her, but Wilden saw they would be too late—a goblin was standing above her, battle-axe ready, and a dozen more of the beasts were only a few steps behind. Wilden began teleporting before he could think about it, fragmenting into a flurry of magic and reappearing behind the attacking goblin.

With two quick thrusts, the goblin was limbless and toppled harmlessly to the ground, dead. Wilden spun and sliced with deadly aim. His scythes flashed through a dozen goblin bodies until he was standing alone.

"Are you all right?" he asked, turning to Tayt.

She wiped her forehead with the back of her hand, flicking blood out of her eyes. She looked up at him, and her eyes widened.

"It's all right, Tayt," Wilden said. "I'm here now, and—"

A sharp pain lanced through Wilden's chest and he gasped. Blood gurgled in his throat and he looked down. Thrust through his chest, stained with his blood, was the end of a dull sword.

The pain became a distant throb and the world became a woozy, indistinct thing. Wilden felt his knees give out beneath him, and he twisted as he fell.

The last thing he saw before he collapsed to the dark grass was the creased, cackling, eyeless face of Anica, and the last thing he heard was Tayt's anguished screams.

CHAPTER

19 FACE OFF

Tayt let the tears run unashamedly down her face. Kneeling over the unmoving body of Wilden, she gently caressed her friend's face in a vain attempt at coaxing life back into the pallid skin.

But she could do nothing. Wilden was dead.

"No," she whimpered. "No no no NO! Wilden, wake up, please wake up!"

Hot breath enveloped Tayt's cheek and soft, white hair brushed against her forehead as Anica put her mouth directly to Tayt's ear.

"Now now, dear girl," she said. "How unbecoming of you, to lose your composure during such dire straits. One *wonders* how you made it this far, being clearly an overemotional little girl and not the little warrior mage you pretended to be."

Tayt screamed out the rage, the sadness, every emotion she'd ever felt and leaped to her feet. She shoved the old woman away, making Anica stumble backward.

Around her, kender fled into the city of Kendermore as goblins fought around the walls. The misshapen, giant mass of red goblin parts that was the Goblin Man roared somewhere near the wall of flame.

Tayt ignored all of it, forgot all about their plans. Instead, she saw only Anica and her lizardy smile cracking her wrinkled face in two, her empty sockets dark with evil.

And then she saw Wilden at her feet, his body pale atop a crimson pool.

Tayt choked on her grief, felt tears sting the corners of her eyes. "You never did look behind you," she whispered at him, almost angry. "You stupid, stupid man."

Anica cackled and rose to her feet. She tilted her head.

"Oh, Tayt. Tayt, Tayt, Tayt." Hands behind her back, Anica strode forward. "You thought yourself so terribly clever, stealing my eyes, freeing my slaves."

Shivering, Tayt sneered and looked Anica directly in her endlessly smiling face. "You killed him," she seethed.

Anica let out a laugh, a bitter, gravelly laugh. "Of course I did, you stupid child! Did you think this was a game we were playing? A little bit of cat and mouse, of the little guy tricking the big guy into its traps?" Anica's thin, white lips rose into a sneer that mimicked Tayt's own. "You knew what we wanted, what our master wanted. You forced our hand. *You* and your little friends brought the kender into this."

Far faster than Tayt had expected, the vile little witch lashed out with her hand. She clenched Tayt's chin, her long nails cutting into Tayt's cheeks, and forced the girl to look down at her.

"Now you shall all die, one by one, until Nuitari's orders are fulfilled and Sindri is brought here and destroyed."

A shudder of dark magic pulsed from the old wizard's palm and into Tayt's jaw. Feeling as though she'd been slammed in the face with a boulder, Tayt reeled backward, tripping over Wilden's still form and landing hard on her back.

Stunned and unable to move, Tayt blinked and looked up. Cackling madly, Anica pulled two serrated daggers from inside her tattered black robes.

This is it, Tayt thought, shock and anger giving way to overwhelming grief. All I thought I did, all that I thought I could be, was just a lie. I'm just a stupid slave. Now and forever.

"One *wonders*," Anica said as she leaned over Tayt and raised the blades, "how you might like it if I tore out *your* eyes?"

Tayt met Anica's empty gaze, feeling hollow. Looking away, not wanting to witness her destruction, she caught sight of Wilden's body. He'd said she and Sindri were his family, that he wouldn't let anything happen to her. And he'd leaped in just in time to save her, putting himself right in the path of Anica's sword.

She would *not* let that sacrifice go in vain.

With a scream of rage, Tayt kicked out, her boots meeting Anica's wrists. The old woman shouted as her daggers flew away, and Tayt leaped to her feet.

Anica sneered. "Oh, you think you can do this again, do you? Well I—"

Tayt screamed again and barreled into the woman's fat chest, shoving her hard against the ground. Anica shrieked and scratched at Tayt's face with nails that had been sharpened to talon points.

Tayt gulped in her rage and balled her fists. Her punches flew wildly, hitting the old wizard in her ribs, her gut, her face.

"*Imbas ke tanda!*" Anica cried.

A cloud of shadow enveloped Tayt, tightening around her and restricting her breath. Tayt gasped for air and fell to the grass as the old woman cackled madly.

No, Tayt thought again. Wilden did not die in vain!

"*Ah . . . api—*" she gasped out, aiming her hands toward Anica's face.

Anica got to her feet, brushing off her tattered robes and watching in glee as the shadowy magic constricted Tayt even tighter.

"You think your pitiful, self-taught magic can stand up to the power given to me by Nuitari?" Anica asked, almost incredulous. She reared back her head and cackled again, an infuriating, sinister laugh.

"*ASPARAH API,*" Tayt screamed, finishing her spell with the last breath left within her.

Anica's laughter turned into a high-pitched squawking as her poof of white hair burst into flame. She flapped around like a frightened chicken, slapping at her head. As she stopped paying attention to Tayt, the spell surrounding Tayt fell away.

Gulping for air, Tayt didn't waste a moment. As Anica spun in frantic circles, Tayt ran to her, pulling free the dagger from her boot.

Gripping the woman by her shoulders, Tayt forced Anica to face her. Without saying a word, she shoved the dagger deep into the old woman's gut. Blood ran free, soaking Anica's dusty, ancient robes.

Anica's screams turned to surprised gurgles. Trembling all over, Tayt pulled her stained blade free and shoved Anica away. The rotten sent of burning hair filled the air as the vile old wizard landed against the darkened grass, very much dead.

Swallowing back the bile that had risen to fill her throat, Tayt turned away from her old master, dropping her dagger in the grass. She managed to make it back to Wilden's fallen form before her legs gave out on her and she collapsed.

Tayt heard the flap of vast wings from above, but she ignored it. The shouting of the fleeing kender and the cries of the goblins disappeared. Nothing mattered now. For Tayt, everything had ended here with the deaths of Wilden and Anica.

Hugging her friend's cold body, Tayt let all of the emotion she'd taught herself to hide for so many years finally flow free, and she wept for all that had been lost.

Auren landed at nearly top speed against the cobbled main street of Kendermore, his talons skidding across stone as he did his best to avoid barreling into the crowd of kender gathered there. Immediately, his passengers disembarked, dashing up a flight of stairs to the top of Kendermore's surrounding wall in an attempt to decipher the madness occurring in the darkened clearing outside.

Most of the kender were fleeing the somewhat-diminished army of goblins, exchanging bloody blows and struggling to hold their ground as they made their way slowly but surely inside the walls of Kendermore. Though no longer overwhelmingly superior in numbers, the goblins were instinctively better trained for combat than the kender, and were pushing steadily ahead.

And, of course, they had Arvin.

Sindri stared in disbelief at the hulking mass that was once the Goblin Man. Now easily eighty feet tall, Arvin's every step punctured the ground and shook the very walls of Kendermore. The resulting shockwaves knocked kender and goblin alike off their feet, offering brief reprises from the otherwise constant combat between the two.

"That is definitely something to see," Sindri muttered to himself.

Davyn and Rina didn't hear him as they raced down the inside of Kendermore's walls to head out the gates and join the fray.

"Kender man," Rizzek whimpered from within Sindri's cloak. "I no help. I sorry."

Sindri tugged open his cloak and caught sight of the furry head of his little companion. "It's all right," Sindri said. "You helped a lot, Rizzek. You go hide." Looking down over the palisades at the retreating kender and the ghastly goblins racing through the wall of flame, Sindri narrowed his eyes in resolution. "I'll handle this."

Rizzek yowled and leaped from Sindri's grasp. He bounded to the main street of Kendermore below, where crowds of kender were jumping to look over each others' heads, enraptured by the amazing sight of the gold dragon that had landed in their midst. They poked and prodded him, oblivious to the fighting outside, questions running rampant from their curious lips.

Sindri raced along the top of the wall, his cloak fluttering behind him as he dodged kender standing guard or spectating, then bounded down the steps that led to the streets below. Shoving past the excited kender, Sindri made his way to Auren's side.

"Auren!" he shouted. "AUREN!"

The dragon lowered his massive head, his eyes clearly bewildered by the little people crawling over him. "Sindri," Auren rumbled, "your friends and the kender seem to have killed most of Arvin's army, but . . ."

Sindri nodded. "I know, Auren, I know. I know what I need to do. You can help, right? Can you help take out the rest of the goblins?"

Auren closed his eyes, then nodded. "Of course, Sindri. But hurry. I fear if we wait much longer the Goblin Man may make his way through the gates of the city."

Sindri didn't wait a second longer. He pushed through the kender men and women, apologizing as he stepped on toes and scanned the dark crowd for faces he recognized. By the hazy light of the lamps that had been lit in the sudden darkness, he caught sight of Aunt Moonbeam standing on a cart and shouting out orders with her hands on her hips and her blonde topknot lashing about with each sharp turn of her head. Sindri smiled in relief when he saw his mother wringing her hands nearby, no doubt half in anxiousness to see the fighting and half in worry about her little boy.

"Don't worry, Mother," Sindri whispered to himself as he focused on making it to the massive gates of Kendermore. "I'll save us."

As Sindri neared the gates, for the first time he heard its giant metal hinges creak: The gates were being pulled shut! All kender left their doors and gates wide open, and even though Kendermore was surrounded by a wall, the city itself left its gates open wide to welcome anyone who should come visit.

But not on this day.

Sindri reached the gates just in time to see the last of Weave-willow's refugees dart through. Some of the older kender who had been appointed guards ushered the writhing kender crowd back, as the stronger, younger kender heaved at the gates. The giant wooden doors shuddered, dragging through hundred-year-old dirt that had piled up in front of them.

Beyond the gate, the field in front of Kendermore glowed orange from the wall of magical flame that still blazed at the forest's edge. What goblins were left—seeming like hundreds of them even now—paused to rally each other with a war cry, shaking their weapons high in the air. Their piecemeal armor caught the firelight, reflecting harsh shadows on their scarred red faces. Behind Sindri, the kender met the goblins' cries with a chorus of taunts and jeers, unafraid of their smelly foes.

And towering above the goblin army was the Goblin Man.

Whatever had existed of Arvin Derry was mostly gone. He was a deformed monstrosity now, a beast standing the height of twenty men. He was as tall and as wide as the Tower of High Sorcery in Palanthas, his body vaguely in the shape of two arms, two legs, and a head, but with so many twisted goblin bodies surging beneath his red flesh that it was impossible to tell where one part began and one ended.

And his face—oh, his face was a thing to see, a bulbous round thing with a jagged gash that passed for a mouth, and two giant, blank black eyes that shimmered with cold, deadly power.

The Goblin Man raised his massive claws toward the darkened sky and tilted back his head. His manic laugh, so familiar to Sindri from before, now boomed loudly between the clouds.

A gentle wind tugged at Sindri's cloak and his hair, whipping them behind him. Clutching his hoopak tightly in one hand and caressing the golden dragon scale that hung from his neck with the other, Sindri strode forward past the gates.

"Get back inside," he commanded the kender shutting the gate, and something in his voice made them listen. His people all safely within Kendermore's walls, and his eyes firmly on the hulking form of the giant, deformed Goblin Man, Sindri opened the well of power within him.

It began as always, deep inside his gut, a churning of magical energy that felt like water boiling within him. The power spread, filling his veins and rushing to his feet, his hands, his head. Weightlessness overcame him, and he drifted up from the ground, the gentle wind that had met his cheeks growing around him to a furious whirlwind that ripped leaves and grass from their place on the ground.

Gold light seeped from Sindri's pores, his wild magic given form. As the goblin army and its monstrous leader paused in wonder, Sindri raised his arms and thought: Close.

The furious wind left Sindri, swirling out to grab the massive gates. The gates slammed shut, sending a shockwave racing across the grass and making the walls of Kendermore rumble.

Above, Sindri heard the flapping of wings. Auren had escaped the curious grip of the kender and waited for Sindri to make his move.

"Ah, Sindri!" The crazed voice rumbled from deep within the Goblin Man's undulating torso. "Oh, I am so glad my plan worked—threaten your family, and here you are, ready to be destroyed. Oh, how my master will be pleased."

Sindri did not speak, could not speak. More power than he'd ever felt before rushed through his body, energy so strong he felt like a dam holding back the entire ocean.

Silently, Sindri willed himself to float forward toward the Goblin Man.

It was time for him to end this once and for all.

CHAPTER

20   A JOURNEY ENDS

With the tall, dark walls of Kendermore to his right and the inferno of flame to his left, Davyn ran.

Rina was at his side, her strides long and graceful, her golden curls a streamer behind her back. They'd missed most of the battle, but as they left Sindri's side to head out the gates, one of the kender—a woman wearing goggles perched atop her forehead and a blonde topknot—gripped their arms and told them that Tayt, Wilden, and Marten were still outside and needed help.

And so here they were, racing to find Sindri's other friends as behind them the goblins formed into an advancing line at what passed for feet on the creature that was once a horrid, creepy little wizard named Arvin Derry.

"Davyn," Rina said, and she gripped his arm. "I see someone ahead. Tayt, I think. She looks . . ."

Davyn met Rina's eyes, which were wide with horror.

"Rina, what is it?"

"We need to hurry," was all she said.

It was then that Davyn saw the small girl crouched over the fallen form of a pale figure. Wilden.

Davyn thought of Sindri and whispered, "Oh no."

He and Rina veered to the left and both skidded to a stop at Tayt's side. Near her, the witch Anica lay very much dead. Tayt did not look up, clutching at Wilden's body and sobbing.

Rina knelt at Tayt's side and put a gentle hand on her shoulder. "Hey, Tayt," she whispered. "We're here. We—"

A horrific, gurgling scream sounded behind Davyn and he spun just in time to see a goblin leaping at his face. Before Davyn could react, a crescent-shaped scythe lanced through the air, slicing the goblin's head from its body.

"Be on guard. The battle isn't done yet."

Scythes held ready, a tall man with blond hair stepped forward. For a moment, in the darkness of the day and from the shadows cast by the raging fires, Davyn thought it was Wilden. But no, the man was taller, his stride different. Marten, he realized after a moment—and from the way Marten's eyes, so similar to Wilden's, widened at the sight of Tayt huddling over Wilden's body. Davyn then realized how the renegade hunter fit into the story and why he'd been with Garin.

Swallowing, Davyn unsheathed his sword, then stepped next to Marten. "Go to your brother," he whispered in Marten's ear. "Rina and I will guard you."

Marten nodded and went to join Tayt. As he did, a loud slam reverberated across the walls of Kendermore.

Davyn spun around and saw a tiny figure floating in the air in front of the closed gates of Kendermore. It was Sindri, golden power swirling around him.

"So much power," Davyn whispered to himself.

And then, closer to Davyn, a trio of goblins chose to attack. Steeling himself for more fighting, Davyn turned away from Sindri, recognizing that Auren now hovered in the sky as well. With all his hopes placed on Sindri defeating the massive, deformed Goblin Man, Davyn rushed forward to protect Rina and what was left of Sindri's newfound family.

Sindri could no longer tell where he ended and where his power began.

Golden energy surged over his skin, spilling from his pores and swirling out into the darkened sky. The well within him, the source of his power, had burst apart, and now Sindri willed all of his magic to pour free.

More, he thought even as his bones rattled from a sudden surge of extra magic. More.

Sindri breathed deep, his body rising higher and higher into the night sky.

Everything seemed to glow now, Sindri realized. The trees, the stars, the grass—all of it burst with golden magic. Untamed magic flowed through everything and it was so very beautiful.

Everything except the giant beast that was what had become of Arvin Derry. The Goblin Man and his massive, shifting body waited before the wall of flames. He stretched his monstrous arms wide and giggled in his mania. Sindri was like a gnat hovering in front of a crocodile.

"Come to me, Sindri!" Arvin cackled. "Come and feel the wrath of my master!"

Pulsing with his power, Sindri closed his eyes and thought: Stop.

All around him Sindri felt particles of water that had floated in the air stopping in place.

Freeze, Sindri commanded.

Crunching filled the air and cold tingled along Sindri's arms. The water droplets had frozen into millions of tiny bits of ice.

Sindri opened his eyes and thought: Fly.

The pieces of ice hovering in the air zipped forward, forming a cloud made of small, glittering diamondlike bits. They shot through the dark sky so fast they became a blur. The Goblin Man hardly had any time to react before the frozen droplets sliced into him like thousands and thousands of shards of glass.

The Goblin Man opened his gash of a mouth as blood dripped down his shifting red side, and he let out an angry scream that echoed through the Kenderwood.

Sindri clenched his fist and shuddered as another burst of power spilled free from the well within him. More, he thought.

The Goblin Man's scream was met by a triumphant roar. Gold scales reflected the flames on the ground as Auren soared over Sindri. The dragon flew around Arvin's deformed head—even he was dwarfed by the Goblin Man's massive size. Auren roared again, then breathed long lines of fire. Arvin's flesh sizzled.

"This is none of your concern, dragon." The Goblin Man's voice reverberated from inside the shifting faces that covered his chest. "Be gone, pest."

With one swat of Arvin's giant fist, Auren spun away. The dragon regained his balance in just enough time to make a controlled landing. He hit the bloodstained grass and kicked up a cloud of dust. As he did, a dozen goblins swarmed toward him. Auren bellowed, then lashed out with his tail, flicking them away.

Focus, Sindri told himself. I need to finish this.

He closed his eyes, picturing lightning zipping from the sky to explode against Arvin's beastly body.

Before he could make his spell a reality, Sindri felt air rushing toward him. He opened his eyes just in time to see that the Goblin Man had wrenched up two oak trees and had thrown them. Reacting without thinking, Sindri lashed out with his golden power and the trees spun away before they could hit him. Sindri turned to see one land harmlessly in the clearing. The other smashed against the Kendermore wall, sending it shaking yet again. The kender who watched in awe along the wall's top cried out, surprised and excited, as they clung to the palisades, trying not to fall.

"Sorry," Sindri said.

"Oh Sindri." The Goblin Man's voice gurgled up from within his chest again. The high-pitched insanity was still apparent, but his voice was louder now and reminded Sindri of bubbling oil.

The Goblin Man hefted up one vacillating leg and stepped closer to where Sindri hovered before him. The ground rumbled with his step.

"Oh Sindri, you annoying little creature," the Goblin Man said.

Sindri put his hands on his hips. "*I'm* annoying?" he shouted.

The mound of flesh that was the Goblin Man's head tilted back, his laugh wicked. "Oh yes, yes, you're right! Pot calling the kettle black and all that. I always did feel you and I were two of a kind, Sindri. Misfits who no one ever thought was worth anything, but who are now more powerful than anyone could have ever imagined."

Sindri gulped as another wave of magic burst up through his chest. "That's true," he called out to Arvin. "But my magic makes me look a lot better than yours did!"

The Goblin Man's massive mouth curled down into a dripping frown. "That's true, that's true. But I'm bigger. And I've got a god on my side."

The bulbous black orbs that were now Arvin's eyes flashed with shadow, and the air around Sindri prickled with dark energy. Before Sindri could react, shadowy magic fell upon him from the sky, a torrential waterfall of blackness.

Sputtering, Sindri ceased to float. He was instead blasted toward the ground by Arvin's dark spell. He landed hard against the ground, black magic washing over him like a sea of ink. It dug into the corners of his eyes, into his ears, beneath his fingernails. The oily magic caused a pain unlike anything Sindri had ever felt before, and it would have been interesting if it didn't hurt so much.

Forcing his arm to move, Sindri gripped the golden dragon scale that hung around his neck so hard that it cut into his palms.

It felt like ages ago, but he'd used this scale to fight Anica's shadowy monster back at Cairngorn Keep. The golden, wild magic had burned the creature into a shriveled heap, and that was when Sindri realized part of the reason Nuitari was so bent on his destruction— whatever this wild magic was that welled within Sindri, it was stronger than the dark magic wielded by Black Robes.

Even as Arvin's spell dug deeper into him, Sindri willed for even more magic to pour free from his insides. Burn, he thought.

Golden tendrils of power lashed out from Sindri's body, tunneling through Arvin's black magic spell. Anywhere the golden magic touched, the shadowy magic burned, flaking into ash that soared away on a gentle breeze.

The Goblin Man's magic dispelled, Sindri climbed to his feet, dusted off his trousers, then put his hands on his hips. He looked up at the massive form of Arvin towering above him, and Sindri laughed.

"That the best you got?" Sindri shouted. Behind him, he vaguely heard the kender assembled along the wall cheer.

Arvin's endlessly wide shoulders slumped. "Oh dear," he rumbled from deep within his deformed body. "I can't believe that didn't work. I was so sure I'd get it right this time." Then, shrugging, he bared massive goblin fangs that had been hiding up till that point. "Perhaps I should just go back to basics."

The Goblin Man raised one massive foot, then brought it down. Sindri dived out of the way just in time as Arvin's house-sized foot punched a hole into the ground right where Sindri had just stood.

The Goblin Man peered over to see how he'd done, then frowned. "Oh dear, I missed." Then, raising the other foot, he stomped again.

Sindri dived between the Goblin Man's legs, rolling in the grass. He ended up dangerously close to the wall of flame that still raged, rising up toward Nuitari's darkened sky.

"Sindri, get on!"

Sindri turned to see Auren standing behind Arvin as well. Beyond the gold dragon, the rest of Arvin's goblin army lay dead.

Grinning, Sindri raced to Arvin's side, climbed up his leg, and settled onto his back. "Let's go!"

As the Goblin Man continued to stomp uselessly on the ground, Auren spread his wide wings, bunched his back legs, and leaped into the sky. "Sindri, what do we need to do?"

Sindri looked over the clearing beneath them and swallowed. He saw the bodies of several kender, and over near the Kendermore wall, several humans—his friends—crouched over someone's fallen body.

"Oh no," he whispered, and tears bit at his eyes.

Wiping his eyes furiously, Sindri looked up at the dark sky. Nuitari sat in front of the sun, still watching and waiting to see how this battle would play out.

Sadness washed over Sindri, and he looked down at his glowing golden hands. The power hadn't stopped gushing from within him, and as always, it was a heady, intoxicating thing that he never wanted to stop. But his magic had also inadvertently brought about so much death and destruction. And from what Sindri had seen of the past, if more people were granted access to the incredible power people like he and Arvin now wielded, so much more devastation could be wrought.

Though the thought of what he was about to do made Sindri want to curl up into a ball, he knew it was time.

"Auren," Sindri said and patted the dragon's side. "Bring me to Arvin's head."

Auren rumbled his consent, then made a wide arc in the sky. In front of them now, the massive Goblin Man stopped stomping uselessly in the clearing. He smiled in glee as he saw Auren and Sindri heading straight toward his head.

"Why, hello there," Arvin thundered, still laughing maniacally.

Sindri didn't answer. Instead, he pulled the dragon scale from his neck, gripped it tightly, then carefully climbed to stand on Auren's back. As the dragon came close to Arvin's wide head, Sindri leaped into the sky.

There was an audible gasp from those watching in Kendermore, then applause as Sindri landed. The top of the Goblin Man's head was slick and greasy, the flesh spongy as though waterlogged.

"What are you—" the Goblin Man rumbled from beneath him.

Sindri stabbed down with the dragon scale, piercing Arvin's

skin. With one hand holding the scale tight to keep himself from falling, Sindri placed his other hand against Arvin's head, closed his eyes, and thought: Destroy.

If Sindri's power were a river raging through him before, now it exploded into an ocean angrier than the Blood Sea. Golden power flooded from within him, tearing through Sindri's body and feeling like the peak of pleasure and of pain, all at the same time. Sindri gasped at the untamed joy of his wild magic as it flowed to overtake Arvin.

Then the golden tendrils pierced Arvin's skull, and the Goblin Man screamed.

More, Sindri commanded. All of it, all I could ever have had—destroy.

More power came, making Sindri feel like an overfilled water skin that had finally burst apart. As with the dark beast at Cairngorn Keep, as with Arvin's shadow spell only minutes earlier, Sindri's power tore apart the black magic monstrosity that was Arvin. The Goblin Man's red flesh cracked, golden light seeping through as it burned apart the roiling goblin body parts and the shadowy magic that had come together to make his beastly form.

"Oh!" Arvin wailed, the sound echoing between the trees and the walls of Kendermore. "Oh, I've failed yet again. I suppose I should have expected—"

He didn't get to finish. At that moment, Sindri willed his last spell.

All of it, Sindri thought. Go into him. Destroy him.

In an explosion of embers and golden light, the Goblin Man burst apart. Sindri tumbled through the air as ash floated throughout the clearing, falling like black snow.

"*Pfeatherfall!*" Sindri cried out. Nothing happened.

Sindri landed hard in a pile of charred goblin flesh that was the Goblin Man's remains. His spell hadn't worked.

As well it shouldn't. What Sindri had decided back at the last temple, the conclusion he'd had to come to was this: He needed to give up his wild magic.

It was gone. All of his power was gone, drained free, and the conduit that had let it into Sindri in the first place sealed forever.

Sindri felt hollow, his mouth dry. He should have wanted to cry, or yell and stomp his feet, but instead he felt, for a moment, grateful. The power he'd experienced, the magic he'd wielded, was unlike anything anyone had experienced in thousands of years. He was, for now and always, the only kender wizard on all of Krynn. For a few glorious years, he'd been special.

Wiping black ash from his cheeks, Sindri looked up at the dark sky. Nuitari was still there, watching.

"It's done!" Sindri shouted. "I gave it up! It's all gone, just like you wanted! Now leave us alone!"

Slowly, the black circle that was Nuitari retreated from the sky. Buttery yellow sunlight washed over the clearing, revealing the carnage left in the Goblin Man's wake. Goblin bodies lay everywhere, the ground was covered with potholes, and what grass lay between the clearing and the Kenderwood was scorched black. A thin layer of ash coated everything, like an old house that hadn't been dusted in a very long time.

As bright, harsh daylight overtook the clearing, Sindri closed his eyes. Cheers overtook the air as all of Kendermore rejoiced in this victory, but Sindri couldn't join it. With the return of the sun, realizations of what had just happened washed over Sindri.

Exhausted and sad and joyous all at once, Sindri drifted off to sleep.

CHAPTER

21   THE GREATEST KENDER WIZARD WHO EVER LIVED

For weeks, Sindri did little more than sleep.
The cleanup of Kendermore and Weave-
willow in the aftermath of the attack by the Black Robes Arvin
and Anica and their goblin army lasted for many of those weeks.
During the moments Sindri managed to will himself off of his
mother's sofa, he helped—there was much to do. Ash needed to
be swept up, goblin bodies needed to be disposed of, traps needed
dismantling, gaping holes in the ground had to be filled in, and
grass and trees needed to be replanted.

And there were those who had fallen during battle that needed
to be honored.

Unlike many of the races of Krynn, kender do not fear death.
The Gray, the realm beyond death where all good spirits eventually
travel, is just another place to explore. To kender, death is seen as
the beginning of the greatest adventure of their lives.

But that didn't make the loss of his fellow kender—and of his
new friend Wilden—any less sad for Sindri.

Though only a few kender fell to the goblin horde that besieged
the Kenderwood, all the kender of Kendermore, Weavewillow, and

other nearby villages came together a few days after the climactic battle to take part in the funerals.

Tales were spun of the adventures of the fallen, tears were shed, and laughter was shared. As night fell on that day of mourning, the bodies of the fallen were cremated along with their most cherished trinkets, and their ashes were scattered to the wind.

There was one person lost during battle who was not part of the great kender funerals: Wilden. No stories were told about his adventures, but those who knew him shed many tears. Wilden was bundled up in Grandmother Trumbauer's finest silk sheets, and his brother, Marten, took him home to the Wizards' Conclave. There, Marten promised to share the stories of what had happened so that Sindri and Tayt would be left in peace.

Sindri stood just inside Weavewillow's open gates after the small funeral, watching as Marten's wagon rolled into the woods. There had been so much he'd wanted to learn from Wilden, so many adventures he'd planned to have alongside the good-natured renegade hunter. Instead, his friend was taken from him far too soon. And unlike past friends who had flirted with death, this time Sindri was quite certain Wilden would never return to the world of the living.

"I never did remember to ask you about your tattoos," Sindri said to himself as Marten's wagon rounded a maple tree and disappeared into the trees.

Tayt, who in a short time had gone from a runaway magic-using thief to a recaptured slave to a wizard's apprentice, stayed with Sindri's family after cleanup was done. She grieved, Sindri knew, but the hollow inside him was so empty that he found it hard to speak with her about their shared sadness. Davyn and Rina stayed in Weavewillow as well, both knowing all too well what it was like for Sindri to lose a home and friends. The dragon Auren helped as much as he could before one day disappearing on some unknown business.

More weeks passed, and soon the battle that had proven so fateful for Sindri faded from everyone's memory, transforming into yet another embellished kender tale. As summer neared its end, Sindri, the former greatest kender wizard who ever lived, chose to be alone with his thoughts, feeling less like a kender than he ever had before, even while his friends and family moved on without him.

Then, one day, the gold dragon Auren returned.

"I found it!"

A tiny kender who stood no higher than a grown human's knee darted around Senna's hut, dashing between the sofa and the end tables. Her arm was raised in the air, a stone clutched in her fist, and her short black topknot swished triumphantly.

Sindri, who lay on the plush sofa with one eye opened to watch, grinned as Great-Aunt Chauncey hobbled over to the little girl's side and placed a hand on her shoulder to calm her down. Great-Aunt Chauncey positively towered over the little girl, her face a map of impressive wrinkles and her topknot a silvery gray that hung past her knees.

"Well, let me take a look, dear," Great-Aunt Chauncey said. She took the stone and peered at it with her one good eye (the other having clouded to a pale blue). "Oh, I'm sorry sweet thing, but this isn't the Graystone. It's just not *gray* enough."

The little girl pouted, then turned to run back outside to continue her hunt. As she did, she caught sight of Sindri lying on the sofa. Eyes wide, she gasped and put her tiny fingers over her mouth.

"Is that him?" she squealed.

Great-Aunt Chauncey grinned. "It sure is."

Sindri opened his other eye. Still lying on his side, he smiled and wiggled his fingers in greeting.

The little girl darted to the sofa, kneeled beside it, and put her chin on the cushion near Sindri's face. "I can't believe it's really you! You're Sindri Suncatcher, the wizard!"

Sindri shrugged. "*Former* wizard."

The girl didn't seem to hear him. "I was there! I helped release some of the traps and then we went to Kendermore, and Mama let me sit on her shoulders while we were on the wall so we could see you, and then you used your magic against that big goblin man!" The girl's eyes opened even wider. "You're famous! Maybe more famous than Tasslehoff, or Uncle Trapspringer!"

Sindri laughed. "I wouldn't say that."

The girl leaned back and clapped her hands. "My friends will be so excited when they find out I got to meet you! I'm going to be a wizard when I grow up too, you know. I'm going to travel all over and cast spells and have adventures, and it'll be so much fun!"

Sindri looked down at the sofa. It was green and dotted with pink flowers, which was much nicer than the sofa that had been here in his mother's living room the week before.

"I used to say that too," he whispered.

"Come now," Great-Aunt Chauncey said, ushering the little girl away from Sindri's side and out the open front door. "Sindri needs his rest. Let's go outside. You don't want one of the other kids to find the Graystone before you do, right dear?"

The sound of the two faded away as they disappeared outside, and Sindri curled himself deeper into the sofa's cushions. It had been a strange few weeks, partly because he'd spent most of it in his mother's living room sleeping on her furniture, but mostly because before now he'd never experienced this level of sadness in his life.

All he'd ever wanted was to be a wizard. For a glorious time, he was. Now . . .

"I must have tripped over five kids on the way over here," someone said from the doorway. "And Rina's been carted off somewhere by Cousin Phadri to help set up some games. What's going on?"

Sindri leaned up at the sound of the voice. Davyn stood in the doorway, his mended green armor shining in the midday light and his hair as overgrown and unkempt as ever. The young warrior offered Sindri a smile.

"Hi, Davyn," Sindri said, smiling back. "It's Graystone Eve. You know the story of the Graystone?"

Davyn shook his head, then plopped down on a stool near Sindri's sofa.

Sindri sat up, shaking his arms out to get the blood flowing through them again. "Well, long ago the gods put a whole lot of power into a stone meant to represent all of Krynn. Somehow this stone got set loose, and it spread chaotic magic everywhere! We've always thought it was the most fascinating magic item in all of history, so once a year everyone goes hunting for it, and we call that day Graystone Eve."

Davyn tilted his head. "Anyone ever find it?"

Sindri shrugged. "Nope. At least, not that I know of. But everyone always comes home with lots and lots of interesting items filling their pockets, and it's always fun to see what's been gathered. I always wanted to learn more about the Graystone. I meant to ask . . ." Sindri looked down.

"Maddoc," Davyn finished for him.

Sindri nodded. "Yes. Maddoc."

Davyn leaned forward, crossing his arms over his knees. "I've been meaning to bring him up with you, Sindri. That day, the attack, everything was so rushed, and since then you've been sleeping . . ."

"Yeah." Sindri ran his hand through his shaggy hair, shaking tangles free. "Did Auren find out if anything of his was missing?"

"I don't know," Davyn said. "Last I spoke to Auren he hadn't found anything lost. But I know Maddoc, Sindri. And you do too."

Sindri thought back over the last few years. He remembered the battles he fought alongside Davyn, Catriona, and Elidor as they strove to help their friend Nearra regain the memories Maddoc had stolen from her. He remembered how Maddoc befriended him, helped him learn how to use his burgeoning powers. He remembered the months he spent in Cairngorn Keep, working every day with Maddoc to become someone the old wizard would be proud of.

And he remembered the moment he found the burned map and the charred dragon scale in Maddoc's hearth. It was the moment he lost his trust in Maddoc forever.

Sindri fingered the golden dragon scale that still hung around his neck. His mother had mended the silver chain that Maddoc had made for him.

"Yes," Sindri said. "I know Maddoc. He was upset when I told him we should go our separate ways. Do you suppose he's up to something new now that he can't study me?"

Davyn clenched his jaw. "I know he is. I think we should do something about him before anything bad happens this time,

Sindri. I've been thinking. Rina and I were going to go find Elidor anyway, and we can still go there. What if we get Elidor, Nearra, and Catriona, and we find Maddoc and stop him before he does anything worse than he's already done?"

Sindri nodded. "Catriona did say that if I ever started questioning my trust in Maddoc that she wanted to be the first to know. Do you suppose we should get the old group together again?"

"Yes. We've all grown a lot since we first met. I'm pretty good with this sword, Catriona is probably ten times the warrior she was when we first met. From how Rina tells it Elidor is stronger than ever, and Nearra is fast becoming a powerful wizard, just like—"

Davyn stopped speaking and looked down. The hollow inside Sindri felt emptier than ever.

"Sorry, Sindri," Davyn said. "I forgot that—"

Sindri reached out and grabbed Davyn's arm, then smiled. "It's all right, Davyn," he said. "It was my choice."

Davyn swallowed and met Sindri's eyes. "You didn't have to give your magic up, Sindri. We would have protected you from any other attacks Nuitari would have thrown at you."

Leaning back into the plush cushions of the sofa, Sindri picked at a loose thread and looked around his mother's living room. His book about dragons was nailed to the wall again, a reminder of a different time.

"I never really told anyone why I did it," Sindri said.

"Why did you?" Davyn asked.

Sindri looked down at his lap. "Magic was all I ever wanted," he said. "And I had it, and it was amazing. But I saw things, Davyn, visions of how people who had power like mine abused it. I think, after that, I kind of agreed with Nuitari. I didn't give up the magic to keep him from attacking me and my friends and my family, not entirely anyway. I did it because Nuitari and the other gods took control of magic for a reason. And if a kender isn't supposed to use magic, then I guess . . ."

Sindri shrugged and looked up. "But I guess it's not all bad. I'm still good at lots of other things, I suppose."

Davyn nodded. "I understand, Sindri." He reached forward and gripped Sindri's shoulder. "You're one of the bravest people I've ever met."

Sindri smiled. "Thanks, Davyn! Same to you." Sindri sighed. "I guess, I just wish I had had a chance to learn more about all of this. Like why it was foretold that I'd bring about wild magic when I just got rid of it forever."

Footsteps sounded in the doorway. "Because you did bring it back."

Sindri leaped to his feet at the sound of the voice. Turning toward the door he saw the tanned skin and golden hair of Auren in his human disguise.

"Auren!" Sindri cried. "You're back!" Before he knew what he was doing, he'd leaped onto the rug and raced to the front door to hug Auren around the waist. "I was hoping you weren't gone for good!"

Auren laughed and patted Sindri on his back. "Of course not. I wouldn't go through all the trouble to help you just to disappear! And Davyn, good to see that you're well."

Dusting his pant legs, Davyn stood up and came forward to shake Auren's hand. "You as well."

Sindri tugged at Auren's orange tunic. "What do you mean that I brought it back? I thought my whole journey was supposed to get rid of wild magic, and that's why you showed me the temples."

Auren turned to look out at the town of Weavewillow, and

Sindri followed his gaze. The holiday was in full swing and kender swarmed the streets, peering beneath boulders and digging through each other's homes in their attempt to find the Graystone. Despite the battle weeks earlier, the town looked better than ever.

"Look around, Sindri," he said. "You can't see it now, but wild magic courses throughout the bones of the world. It surrounds us all, waiting to be tapped."

"But we can't tap into it anymore," Sindri said. "That's why there are the gods of magic, to make sure that magic is controlled."

"Ah," Auren said, and he looked down at Sindri and winked. "For now. What you were, Sindri, was a catalyst. Your adventures were the start of something that won't play out for years. But one day, when the time comes, wild magic will be a necessary thing. You were important in making it possible for it to be used."

Sindri furrowed his brow. "You mean I gave it up for nothing? That it's going to come back no matter what?"

Auren shook his head, then kneeled to be face to face with Sindri. "Not quite. Now is not the time for our world to know the magic you experienced. You saw in your visions the abuse that occurred. But one day, the world will change again. And what you experienced and what you did will help the world transition to a new age."

"I don't understand," Sindri said.

Auren laughed gently. "Well, I don't entirely myself. But you did well, Sindri. You made a sacrifice very few people—most especially wizards—ever would have made. And that is why I have a gift for you."

Stretching forward his slender fingers, Auren touched the golden dragon scale that hung in front of Sindri's chest. He whispered slithery words of magic and the scale glowed. In a flash of white light, it disappeared.

Davyn looked down at Sindri curiously. "What did you do?" he asked Auren.

Auren smiled, holding Sindri's gaze. "Do you feel it, Sindri?"

Sindri scrunched his face in confusion—but then, he *did* feel it. The hollow inside of him once occupied by his endless power wasn't so empty anymore. A drop of sparkling magic had appeared.

"Oh," Sindri whispered. "Oh, I do. I do!" Tugging excitedly at Davyn's pant leg, he jumped with glee. "Davyn, it's magic!"

Davyn shook his head. "What is?"

Auren stood up to his full height, then laughed heartily. "The magic I gave to him, Davyn! That's where I went off to, to study a way to bring Sindri back his magic. He has the spark now."

"Thank you!" Sindri cried, then hugged Auren around the waist yet again.

"Not so fast, Sindri," Auren said. "It's just a spark. All it means is that you have the *capacity* to do magic. There's not going to be any wild magic shortcuts—you're going to have to start from scratch and learn to focus and remember spell words and spell components just like everyone else. It's not going to be easy."

Grinning, Davyn kneeled down and gave Sindri a congratulatory slap on the back. "It never is. But I know Sindri can handle it. Right, Sindri?"

"Of course!" Letting go of Auren's waist, he did an impromptu jig and whooped for joy.

They all laughed. As Sindri struggled to regain his breath, he saw in the streets someone he hadn't seen in days: Tayt.

"Wait here," Sindri said. "I'll be back."

Before they could answer, Sindri darted between Auren's long legs and raced out into the streets. Laughing children decked out in their finest and brightest clothing darted over the path. Sindri bopped a few on their topknots playfully, and they ran off giggling.

"Tayt!" he shouted as he neared her. "Hey, Tayt!"

Tayt stood with her back against a birch tree that had grown up from the cracks in the cobblestone street. She watched the festivities of the kender holiday with sad eyes, not seeming to see him.

"Kender man!" a voice cried from the branches above Tayt's head. "You awake!"

Rizzek leaped to Sindri's shoulders as he passed underneath the tree, and Sindri laughed. He scratched behind Rizzek's ears, and Rizzek purr-clicked in contentment.

Snapped out of her thoughts, Tayt looked down at Sindri and smiled. "You're awake. And you seem happy."

"I am, Tayt!" he said, and he leaped forward to take her into a hug, surprising her.

"Whoa!" she said, then laughed despite herself. "What is it?"

Sindri stepped back, smiling so hard he thought his face might crack. "Auren's back, Tayt. And he gave me magic! I can learn to be a wizard, a real one this time. We can learn together!"

"Oh Sindri, that's wonderful." Kneeling down, Tayt pulled him into a hug. "I'm so happy for you. And I'm so proud that I met you."

"You too," Sindri whispered, recognizing that even now her tone was sad.

And of course it was. A member of their short-lived family was gone forever.

Sindri stepped back, face forlorn. He met Tayt's eyes, and she nodded knowingly. "Yeah, I really miss him," she whispered.

"I know," Sindri said, and he clenched her hand reassuringly. "I feel like we didn't even get to know him as much as he wanted us to."

"He said he couldn't go back," Tayt said. "The choices he made, maybe it was for the best."

Sindri shook his head. "Never. Wilden never should have died."

"Never," Tayt repeated softly.

Sindri looked back at his mother's hut. She was outside now, dressed in a perky yellow dress and laughing animatedly with Auren and Davyn. She'd no doubt just been given the good news.

Kender were wanderers, Sindri realized as he watched her and the other kender laugh and play in the streets. Kender weaved in and out of people's lives, hopping from one adventure to the next. New families and new friends were formed every day. But that didn't mean that those friends lost along the way would ever be forgotten once their journeys together were done.

Sindri turned back to Tayt and clenched her hand. "You know what, Tayt?" he said. "I think I do know who Wilden was. He was a kender disguised as a human. He was good natured and loyal, and what he never would have wanted was for us to give up our adventures."

Tears glistened in Tayt's eyes, but she smiled anyway. "You're right."

Sindri grinned. "Of course I am," he said. "Davyn over there, he wants to gather my old friends to go see what Maddoc's up to. But I've got a long way to go before I'm ready to run into battle again. What do you say, Tayt? You and me, we should stick together. We can learn magic like we always wanted, and become the best wizards this world has ever seen. Just like Wilden would have wanted. Hey, I have a standing invitation at a wizard school in Palanthas!"

Atop Sindri's shoulder, Rizzek howled. Sindri laughed and patted the little creature's rump. "And you too, Rizzek. You can come along too, though I don't know if you'd be very good at wizarding."

Tayt looked away, scanning Weavewillow's streets, a small smile on her face.

"Yes, Sindri," she said after a moment. "Let's." Grabbing his hand, she pulled him toward the stalls being set up in Weavewillow's town square. "We're going to study, and you're going to become the greatest kender wizard who ever lived."

"Again!" Sindri said.

Laughing with joy even as sad memories of their departed friend Wilden went through their heads, the friends ran off into the holiday stalls to eat treats and play kender games. Maddoc's intentions, Sindri's plans for study—those future troubles could wait. For now, Sindri just wanted to have fun.

Tomorrow, his new journey could begin.

ACKNOWLEDGMENTS

A special thank you to Andrew Hamada and Rachel Morgan-Wall for all the help they provided when I was stuck in place.

Thank you also to Joe Lambert, for putting up with me every day, and to my amazing editor, Stacy Whitman, for being so supportive during the final stretch.

How do you trick a troll?

Do vampires sleep?

Why worry about yuan-ti?

All the answers (and more!)
can be found in

A PRACTICAL GUIDE TO MONSTERS

AUGUST 2007

Written by famed wizard Zendric, this fully illustrated guide is chock full of fascinating monster facts! Discover intimate details about the habits and habitats of each magical beast, pore over maps of their lairs, and find out the best tools and tricks to overcome them.

FOR AGES SIX AND UP

THE NEW ADVENTURES

ELEMENTS
Ree Soesbee

Four Elements

Three Dreams

Two Sisters

One Final Test

New to her magic, Nearra has only recently stepped on the path to fulfill her destiny as a wizard. But before she can take the Test of High Sorcery, the Wizard's Conclave charges her with solving a mystery. With her sister Jirah in tow, Nearra finds herself on a quest to uncover the Crescent Cabal's machinations. Four pillars, each controlling one of the elements, are the key to the mystery. But will Nearra be able to find them before the Cabal does?

PILLAR OF FLAME
Volume One

QUEEN OF THE SEA
Volume Two

TEMPEST'S VOW
Volume Three
FEBRUARY 2008

Join the Knights as they battle monsters, solve mysteries
and save their town from certain destruction.

COLLECT THEM ALL!